INSIDE THE SEVENTH WAVE

G. W. HAWKER

VENEFICIA PUBLISHING UK
https://www.veneficiapublishing.com
Typesetting © Veneficia Publishing
UK September 2019

For Mum, Marion and Lyn
Who kept me on the path

For Lisa and our boys, Luke and Joe
Who showed me the path in the first place

The universe is made of stories, not of atoms
The Speed of Darkness - Muriel Rukeyser (1968)

This isle, this poor isle - I bless it with a curse
Attributed to Joseph of Arimathea (circa 50 AD)

But this Island sucks up everything I am
Odysseus (Homer's Odyssey - Simon Armitage 2006)

Whenever we went from our picnic area by the Fleet over the top to Chesil beach, our parents would always cry after us:
'Beware the Seventh Wave! Beware the Seventh Wave!' *Dexter William (2001)*

CONTENTS

PROLOGUE

In 1971 a family of five decided to explore the coastline of the county. The parents sold it to their children as an extraordinary adventure. One stormy day they found themselves exploring the bank of pebbles which connects the mainland to the lump of rock known locally as The Island - as if it were the only Island in the world or the only one that mattered. There are other names for it, some antique, some derogatory, but mostly mainlanders call it the Isle of Portland.

The beach was not entirely empty of people, but there weren't that many around: a few brave fishermen dotted the shoreline, several afternoon dog-walkers, a handful of holidaymakers. They all shared the sense of excitement and drama as the sea bashed the shore again and again with an immense and uncontrollable force. Despite this relentless onslaught, the waves didn't seem to make the least impact on the mound of stones. The sky itself was trying its best to add to the turmoil with sudden gusts or odd eerie sighs. It took one's breath away. It was live theatre; it was the best play in the land.

The children were running up and down the banks of pebbles, shrieking and hollering, jumping into the air against the wind and experiencing the wonderful feeling of being uplifted and then pushed back and slammed down onto the beach. They found a dead gull smashed with angled wings and a broken neck.

When mother and father tore their gaze from the waves, deciding to go for lunch, they clocked only two of their three children. Against the cacophony of the waves they began to shout; the mother running about in widening circles, the father yelling for the other two to come to him. They all started circling and hollering. Several sightseers joined the dance. The two-year-old was missing. It was obvious he wasn't there, not anywhere, but the group, increasing in numbers and connecting with the panic, carried on with its desperate futile search. The mother ran into the sea up to her waist, pulling at the waves as if they were the sheets of a bed. She fell over, she stumbled under and the father went in and heaved her out. The other children, a girl of seven and a boy barely four, were already in tears and hugging each other. There was no convenient pause in the activities of sea or sky. There was no let up to the push and drag of the pebbles roaring in their collective commotion. Only the supplementary sound of a mother wailing. The boy was gone. He was nowhere. It was the Seventh Wave. The Seventh Wave had taken him.

FIRST WAVE

Compiled from various sources including the account of Eve Hill (née Fancy) dated 1985 from a transcription of a dictaphone recording.

Having a harbour with an area greater than the county town comes with its own problems. Conveniently located on the soft underbelly of England, this harnessed bay is protected by an extended breakwater with channels deep and wide. Naturally, in wartime, this type of sanctuary is going to be used to the maximum. Battleships, frigates and cruisers adored this place. They could moor side by side, await their next instructions and, in the meantime, deposit their cargo of men to the local town. Everyone was a winner until, of course, it becomes a target for enemy activity. The drone of planes from the east was already an all-too familiar sound at night or, towards the end of the conflict, even in broad daylight. The enemy wasn't particularly fussy and would commonly pepper the harbour and surrounding coastline with an array of bomb blasts and machine gun fire.

Bert was on a promise. Eve was that promise. This arrangement had taken forever to engineer. Eve would go to her uncle's beach hut in Deadman's Bay and wait for her lover there. Bert would leave his work as a clerk in the munition's factory at exactly five o'clock and, on his bike, would cycle down to the straight, flat road and make his way to the Island. The plan was simple and valiant and dangerous. After all, the young girl was not quite sixteen yet and he was much older: nineteen. Five thirty in the afternoon was the agreed meeting time.

Bert left work on time, mounted his bicycle and headed off downhill on the main road, whistling all the while with anticipated joy. A raid of enemy aircraft was sighted at just that moment. The sirens wearily went off. Everyone began running in controlled alarm as wardens popped up from nowhere and began ushering the populace into havens deemed safe against a two-thousand-pound bomb. Bert was not a man to give up and, not whistling now, continued downhill towards the causeway. War is not without its moments of pure bliss. One pilot, perhaps bored with the usual glut of grey metal in the bay, decided to comb the surrounding area for victims. His first burst of machine gun fire killed or wounded only four and he went back for more. He saw Bert, swift on his bike and decided to release a bomb as close as possible.

The blast threw Bert from his bike. The force of the explosion didn't kill him - although it did untold damage to the road which wasn't fully remedied until the summer of the following year. The messy fall from his bike didn't kill him either. Some people, including two wardens, hurried over to the man on the ground. He was still alive, but they noticed that his left leg was now in a neighbouring garden.

'Get me to my feet!' he commanded, obviously in shock and still thinking of Eve. 'Get me to my feet!' They tried to explain what had happened to him but, confused by the bomb themselves, they helped the man onto his one remaining foot. Bert toppled over immediately, smacking his forehead on the kerb. And that's what killed him.

Eve waited until seven o clock, still partially undressed, until she cursed his name and left for home.

JACK

Early in 2005, I found myself at a loose end. In fact, to be fair, my whole life was a series of loose ends, so I was constantly looking out for something or someone to tie them together. When I spotted the advert in a regional magazine it restored my faith in serendipity. This was a perfect opportunity to conduct research into the folklore associated with an Island you may or may not have heard of. Basically, they were looking for someone to pull all the stories, folklore and myths linked with the Isle of Portland into one neat set. Portland is that lump of ashen rock tagged onto the coast of Dorset. It's only three hours out of London. Some say - and I would probably include myself amongst them - three decades or even three centuries would be a better gauge of the distance.

Coming across the advert was unusual in itself. This work was not only in line with my experience, but I actually had a connection with the Island. My grandfather was born there in 1899. I never met him - he died years before I was born. For that matter, I can hardly remember my father as he vanished from my life when I was five years old. For all I knew he may have died there too. I had no recollection of the Island whatsoever, although Mother told us later, we had visited several times as children. My sister, Rosie, remembers more, but she refused to talk about our childhood. Then she refused to talk to me about anything - I haven't seen her for years. I do remember possessing a secret photograph of my father at one time until, that is, I came home from school to discover Mother throwing it on a garden fire with other reminders. 'The past is dead,' she said, taking another sip of pinot.

When I try to fathom what life was like then, not surprisingly I arrive at a black hole with a deep unspecified sickening feeling. The only thing I recall from the photograph is that he had huge anachronistic Edwardian sideburns. It's a sort of memory of a memory.

Up to his disappearing act, we had lived in Christchurch but, after my parent's separation, my mother went mad and took us kids, Rosie and me, on the road. Mother dragged us around the country, scribbling a random path between towns and cities south of the Watford Gap. We ended up settling in Warminster. A pointless little town on the Salisbury Plains, famous for its excessive sightings of UFOs and infamous for the collective boredom inflicted on its teenage population. Even then I knew I was missing something. I had been dumped in a place I neither belonged to nor had any relationship to. It took me to nearly twenty years old before I realised what exactly I was missing. One of the things I identified was that I wanted to be on the coast. I missed the sea.

So, when it came to my first real choice in adulthood - the choice of university - I had to choose somewhere by the sea: Aberdeen, Southampton, maybe Brighton. In the end I plumped for Plymouth. I always had a fascination for mysticism. It's hard for me now to think why I went for this, but not knowing I suppose was all part of the irony. I began by studying western religion, then comparative religion, then primitive religion and finally folklore. I had quite a reputation for changing courses. That was 1986; the year mother was diagnosed with breast cancer.

Mother pointedly refused all treatment. Throughout her brief sickness, she was remarkably calm and quiet. This was extraordinary for her. In all my childhood, I had never seen her like this. She had always been an emotionally driven woman. After Dad's disappearance, she kept forming dubious relationships with dubious men. She went for losers, boozers and cruisers. She finally settled with Nigel, a sycophant, who adored her despite never being loved by any of us, including my mother.

It may sound outrageous, or is it common enough, but it was almost as if she wanted cancer. It was almost as if she had had enough and wanted to die. When the inevitable did happen, she died in agony, refusing any pain killers, saying that this was her rightful punishment. Nobody, least of all me, could understand why she chose this or why she deserved to be punished. She allowed herself to be slowly consumed by the illness. Her death was terrible. She never gave me any explanation as to why she wanted to suffer although I could tell that she was thinking of a specific event, action or regret. One sad clue was that she called out the name of my father on the day before she died. The last word she said. Maybe, this was what it was about.

Her funeral was a gloomy affair as I suppose it should have been. Everyone wore bright clothes as she had requested, but the service was dismal and the hymns inescapably final. That was the last time I saw Rosie. I always felt there was something *wrong* with my family, something ill-fitting, unbalanced, unchecked, as if I had been born into it by mistake. The whole pantomime of the funeral merely served to confirm it.

When my time in Plymouth came to an end, I was left with the feeling of celebrating alone. I got the odd card from an aunt or two congratulating me, but it did very little to shift a sense of futility. The success of completion should have been followed by the thrill of independence. With independence came the utter poverty of not knowing what to do with myself. Despite all my studying and manoeuvring between courses, my degree was useless and prepared me for absolutely nothing.

The gods must have heard me on this occasion. When us students reconvened for the graduation and the associated parties, I met Trish. I had seen her before but had not had the motivation or opportunity to talk with her. She seemed OK enough from a distance, but not OK enough to make the effort to make a move. Our social worlds had skimmed against each other but had never collided. Hello, post-course celebrations. The world had emptied into the Barbican and the world was having fun. We were collectively *going for it.* We signed up to an excess of all things. Mostly it was an excess of alcohol.

Later that night, I found myself in the same toilet as Trish - I can't remember if it was the males or females. We were both trying to achieve the same thing; I was thumping the shoulders of Mike Fisher and she was stroking the back of Wendy Brake. She was actively encouraging her charge to place a forefinger down her throat whereas Mike needed no such encouragement and was throwing up his internal organs. In this unlikely situation, the two of us met and so began a decade or more of vicissitude; a permanent state of impermanence. *Off and on* was how we described our relationship to strangers.

For no particular reason I can remember, we decided to settle in Exeter. We had two episodes of living with each other, one of eight years and a second sad period lasting fifteen months where we tried to rekindle an imagined former happiness. There were phases where we were literally consumed with one another. There were phases when we couldn't stand the sight of one another. During these endeavours, we both experienced other relationships, all equally as unsuccessful as the one we had together. We even did a foursome, partly out of curiosity, partly to jump start a failing story. Eventually, we had to admit defeat. We confessed to each other that it had been a toxic cocktail of joy and anxiety. In hindsight, it was probably less of the former and more of the latter. I am, of course, cutting a long story short. The whole thing ended with a whimper; she returned home from a weekend with her Uni friends. She came into the garden, holding the gate handle. I was reading the newspaper.

'How many times have I asked you to fix this.'

'Hi and how are you too.' I said, rolling my eyes.

'It's over, Jack. It's over.' I looked at the rusty old gate handle, lying on the garden table, and knew she was right; it was over. Saying farewell to each other was actually more difficult than I thought it would be. I had discovered a stable dysfunctional relationship of sorts gives your life shape and meaning. Even when it loses meaning, at least you still have the shape. Then when the relationship ends even that is lost.

Probably the way I bounced from one job to the next hadn't helped our relationship. The standing joke among friends was being greeted with the question; 'So, Jack, what are you doing this week?' I discovered I had the knack of getting a job but crap capacity at maintaining it. Over the years I have been a travel agent, a gardener, a plebe in an employment agency, a drone in a call centre, an art gallery attendant and a surveyor for an electricity company - you get the picture. Like I said, my education was a total waste of time in the real world until I saw this advert in a crumby magazine. Maybe, just maybe this was what I had been looking for all these years. Time would tell, yet even I was suspicious of my own positive spin on things.

I applied and got the job, learning much later that no one else had gone for it anyway. I should have been wary as the brief interview was over the phone and carried out by an employee rather than by the man himself. I was told not to worry. They had my CV which was "excellent" Really? Then I thought, Hell yes. I was perfectly qualified: the degree, the connection and, at the end of the day, I had the time; plenty of it.

*

I was not sure what I had expected but coming to the Island was disappointing. No part of my memory lit up when I first saw it rising above the causeway. It was drizzling and the air damp and stifling. The whole scene came across as dreary. A long beach road, the sea each side, leading to the gloomy Island standing with its head in a mist, somewhat forlorn. It dawned on me that if this Island had been anywhere else, everything about it would have been different. If it had been anchored off in the Aegean coastline it would have been a place for summer visitors, packed high with white houses and a church on its summit - rather than a prison. If it was in the Adriatic, it may have been a playground for the rich with expansive mansions grafted on its flanks and large cruisers moored in its harbour. If it was lost amongst the Scottish isles, it may have been a holy Island, a destination for pilgrims with a shrine to some sixth century saint at its centre. Or even in the mid-Atlantic, its insolence and stamina would have been recognised and respected. It would have served as a stopping station for sailors or navigators complete with an add-on airstrip sticking out like a tongue of defiance. Imagine it in the Caribbean, a tax haven, a cruise stopover, beaches with cafes or outlets, where you could hire ski boats or kayaks for an extortionate hourly rate. Instead, it is a grey barren rock, seemingly forgotten by the rest of the world. Other than the beach, there is this one road jumping over the mouth of water at the entrance to a lagoon called the Fleet. In its history, I learnt later, of a rough ferry, which had a healthy reputation for keeping most travellers afloat, was used to cross over the narrow strait. Eventually, a bridge was built. Having only one road though could be convenient. If a prisoner happened to escape from one of the prisons - not that common or likely - the police had the easiest job. They sealed off the causeway road in one direction only and they waited. There's nowhere to go. It's as robust as Alcatraz was in its day, but sadly, without the reputation or the notoriety.

I soon found out that it was great to *look at*, great to look *from but n*ot so good to *be* on. Largely discarded by the mainland, when God made the coast, one myth goes, he put all the beauty on one side of the causeway and dumped all the crap on this side. The Island was far too small to have any real impact on the mainland and it was far too big to be called an islet. Technically, it wasn't an Island anyway. An Island is meant to be a free-floating entity surrounded entirely by water. This "Island" was joined to the mainland by a slither of pebbles, which acted as its singular chain stretching thirty kilometres to Abbotsbury.

So, this tatty Island is actually best described as a tied Island or tombola like Karystos in Greece or Monte Argentario in Italy or Chappaquiddick in the States. The word comes from the Latin meaning for a mound, with the implication that it is "almost an Island." I would probably be burnt alive if I dared to mention such a notion to an inhabitant.

*

Alex Weller was a heavy man, thick set and overweight, pale, freckly and exceptionally ginger for these parts. I found Weller to be a man characterised by constant sighing coupled with an air of bemused boredom about him. Although he didn't come across as especially interested in his own project, I could tell that this was a man who was used to getting his way. Everything and everyone were beneath him; including me. I'm sorry to say, but I instinctively didn't like him.

'You are to stay in one of my cottages down by the beach: here's the address. You must have passed it on the way. You can move in whenever you wish. You have access to my library - by appointment, of course. Mrs Weller becomes anxious if people turn up uninvited. Here is the pile of notes and papers my father collected. You will see that I have added my own thoughts. Be sure to include them in your final draft.' He slapped the bundle of papers - a foot thick - on the table in front of him. They were fastened clumsily with string and looked tired and dog-eared as if they had been thrown disrespectfully from a passing aircraft. I concluded that he had held on to this idea for some time and now guilt or age, or both had forced him to take action.

Without prompting, he began to tell me random snippets about his family. He was convinced that he had a historical mandate to complete the task in hand. He obviously didn't pick up the irony of the fact that he was giving it to me to finish. Weller appeared to exist in that charming zone of life only allowed for the rich or the mad, both of whom, to some extent, have that wonderful knack of losing touch with their own mundane reality. He told me his family had settled on the Island back in the Middle Ages.

'So quite recently, really,' he added. I laughed a bit too late, when I realised, he was making a joke. It followed that his father had been born on the Island but, unlike mine, he had stayed in the family beyond Weller's fifth year and went on to become the Island's most successful fisherman. In its heyday between the wars, he owned a small fleet of five fishing boats. When the Second World War came, he became a councillor, a man respected for always speaking his mind. More than any of these facts, Weller informed me, he was known as a teller of stories. It was this skill that had planted the seed of the idea now coming to fruition in his son's mind. His father had long 'passed over' and Weller had been struggling to think of ways to honour his life. Enter stage left, yours truly.

'Yes, my father was a great man, an enterprising man in life and indeed in death…' He left the point hanging in the air. 'I shall share with you one fact and one rumour which may explain my drive. You never know, it may, indeed, lead to an inclusion in our magnum opus.' Maybe he was trying to whet my palate, but I sensed a well-rehearsed story coming on.

Early in 1979, the Island experienced its own mini tsunami. As part of a drama elsewhere, the tail end of a hurricane whipped up a hullabaloo some thousand miles south west. Instead of being mollified, checked or otherwise quailed by fellow waves or contrary currents, one egocentric wave gathered them up into its wake with colossal appetite, eventually mounting into an unadulterated hillock of salt-water. As his character dictated, Weller Senior went down to witness the phenomenon. Weller added quickly that there is no better story than one founded on the truth. Weller Senior spotted the wave on the horizon and decided to stand his ground against the wind and the approaching wave. His companion chose caution and hid behind a boulder of stone, an act which unquestionably saved his life. Apparently, Weller Senior stayed, laughing at the storm. His last words were said to be "Wind Whistle Do!" A well-known phrase of defiance offered up by any fisherman battling in a storm. The wave crushed him down and then lifted him up, carried him along and threw him into the first-floor window of an adjacent house. He landed on the bed of the couple who lived there. He always said he would die in bed and not at sea. In a way, he was both right and wrong at the same time.'

There were also rumours circulating about his father's alleged "smuggling activities." This was the county of Moonfleet after all, Weller beamed with questionable pride. 'Smuggling had been a preoccupation of the Islanders for all time and was historically fourth on its traditional list of professions after fishing, sheep farming and quarrying. Booze and fags were the usual perennial favourites which found their way into the local economy via choppy exchanges mid-channel or swift sailings to the Normandy coastline. The trade suffered with the outbreak of war; La Manche just became too damned busy.'

Why he chose to tell me these tales I couldn't really say, but he was trying to give me a message of some sort. I suppose Weller was driving some point home about himself, though it was not clear how. One story depicted a defiant, but foolish courage, the other was the beginning of the family's incredible, if not illegitimate wealth. Who was I to spoil the way Weller saw the world. After all, he was offering me a position which was poorly defined, over-paid, somewhat pointless and absolutely ideal.

'Any questions?'

'Many,' I said quickly. 'Only one which is important to me at the moment. How long have I got to complete?'

'Inclined to say take as long as you like but that would be wrong. Shall we say that by the Autumn Equinox I want to see the first complete draft. Yes, the Autumn Equinox. I like the sound of that.' He smiled at his own inspiration; which was interesting in as much as I didn't know when this was and suspected that he didn't either.

I didn't care. It was late in the year, at least some six months from now.

'Don't forget I want it all: tales, histories, stories, folklore, anything and everything. In short, I want a comprehensive picture of this Island from time zero to the present day.' He got up to shake my hand, using a stick I hadn't noticed before to propel his frame forward. I thought his movement seemed more theatrical than necessary for a man of only sixty or thereabouts.

I left the house somewhat puffed up with self-importance, the bundle of papers snug in my rucksack. The notion of the task was impossibly vast, but six months. Six months of research was a fantastic privilege for someone in my situation, someone who basically had nothing to do with his life. I could already see the heavy tome in my hand, the picture of the island on the front, possibly a follow-up, with volume two or even three, perhaps leading to a lecture or two in the county university. The phrase which came to mind was the probable response from my old friend, Ellis: 'So it's *fannying* around for six months then is it?' Yes, I'm happy with that, *fannying* is the verb which seemed to fit the bill; it was a gift, or so I thought at the time.

*

I could see why the house was rent-free. Going from the stains running down various walls and the unremitting stench of damp, it may have been roof-free as well. The name of the cove it was in didn't help: Dead Man's Bay. Mine was the third house from the road in a detached terrace of four. Put another way, my place was the second closest to the sea. About two hundred metres of pebbles away and there was the mighty ocean. All the other houses were inhabited, I was told by the woman in the corner store. None looked in a good state of repair. Probably all owned by Weller I surmised, and all left to rot.

More or less, as soon as I entered the house, there was a knock on the door. It was Eve, the elderly woman who lived in the end terrace nearest the road. She thrust a tin towards me and informed me it was homemade, as sweet as a sixteen-year-old girl and an excellent example of 'dump.'

'Excuse me?' It's a type of fruit cake, she informed me, a speciality of the Island.

Somehow, she already knew why I was there and for how long.

'Have you any roots here?' she asked. I told her about my grandfather having lived here. Interesting was the word she used.

'Have you heard of him? do you know him?' I asked her. She reflected.

'No, never heard of him.' A tad thrown out, I insisted that he had lived here.

'You're wrong,' she said emphatically.

'He's never lived here. If I haven't heard of him, he didn't exist. At least, not on this Island.'

'Are you sure?' I repeated, reminding her of his name and birth date. William Powys, 1899.

'I am sure - one hundred percent.'

Eve dropped the subject and started to put me in the picture about the other residents in the block. She described them all - including herself - as an "odd bunch."

'You will probably fit in well!' she added. Next to me seaward was Rowan, a woman about thirty, who was as "mad as a box of frogs." Eve informed me that I would be lucky to get two words out of her and probably would hardly ever see her anyway. Outside her little "episodes" she's a dormouse. Between Eve and myself was Claude Mayfellow. Nice enough in most ways, bit of a rascal, having been in prison twice for fraud or some such thing. Nobody knew how he made his money as he did hardly anything other than fish and drink.

'Sounds perfect' I volunteered.

'Sounds a waste,' she snapped back. 'But it's his waste, not mine. No, I think you will find it quiet enough here. This may be a doddery terrace built on shaky foundations, but you can't beat the location, can you.'

'What do you mean by shaky foundations?'

'Just what I say, Jake.'

'It's Jack actually,' I interjected to her obvious annoyance.

'When the Victorians threw this lot up, they wanted to house workers responsible for transferring the local stone onto the ships moored just offshore. They built these houses far too quickly. The foundations are half as deep as they should be. In bad weather, you can feel the place moving under your feet. We're always having trouble with burst mains here or pipes snapping in two. The Council would love to condemn them, but they haven't found a good enough reason yet. Any rate, Weller is still too powerful here abouts.' So, it was as I had thought, Weller was landlord to all four of us. Just as Eve was about to leave, she told me never to mention a certain rodent. She indicated the one with the pointed ears.

'I don't think technically it is a rodent. Rab...'
She hushed me crossly.

'I'm not interested in the technical side of things. You don't speak their name on this island. Is that clear.'

With Eve gone, I decided to ignore the news of my grandfather's non-existence. My entire life had revolved around his son's invisibility in any case and I wasn't going to let him spoil my enjoyment. No, instead I tried to put a romantic spin on the place: I was living within ear and eye shot of the sea, close to the local pub on the shoreline, a corner store within a minute's walk and more than that, I have been charged with writing the history of the Island in the context of its lore and myths. Perfect. Considering that during the last long year, I had been dying inside, frightened of my own shadow and holder of a phone with speed dial to the Samaritans, I allowed the feeling that I had landed in heaven to overwhelm me. This was indeed a new chapter of my life. I was shaking loose the chaos of the past and a new phase was emerging.

My first task was to walk out onto the beach, crunching the noisy pebbles underfoot and gathering driftwood for my wood burner. It was the first time I could contemplate the beach in its entirety; miles of pebbles sketched in an arc rising to the red cliffs around Seatown in the distance. Not surprisingly, the scene struck me with an ominous feeling. This was an awesome coastline. Somewhere in my brain there were buried memories of the place, but none were coming back to me. With the sun lighting up the water into a dazzling brilliance, I basked in the sheer beauty of it all. 'This is fun!' I told myself when I got back to the house, the flames starting to dance on the wood. This is *real* fun and it dawned on me how long I had lived without feeling anything like happiness. To celebrate I had a cup of tea and a little dump.

ROWAN

I, Rowan, have never spoken of Him before. Now I realise that I must admit to His presence. Or I shall never be free. He's not going anywhere. He is as much me as I am. The space between where I stop, and He starts is a hair's width.

He first came on a December's night. It was a long, long time ago now. I was high in my attic bedroom, looking out to the dark shadow of the hill fort. The sky was this weird inky mess. I could hear the wind blowing hard across the window, like it wanted to come in. The skies were too harsh and too murderous for me. The mounds of Maiden Castle were rising and falling like waves. The whole thing was on the move. People would die that night, I thought.

I knew it even at that time, a young girl of only twelve, that my life was marked in some way. Something was different about me. Of course, I didn't know what was happening to me. I felt suddenly hot and sort of transparent. It felt like I was transforming into another type of human. I was both surprised and not surprised at the same time. My skin was tight but sponge-like as well. My pores were open and exposed. I don't know why, I took my clothes off, all of them. I laid my them out in a pile, carefully like I had been taught to. I stood in the window and watched the night pulling in and as I did so I could feel another darkness building in me, rising up from me to meet the darkness outside. I felt Him for the first time.

How do I describe Him? Better to describe my experience of Him. A violence, a brash force, shifting this way and that. I felt I could throw up. I could sense Him as a dark strength forming inside and when formed, I immediately knew its nature. His presumption that I was now a mere servant, an empty vessel for *His life* rather than for my own. The nearest I can come to describing him is as a wolf. So, Wolf He shall be.

I began to cry without any real passion, just a soft quiet weeping. The tears fell down my face. My mind was alarmingly clear. I felt as if I could see everything. I tried to shout out for help, for someone to come and save me. No words came. I knew that all I had to do was to walk over to the door open it and cry out for help. Or I could have opened the window wide and allowed myself to drop silently into the night. I couldn't do either. I just couldn't. I was standing there stunned, hypnotised, helpless, waiting. He began pressing on my skin, pulling it this and that way. The Wolf was trying to tear out of the flesh which imprisoned Him. My body was shaking with the cruelty of His demands. He wanted freedom above all things, above my own self; above the needs of the host who sustained Him. I smashed a glass I had on my dressing table. I cut deep into my arm from the wrist to the elbow. The blood flowed everywhere, onto the floor, over the carpet, onto my bed, the wall. I had stopped crying. I watched the blood spill. I even managed a smile. I could hear Him howling. I knew He was free.

I would like to say that was another life, but it wasn't. It is the same crazy life I am still living. Everything is the same. Everything is different. I am at home now and living next door to that other lunatic we call the sea. The Wolf remains with me, but I know Him well now. We are familiar now.

*

I deliberately chose to return to the Island. When I left Dorchester at sixteen - I couldn't wait to get away - I moved to the topside of the Island. I wanted to get back where I belonged. Up there on Tophill, I felt one-step removed from the action down on the shore. So, when this place became free, I jumped at the chance. Of the four-house block in which I live, I am the envy of them all. I am the closest to the water. At night, there seems nothing between us. There really isn't much, a bank of stones and wham-bam it's the ocean. The house sways with the incoming tide. It creaks in the wind. Even on the mildest evening, I hear its sleepy lullaby as the waves nestle into the shore like a tired lover. When it rages, boy-o-boy, I feel I am being beaten and battered and thrown around the bed. Rowan, the rag doll, tossing from side to side, like being rolled around by the sea. I love it.

I spend most of my time in my house or walking the beach. Occasionally, an old friend will visit, but I have learnt to keep contact to the bare minimum. Safer for me, better for them. Katie however can come whenever she wishes. I do not say this lightly. In some ways she is as fucked up as I am, but only she realises what has happened to me and recognises who I am and accepts me as I am. Whatever the rest say about Katie, she takes me as me. I find this experience unusual. The rest of the world are bastards, largely. They do not understand, cannot understand, will not understand. So, I have made my world accordingly; I have made it small, protected, isolated, safe. This seems to be the world's definition of madness because, on three occasions now, it has come knocking and carted me off to the local nuthouse. The first time - not at all funny when it was happening was hilarious looking back. Two police cars arrived and out poured half a dozen cops. I led them a merry dance along the shore, running into the waves, running up the steep banks with all these men, twice the size of me, in chase. At least two got a soaking. I was drenched anyway and didn't care. When they finally did get hold of me, they used far too much force. One deliberately thrust my arm behind my back with spiteful strength and called me a crazy bitch. He wasn't that wrong, but the words took my breath away more than the violence. My laughter died in an instant and, much to their relief, I began to cry.

When I arrived at the nuthouse, to my surprise, my aunt was already there. I couldn't understand how or why. She rushed towards me and held me firmly, despite the coppers taking a dim view of this show of affection.

'My God!' my aunt cried. 'Why has this happened to you? Why you, Rowan, why you? Where did we go so wrong?' I had no idea why she was asking that question she knew exactly where it all went wrong.

*

I call her Katie My Saviour. My rescuer: Santa Katia.
It is true that at first, I did not trust her. The exact opposite, in fact. When she turned up on the doorstep in her long multi-coloured dress, I thought here we go. If all else fails, send the hippy to the loony!

'I have been allocated your case.' Her first words to me.

'And what the fuck does that mean?' came my speedy reply.

Apparently, it meant she was key working me (what?), that she was there for me (Oh, yes!) and that she was charged with assessing my needs. I told her to piss off and address her own needs, starting with her choice of clothes. She burst into tears and informed me that it was her first week in post. I told her to piss off again and told her I hoped she wouldn't make her second. I slammed the door on her and went to smoke a joint. An hour later, I happened to look out of the bedroom window. She was still there, sitting in her car, still clearly upset. One to me. I laughed. Please understand that it is not the pseudo-compassion which drives me insane. It is not their professional angst to justify their time and energy that makes me want to puke. It is the sheer arrogance. It is like these do-gooders, earning several times what I get, look down on my life, searching for flaws and defects. They look for what is missing and not what is there. They peer over the fence of their mansion into my shed and then arrive at solutions where no solution has been asked for. The fucking nerve. Like they are looking through a keyhole into my life and making a judgement based on their own warped view of it, completely unaware of the horrors and the nightmares happening immediately outside their vision.

An hour later she was still there so I went out and tapped on the window. This made her jump out of her skin. I invited her in for a smoke. Ha! She gave the impression of being too grateful and smoked most of the two joints I shared with her. She told me about her life, thankfully leaving me with hardly anything to say. She drove away on the wrong side of the road and it took an on-coming car to waken her with much hooting of the horn and flashing of lights. I didn't see her again for weeks after that.

It was around about the time Katie started to visit that, on top of everything else, I began having visions. All came from the sea. Most came at night when the world stopped breathing, in the hours before sunrise. Some came in broad daylight and these were the most frightening. Sometimes, I heard them whispering, talking amongst themselves, murmuring my name. At first, I thought they were regular people who had entered my house and were searching for me. They hid in gloomy corners or in any of the rooms I was not in. When I went to investigate, there was nobody there. Or they were mere shadows loitering on the edge, canny and flimsy and having the sneaky ability to move from place to place without noise or notice.

I saw a sea monster once and, thank fuck, only once. Think me mad. It's true. I was walking the shore, looking out at the horizon, treading as close to the sea's reach as I dared. I thought it was a sailing ship, an old schooner with its white sail cutting a tear in the sky. It appeared to change under my gaze, until the sail was clearly not a sail but a grotesque face with wide all-seeing eyes. With tentacles reaching either side, it was swimming toward the shore at great speed. I was totally and utterly exposed. The cold wind pierced my skin and emptied my soul until only the Wolf remained. Rowan was no longer. What terrified me more than anything was that I could feel that even the Wolf was afraid and shaking. He let out a desperate, piercing howl.

I ran to the house, bolted the doors and pulled the curtains of every window, afraid to look out. I found a corner and huddled into it and stayed there for two days, not eating or drinking. I wet myself and I shat myself. I kept myself from sleep by criss-crossing a razor blade across my forearms. Eventually, I settled. The Wolf returned, loving the spilling of so much blood. He had forgotten His fear. And, in a gesture of shared sympathy, I was glad He had.

I have been told I have an illness. Dr André Komsky told me. A great name for a shrimp of a man, don't you agree. He told me there was no cure for this condition. It could be treated. In theory, he said, I could live a normal life. What the fuck is that? I asked him. He ignored that comment and told me that it took a combination of medication and insight.

'Rowan, I shall tell you frankly. It would have been better to have cancer than this as cancer is easier to cure.'

'Can I swap then?'

'There are, however, a few things we can try.'

'That's good,' I said.' Otherwise, you would be out of a job, wouldn't you?' Dr André Komsky smiled at that.

'What are you thinking, Rowan?'

'I'm thinking you're wrong.'

'Wrong about what exactly?'

'About it all.'

'Well, that attitude may make it more problematic. Don't forget you need medication *and* insight.' He said, not smiling anymore. 'Insight is the hard bit.'

I left it like that. No point in an argument I wasn't going to win. Dr André Komsky and the like would always win. I wasn't even twenty-one and had been through all sorts of shit he didn't know about or ask about. Didn't ever mention my parents. Not once. Let me tell you that it doesn't feel like an illness. It feels like a me.

CLAUDE

My sole wish was that I had had children. Is that too much to ask? Sweet Jesus. I had the misfortune of marrying three times and, yet, I was cursed with the misfortune of not delivering even one offspring into this sad world of ours. What are the chances that I, as fertile as a man could be, would marry three women all of whom were barren? All of whom were unfruitful. Over the years, I have battled with the statistical improbability of this happening and, although it would be the easiest thing in the world to consider myself jinxed, I chose to believe it was fate. One of those things that was simply not meant to be. I take it as God's way of recognising that the women in my life were lacking or deficit in some unknown fundamental way. Given the frailty of their nature, they probably could have never coped with the inevitable turbulence of yearlings eager to experience life to the full. As a father, I would have worshipped the little ones and made sure that nothing, but goodness would come their way. When my last wife, Elise, miscarried at five months, I don't mind you knowing that I wept like a baby. I took the tiny human in my left hand and held it aloof in order to drink in her full beauty, hoping beyond hope, that any minute a flame would burst her into life. How could it be? *How could it be?* A girl as well, I christened her Anna. My Anna. Through to my core, I know I could have made this little woman happy.

We buried her in the garden of the house in which I live to this day. Being a fundamentally law-abiding person, I did it all officially by informing the Coroner. We did a wee service of our own during which I made my mind up to get rid of Elise as soon as decency allowed. She is long gone now.

Thankfully, she has melted away with the passage of time. I am left with a growing cherry tree whose roots are fed with my lovely progeny: never to breathe, never to speak, never to love. Every birthday, Christmas and Easter, I remember her - Anna, that is, not the bitch who was her mother - and I murmur words to the wind. I place a posy at the foot of the tree and try to remember what should be forgotten and to forget what should be remembered.

It is a remorseless pity, virtually a crime to reach my age, half a century or so and not to possess what must be the right of every man. I have not given up hope. My seed is as robust as it ever was. Jesus knows - and I must say this with a certain degree of pride - I have nurtured a sort of natural resilience. I have had to through all the diversity of my days. Despite having to trample over other people's shit, I have kept going, boosting myself up where I have been able, celebrating modest successes and appreciating casual encounters when they come my way. Wherever possible, I have shared with others what I have learnt, what was helpful, what was not and most importantly, what I may do differently if I were again confronted with the same set of circumstances. When I fell afoul of the law - not so difficult to do in a land where to fart twice in a row may amount to a minor misdemeanour - I have worked on myself. Not easy to do. I have had to look myself in the mirror and face head-on my own distress. That, ladies and gentlemen, is never a straightforward thing to do. The hardest lesson of all is simply and unashamedly to forgive yourself and find release from the burden of the past. Wave farewell to regret, recognise your wrong-doing and set the thing aside deliberately and with purpose. Excuse my boast, for which I will most likely need further exoneration, I have been able to refine the process of forgiveness into an art form. In short, my philosophy is summarised thus: if you wish to move on, pardon yourself unconditionally, let go and apply yourself to the life you have left. You'll see what I mean later.

*

My parents prepared me well for the world. Resilience is not a gift; it is something to be developed and worked on. I can blame my father for nothing; he did his best. To think of it, my mother tried as hard as a loving mother could to make me fit for purpose. Yes, they were unsurpassed given the circumstances of the time and the place and the culture they found themselves in. Certainly, they did their utmost given their perception and their values. Doesn't every parent give of their best? Does any parent really act out of evil? Does any mother or father purposely attempt to ruin another fellow human being? Who knows? The jury is out on this. If one does act in a calculating and contrived way, you could say it is merely an understandable, and in its way, perfectly reasonable thing to do. You could say, it can be none other than a legitimate response to the experience produced by the life they have been provided with. Think on it and report back.

It was the 1950's for God's sake. What do you expect? The war was still throwing its long shadow. Everyone, bar the very young, held a living memory of the conflict. People were still in turmoil, unable to make their minds up as to whether they should be imitating the past or facing up to a changing future. There was a prevailing and strange sense of grief and loss at odds with a heady air of anticipation.

Looking at our dear country, it was as if we had lost the war and the enemy had triumphed and condemned us to an impoverished and grey existence. The country was tinted grey. Let's face it. This very Island with its leaden bulk, sitting sterile in the sea, pallid and lifeless, washed-out and treeless, personified the entire country. My father, exposed to this hostile climate, had little choice but to exercise a discipline which tempered me into the man you see before you today. As soon as I was able to understand, I became painfully aware that I could readily find myself guilty of what my dear father called a 'transgression.' At first, I was slow to learn. Then I wasn't. One sweet day, it just clicked. Indeed, I, the young Claude Mayfellow's rate of learning accelerated alarmingly until I could read my father before he had articulated one single word. Quite a talent. Let's have an example. Staring at my father for longer than a second, even when waiting for a response from him, was considered a transgression. His punishment was always fitting and related in some way to the felony in question. The cruelty of it was pure genius.

'What are you staring at, Claude?'

'Nothing, father.'

'So, I am nothing - is that what you are saying?'

'No, not at all, Father, not at all.'

'Yet, you continue to stare.'

Conveniently, he had one of those contraptions in those days favoured by opticians. He generously reserved the punishment to one eye only, applied the device and left it in place for an hour, one eye blinking madly, the other unable to do so and both weeping a mixture of tears; tears of sorrow and tears of pain. In line with my father's military upbringing, exactly on the sixty-minute mark, he cheerfully removed the gadget to reveal a sore, unfocused, reddened and unseeing eye. He put his arm around me and put on a Sinatra record. A love I share with him to this very day.

Lesson learnt. Thanks Dad.

*

JC, what is it with people? What is it about the human condition which makes most of the contact between members of the species basically insufferable? Inexplicably, we crave relationships and thirst for connection. When we finally have it, we go through this impossible task of crushing the true self as we worry, fret, fuss and endlessly compromise. We try to fit in with, adjust to and/or accommodate some bastard or bitch who don't even know themselves let alone know us. I love my life, for sure, but I am surrounded by losers. Case in point, a new clot has moved into number 3. Apparently, he is "investigating" the folklore attached to this austere and magical Island. Weller, loser times a hundred, tosser times a thousand, has asked him to compile a record of all the myths, legends and stories arising from this bleak stone some of us call home. I haven't met the man - only seen him at a distance - but Eve has spoken of him. Are we meant to be grateful for his presence? I don't think so. Why did Weller choose a stranger anyway when you have locals whose blood is saturated in the traditions here? Moi, for example. Born and bred, on the Island. Like my father and his father and his father, going back centuries. True, I had some years out when father was posted to Gibraltar in 1960, but I came back. Of course, I came back. I belong here and always will.

Locally, rooted and booted, as they say, and knowledgeable from experience and through heritage. This Jack character has a *Masters* no doubt in some bollocking subject, but is he master of his own destiny I ask? From what I saw and what I am hearing, he may find falling over difficult. I will watch him. I don't want or expect any interference in my lifestyle or, indeed, into a particular scheme I have been harbouring recently. I shall see. I will be on my guard. I shall be cautious.

Since the unpredictable routines of my early years, I have attempted to structure every day carefully. It starts from a known place and it ends safely in a foreseeable and desired manner. Thus, I have lived here in this same house for over two decades already.

I love it with a passion. Even the mad cow on the end has her assets, assets going to waste, if you get my drift. So, I don't take kindly to new folks becoming my neighbour. I simply don't like it. People with *agendas* and *remits* - for Christ sakes!

*

I try not to think about the period of my life wasted in the clink. On the second occasion I was unjustly sent down as I honestly denied charges, I was clearly not guilty of. The jury was unduly influenced by emotion and sensationalism and more influenced by the headlines in the newspapers than by any real sense of justice. The world is unjust as we all know. A little movement of a little money and suddenly I am accused of fraud. I do what I can to adjust to a capricious world and, damn it, I am accused of tax evasion. Then they tagged on a minor charge to do with some so-called illegal (please!) DVDs I was passing on to some friends. Because I am of a certain age, because I chose to live alone, because I have now chosen to adopt a solitary lifestyle, I seem to fit a category of human being society appears reluctant to accept. This is prejudice in the extreme.

When I was taken away from the court, unnecessarily handcuffed, I was unaware how my basic human rights were about to be infringed. Dear Jesu, I put on a brave face. On the first incident I came up against the law of the land, I had yelled at the judge as he volunteered his opinion and issued the sentence. I gave him the bitter tip of my tongue and, as I had nothing to lose, thought nothing about restraint. The second and last time, however, although I had more good reason to cause an uproar, I stayed calm and remained as quiet as a veritable Julian of Norwich. I deliberately kept up a semblance of unshaken innocence. When they were roughing me up on the way to the horse wagon, they use to get prisoners from A to B, I maintained my cool.

'A year is hardly enough, you scum!' Words from the highest-ranking guard there - a man who was supposed to set an example and really should have known better.

I had a cell of my own - which was a good thing and entirely correct. I had a TV and my own bog and sink. My first thoughts were OK, this is what I paid taxes for. Yes, I can make this home. A year is only a year. Good behaviour: half, or less. The first thing I did was to have a shit and luxuriate in the familiar stink of my good self, my scent having been fittingly sprayed. On the following day, my cell door was left open and in came three thugs. Initially, I thought I was going to get away with a mere bad mouthing. It wasn't to be. Two held me down while the other one pulled down my pants and kicked me as hard as he could in the groin.

Once would have sufficed. Three times. Mercifully when they tried to force a bar of soap down my gullet, I partly lost consciousness and the guards waiting outside came in and made a little show of pulling the stooges off me. J fucking C, medical intervention was not afforded me nor were there any words of consolation or remorse given me. The offended organ turned a pitiful black and proved completely unusable for seven long, unhappy days.

EVE

Two things you should know 'bout me. The first is, that like Old King Henry I have been married six times. The second thing is that I know I am dying. It is around these two things that you will discover the main drives in me life lie.

How?...

First and foremost, I want to marry once more, a final finale, a seventh time. Put blunt, in these closing years, months, weeks, whatever I got left, I want to find love. Me second goal is to stay alive as long as I can in order to achieve the first goal. I will spell it out straight, I am no way ready to leave this good earth. I am nowhere near ready and I am pretty much determined not to go until goal one has been scored!

Every husband I have had, I have conjured. I have seen them before I have met them. In a dream, in a flash in me mind or a sudden vision. I have always known them before they have known me. Some I have spoken to and joked with way before they had been awakened to me. This is me bag. This gift is mine.

But, for the seventh contender, something has gone wrong. Me head has gone blank and me brain is as empty as a wartime pantry. This skull of mine is vacant as the sea outside this window. I cannot see the seventh man or sense the coming of 'im. Time is running out. The cancer, or whatever it is, advances every single day and I am worried that it will beat this seventh man to the finish line. So, this is a time for extraordinary means. I will do everything and anything to achieve them goals. This is clearly me last chance. Seventy plus years of age and I can already feel me soul moving this way and that within this body, bruising me from the inside and hard looking for a way out. I keep to me ways and will never have a doctor involved. For other people, it is fine. For one like me, it is forbidden and to this day, a doctor has never placed a finger on me person.

So, I am devising a plan - or plans I should say - to turn me fate from staring north to one which is staring south. This cannot be done on a whim, not by science or medicine or by wishful thinking. The usual cocktails and remedies are not good enough. This is a matter I must draw on all me experience and power in order to fix. As you will see, this is a dangerous course, a fickle thing and doubtless on the perilous side. All of me life, all the learning from me life, all the teachings of me own grandmother will need to be called upon and brought into force. If I really and truly wish to run down this path, this much is obvious and this much will be totally necessary.

*

There is, in fact, a third motivation I got the grandchildren Rachel and Tom. These are the children of me third child, Harry. He is the only child who has remained on the Island. Is it an evil for a mum to say that the other two just as well not exist for how much I see them. Paul emigrated to the mainland as soon as he could and is now a banker in London. I see him twice a year and still no kids. The oldest, me daughter Kaye, who should be right here to help her mum in her dotage, emigrated further than the son and owns a ranch in Oregon, a place I have not seen nor want to now. I did have another daughter, but she is with the Angels, as they say elsewhere. Here, on the Island, we say she is in the Sea of

Souls. Simone died without making her first year. No amount of magic could save her. I think I was too old, too greedy for more, too arrogant, too foolish, too something. Her ashes we gave to the sea, thrown from the beach on a calm trouble-free day when the waves were gentle. We threw roses after her. Red roses drifting away in a bright crooked line.

Harry stayed. He stayed and bought a Tudor cottage on the curve of the road which leads to the top of the Island. There he lived with the children and his wife Pippa, until, that is, she ran off with the local vicar. Appears the vicar was one of the few left in the English Church who believed in the power of the confessional. Pippa's confession, I found out later from Harry, was particularly graphic and so the required penitence of a similar nature. The pair disappeared on Ascension Day. You really couldn't make this stuff up!

Pippa obviously liked uniforms because Harry is also a man of uniform. He's a policeman. He's a copper, who, though his station is on the mainland, his responsibilities have always remained on the Island. They call him a locality officer. Sounds a tad formal but I think is nice. It ties him to the Island and the Island is where he belongs. When Harry goes off to work, mostly the children are at school, but gaps often show in their week and that's where Nanny Eve comes in. I love them coming here. Despite them getting older - Rachel is twelve, Tom is nine - they still enjoy coming to me. Needless to say, I spoil them. I consider it me joy and duty to spoil them.

Goes without saying, both children are wonderful. Tom is a breeze. He is a lively lad who leaps about like a kitten with a ball of wool. Not sure if he has a thought in his lovely head, but that hardly matters, does it. His heart is as big and as soft as a ripe melon. He throws himself at life and seems to enjoy every little thing which happens his way. Everyone loves him. Rachel is altogether different. Much more of a thinker. A cracking beauty as well to be truthful. Long black hair, perfectly shaped face, dark eyebrows which draw more attention to her dark brown eyes. The family joke, based loosely on the truth, is that a Spaniard, shipwrecked from the Great Armada, was washed ashore and coupled with one of the local babes, casting a Mediterranean strain into the blood of the Islanders. It's a good story. More than this, there is a quality to Rachel, an air of detachedness and calm. Not like being distant or remote, more like being strangely reassuring. This will sound odd but weirdly, I feel safe when she is around. Shouldn't it be the other way about? She is a gem for certain, a genuine precious stone and if I hadn't promised, I would definitely be passing all me knowledge onto her.

*

The history of the Island has forever been steeped in magic. The rumours of its beginnings were always edged with the supernatural. Some say that this Island of ours should have never existed. It's a quirk. Some call it an oddity, like it's an offence against the mainland. We stick out like a carbuncle on the rump of England. For eternity, they have despised us. They're suspicious of us. Our differences stand us apart. We wouldn't have it any other way. We have grown a thick skin of armour against the elements of the world. Mostly, the human elements!

Like all Island peoples everywhere, we are surrounded by an endless ocean under a sky vast as heaven itself. We

Island folk are made not by what is there, but by the nothingness around us. This describes the soul of the Island well enough. This given, or despite this, we have to build up our inner reserves and look for ways and means to control this mad world and explore how best to check what is clearly unbalanced in favour of death and bedlam. What am I talking about?

Magic. I'm talking magic!

Magic fills that gap between the seen and the unseen. On this rock we have always courted the old ways. It goes back centuries, before the time Joseph of Arimathea was meant to have dropped by these parts. We are talking a long way back. You could say magic takes the best of the church and puts it together with the best of nature. It doesn't matter what you say really. To me, magic takes a leap across that river between the heart and mind. It's all contained in the Book, which is safe enough, but nowadays outside me reach.

Anyways, those days have gone. Belief in magic is pretty much dead. The spilling of blood has become an unnatural taboo. Some round here would say the spilling of semen has taken its place. Everything has been explained away. Even the mysterious clout of all things sexual, has all but gone. In me early years, it was still common practice to not marry unless you were with child. Barrenness was worse than death. Before the sacred act, there was a simple incantation to say and everyone would say it. That is, the women, never the men. The ash from shipwrecked wood was drawn in the crevice of your most intimate part and mixed with two sentences I cannot say here.

Times are changing. Might the old days be returning. Are we moving backwards or forwards? We may be being thrown back to this past age. I hope this to be true.

Already, a portent made itself known to me just the other day. A lifeless dolphin was washed up on Deadman's Bay. That's bad, that's very bad. No storm to confuse it, not a gale driving it off-course. It lay there under a perfectly blue sky, an untouched and perfect creature with not an ounce of evidence to suggest foul play, cruelty or calamity. The lads buried it in a shallow grave on the cliff side and someone used the old magical symbol to mark its body. Not the cross of driftwood but a holey stone - one with a hole right through it - and a white feather set in it. It's a worry.

*

Forever on the lookout for other signs, I tally every minute change. I bring them altogether for me scrutiny and I tries to make sense of them. One change is that we have this character showing up: a stranger called Jack. He is studying our fair isle for old Weller's convenience. Weller has had this unhealthy attraction towards our folklore and the stories arising from this patch of earth on which we spend our time. Weller inherited this fascination from his father, who, unlike his insipid son was a story all by himself. Doubtless, we shall have this Jack snooping about and sniffing around. This worries me. Especially in these doubtful times. I sense the dolphin on the shore has started something. Its appearance gives me the spooks. I feel it in me bones. And this Jack. Looks like a puppy who has lost its tail. Perhaps I am being a little over-sensitive or guarded, but I think not.

I did try to be welcoming and 'ospitable. Me dump isn't made with anything like ease, nor does it come cheaply.

To give it to another is a real gift of some worth. He says he is from here by birth via his granddad. I cannot see that this is the case. I know all the residents here, Tophill and Underhill; I can go back at least four generations. Jack is either mistaken or slightly befuddled. Time will tell.

So, the four houses in our quartet of living dwellings are now full. In some ways, I favour it. Houses should be lived in. An empty house is a shame on us all, but it's a motley crew. Looking at them, a thought comes into me head. I cannot help it, I'm afraid. Sorry for one of me wicked thoughts. Looking at the three occupants, is it not the truth that we have the Mad, the Bad and with this new one, the Sad!

No sooner had I thought this than I hears an unnatural crash coming up from the beach. I peered out of the window. Fishermen were scarpering up the mound of pebbles. One had lost his rod and one his cute fishing stool. There is a boat a few hundred yards out keeling dangerously, the men shouting at each other in total confusion. "Oh dear, I am thinking," the Seventh Wave no less!

THE SECOND WAVE

Various sources - including Alexander Weller's Notes (1993)

In the beginning there was the Island, or so the myth goes, and the Island was the world. The Island drifted alone in the vast ocean of the world. The Island was so good that, after millennia, it spawned others of all different shapes and sizes. Some were huge, some were mere rocks, some became islands within islands. Yet this Island, the Island we call home, was the most important of all because it was the first.

This definitely didn't happen.

There remains a few who still believe in the sanctity of the Island. One native put forward the theory that the Garden of Eden had actually been located on the highest point of the Island. Unfortunately, he spent his final days telling this to his fellow residents in the County Asylum. Druids loved the place and carved it up into solar and lunar alignments, claiming that they reflected a cosmic reality whose essential teachings were sadly lost. It is also said that no less than Joseph of Arimathea docked here on his journey from the Holy Land on the way to Glastonbury where he planted the sacred thorn. The Druids had been waiting for a sign. When Joseph and his entourage landed on its beaches, they embraced the new faith, betraying the ancient "understanding" as if it had meant nothing and without bothering to employ their usual powers of discernment. So, the Island, we were told as children, became the earliest place to embrace Christianity north of the Sea of Marmara.

None of this probably happened.

Likewise, there are too many stories relating to how the thirty kilometres of beach which tethers the Island to the mainland was created. One theory alludes to an almighty storm which arose about ten thousand years ago. In one night, the sea contrived to gather billions of pebbles west and east of the Island. Dragging this tremendous bounty around the channel, as soon as it hit shallow water, it deposited its cargo. Thereafter, the wall of stone was assembled by the sea spitting shingle with extraordinary violence, pebble mounting pebble until the beach was formed.

This probably didn't happen either.

One myth talks about the Island as a floating fortress adrift in the channel, pilotless and pointless in its random sailings along an indifferent coast. The beach was in its infancy and loosely hung from the mainland like a finger pointing south. One day, if it is to be believed, the Island drifted too close to shore and became caught at low water and thus became snared to the spit of land. As soon as this occurred, the beach began its slow build, ensuring that the Island would never break free to drift again.

This, of course, contradicts the original myth and is probably even less likely to have happened.

Probably this happened: The earth became colder and the great ice age came. Everywhere, water was choosing its solid form and bound itself into blankets of ice of unbearable thickness, sucking up the seas and oceans, reducing their viability and exposing land hitherto submerged. After this incessant winter began its demise, the ice began to shift, starting its sluggish melt. The Island of stone emerged above the new waters. Manipulated by the collapse of the ice and the aggressive gestures of a newly invigorated virgin sea, mounds of earth, debris and shingle gathered in certain places. One of these places was this beach. Like an anchor's chain, it ultimately fixed the only sure route on to the Island.

And so, we have the Island: dangling like a bunch of grapes into the mouth of the channel. Let's be frank, it essentially has no purpose over and above the fact of its own existence.

History marks it out for its stone and as a safe haven for sailor and smuggler alike. Despite its proximity to the shores of England, the Island celebrates its inimitability and its isolation. There is a saying amongst the Islanders told to strangers moving there: "the first five hundred years are the most difficult."

JACK

There was a period in my teens when I experienced a series of religious visions. I kept seeing Jesus at the end of my bed, at least, that's who he said he was. This was way before I discovered LSD. I made the mistake of telling mum who, being the lapsed but hopeful catholic that she was, went to church for the first time in years and told the priest. They seemed very pleased with themselves and I had the feeling that for both it was some sort of solution. I was duly interviewed by two other priests. I hadn't much to say. Jesus smiled a great deal, told me his name, but failed to offer any tips for living or quips of wisdom. Before I could be assessed for sainthood, the visions stopped as abruptly as they started. The Catholic Church quickly lost interest. Mum had lost interest ages ago. That was when I actually began taking LSD.

I tell you this because it amounts to a metaphor which sums up my life. Something or someone happens which seems to hold a promise. Then something or someone stops happening, and the promise is lost. Hence, at one point, I thought I was a Taoist. The following month I was a frustrated Buddhist. I was both for a while and just became baffled. I was going to throw my hat in with the Quakers, but then decided to keep my hat firmly on my head. I struck on an idea to go eclectic and call myself a Berq. This was a deliberate ironic take on the word berk as it seemed so idiotic, I thought it might work. Berq stood for Buddhist Existential Reformative Quaker. I was its sole member and it began on a Tuesday and came to an end on the following Saturday.

Trish always struggled with these "musings" of mine.

In our endless break-ups, this was fertile ground to score points from me.

'You're never content with anything. You're forever looking for the next best thing, blind to what is right in front of you!' she said, pointing at herself. 'You are looking for solutions everywhere but here!'

These arguments usually ended in me exploding inside and smashing some item of furniture. Why did I do that? Well, needless to say, it wasn't because I hated our furniture. It was because I knew she was right. There was nothing solid in me. On one level, I could fool myself that a new worthy investment in some project or other was a way of trying to find the something I was obviously missing. I was hoping that a new challenge, a different challenge that I could get my teeth into, would lead to that essential missing piece of the jigsaw. A challenge which will sort me out, once and for all. In my late thirties already, I should have been preparing for my mid-life crisis, but I'm clearly not qualified for that as I haven't really lived the first part yet.

*

With the magnitude of the assignment before me, it was important to establish a routine most likely to meet with success. I work best in the morning. I tend to dip after lunch and, if the morning has been productive, I reward myself with a short nap, followed by a bath, a breath of fresh air, followed by an additional two-hour window of creativity. At this point I can justifiably relax and enjoy the remainder of the evening. Time for a treat: a book, a paper or maybe the pub.

To date, it hasn't quite worked like that. I am not sure whether it is the excitement of my new venture, the peculiarity of the place or the open-endedness of my stay, but I find myself uncannily resistive to any coherent routine. The first day I set the alarm for seven. I slept until ten. How did that happen? For years I had been sleeping terribly, waking up at three in the morning and huffing and puffing through the final hours of darkness. I move into this old house and I sleep a deep dreamless sleep from which I struggle to emerge. I eat my porridge - part of the aspirational routine. I go out walking the shore, studying the sky for change, scanning the shoreline for debris. I watch the waves which take a lot of watching. I time them as if it were a patient's pulse and am trying to guesstimate their current level of health. After coffee, usually an industrious crest for me, I end up popping down the pub and bar-flying my way through a prolonged lunch break. A chap called Mitchell was always in there looking for someone to chat with. This means an early release of my latent fatigue. I take to the bed, soothe myself to sleep with some humdrum fantasy and wake up at teatime. It's far too late for any meaningful application to my work. I may make a list or a plan for the next day. I may write a letter. Generally, I fluff about, watch television and the like, until I go down the pub for a second session of real ale.

Over a week has passed in this way. Largely, it's been a relaxing and a calming time. The closeness of the sea is something you can't take for granted. It's a presence you can't ignore. It demands your attention. Sometimes, I felt its pull and, before I knew it, I was out of the door drifting in that direction like I had been hypnotised. I wanted to throw myself in and give the sea a big hug. Other times, I sensed its crazy nature and wanted to stay away and give it some distance. The sea, in any regard, provided a good excuse: I had hardly written one word and hardly read one either.

I craved distraction and found it everywhere. Often the electricity failed, and the computer went down - hooray! Another excuse to go to the local for refreshment or go and chat to Henry, one of the locals who was always fishing offshore. I was half hoping Ellis would buzz down. That would definitely waste a weekend or more. It wasn't going to happen as he sent me a text saying he was going walking in the Dolomites with his new love-interest Fran. Then, out of the blue, I saw something which inspired me, though not quite in the way I expected.

I was getting up from my afternoon nap, feeling a little self-important, telling myself that I will reshape my strategy by nightfall. My usual thing. As I parted the curtains, I noticed Rowan, the "mad" neighbour living next door, as yet, not seen or spoken to, in her backyard with nothing on her feet, wearing a pair of jeans and a tee shirt, she was unrolling some sort of patterned rug. Hesitant as what to expect from this deranged individual, I quickly noted how attractive she was. Petite, slim, long black hair, rather pale, there was something pre-Raphaelite about her, which happens to be my favourite sort. I stepped back from the window slightly and began admiring her from the concealment of my darkened room. I was about to remove myself, suddenly feeling voyeuristic and slightly pervy, when she swiftly took off her top and her jeans and sat cross-legged and naked on her mat. Wow! She was sitting away from me towards the cliffs overlooking the sea, so from where I stood, I could not see her in her entirety, but could make out a cute ass and the swell of her breast under her arm. I was at once shocked and turned on, and managed to suppress my previous puritanical reaction. In short, I stood my ground. Please do not forget my sex life had been an entirely a one-handed affair for some time!

After what seemed to be an age, possibly twenty minutes, I once again tried to talk myself away from the window - *'you are a sicko, infringing on a private moment, guilty of a crime etc.'* When she finally completed her meditation, she saluted the air with a prayful gesture and got to her feet. She turned around and looked up almost immediately. Had she had known I was there all along? Lasting no more than a fraction of a second, I saw the whole of her beautiful body and she saw my opportune depravity. I stepped back into my room. At the very same time, I was transfixed by both her looks and horrified at my own behaviour. If I had, say, a knitting needle handy I would have directed it neatly into my own eye. With no such weapon in reach, I went downstairs, head bowed in shame and drank a bottle of red.

After this, a change came over me. Not much of a change, but a change nonetheless. A switch had been turned to "on" and I woke up. It may have been fuelled by guilt or embarrassment, who knows. Within an hour or two, I had started organising myself. Initially, I tidied the house, emptied the boxes in the hallway, found a place for the books and the trinkets and all the other surviving remains from my former life. Still energised, I polished the writing desk, filed the papers roughly into sections. I fired up the computer, deleted and created files, cleaned the hard drive, avoided looking at porn, defragged the C drive and ordered the relevant literature on the Island's history. By eight in the evening, I was pretty exhausted and pleased with myself so went to the pub as a reward. Who did I bump into as soon as

I stepped into the place? My other neighbour, Claude.

Up to this point, I had not met Claude either. I had heard him singing some Frank Sinatra ditty in his yard, but I hadn't met him, only waved to him from a distance. At the time, I thought he stuck his two fingers up to me, but I was obviously mistaken as he greeted me like I was a long-lost friend who had unexpectedly returned. He placed his arm around my shoulder, pulled me to the bar and bought me a pint of Cornish ale. He was loud and jovial, introducing me to his "mates" as the 'new boy on the block.' Which I suppose I was.

'Come and tell me all about yourself, young man!'

Although there was possibly only about fifteen years or so between us, his manner was that of a benevolent uncle; I was an eight-year-old who had just returned from Disneyland. He ushered me to the table in the corner where he eagerly bombarded me with questions. Although he inquired into this and that and I answered without reserve, I kept thinking that what he asked was more important to him than how I answered. He bought a second pint and kept up the deluge of questions, all of which were relevant and inviting and pulling me in with his enthusiasm. He called Weller a wanker and a money-grabbing landlord. He said Weller was using me to "mythologize" the Island in a way which suited his distorted view of the world. He may have been right of course, but Weller was the one paying the bills so, I decided to let it go. He also added that he should have employed a local as bringing in an outsider was 'a little controversial if not inappropriate.' I tried to outline my qualifications, but he wasn't interested. As a fallback position, I told him of my grandfather, Island born and bred.

'His name?'

I told him.

'Never heard of him,' came his chipper response.' You sure?'

'I know the name of my grandfather.'

'You sure?'

It would have been natural to become indignant. My grandfather had been denied twice in as many weeks, but another pint was forthcoming; cleverly and precisely the very price for swallowing my indignation. The evening melted on. Locals came and went, walkers popped in for refreshments and left refreshed. As some schools were already on holiday and the evenings growing light, the odd family came in for over-priced food and cheap wine. All was good. I was enjoying myself. I felt a sense of connection and belonging and convinced myself that this was all beneficial and contributory to my primary task.

I found out that Claude had been born on the Island, a stone's throw from where we were now sitting. He had been married three times.

'Not married now though?' I asked.

'Free as a bird, my friend. I should never have got entangled with any of them, truth be known.'

'Any children?'

'Sore point, old son.'

By now I was trying to stop myself swaying from side to side, but I was not too far gone to realise not to push the subject. I quickly asked him if he had any stories to tell which may help me in my task. This was all that was needed to start Claude launching into a plethora of stories and anecdotes.

'My Jesus. Look at her!' Claude declared in mid-conversation. I looked around and couldn't make out who he was referring to. 'The blonde one, the blonde one, man. Can you not see? Are you blind?'

I looked around again. I saw a family only, parents with two kids, a boy and a girl. The girl was blonde.

'A little young,' I laughed, trying to join him in his joke.

'How is she young?'

'Well, how else? In her years, of course. She must be younger than sixteen.'

'My god, what is wrong with you, man. Is she attractive or not?' I turned unsteadily round to her.

'Yes, I suppose she is.'

'Good man. Let me put a scenario to you. If a girl is nineteen but looks like a fourteen-year-old, would it be right and proper to fuck her should she wish it?'

'Yes, she is over the age of consent.'

'Ok, let us say she looks like a thirteen-year-old and has the maturity of a fourteen-year-old. Is it still right to fuck her?'

'She is above the age of consent, so yes.'

'So, you are saying that her chronological age is more important than how she looks or how mature she is? OK - so put it a different way. Let's say we have a fourteen-year-old girl who looks nineteen and has the maturity of a nineteen-year-old. Shall we fuck her?'

'No, not at all, her age - she is too young. It is as uncomplicated as that!'

'She is beautiful, she really wants it and she has had lovers before yet, you say no. Yet, you are happy to fuck the immature nineteen-year-old who doesn't know her up from her down?'

'Yes, I am!'

'Then sir, you really are a bit of a pervert!'

In my drunken state, it was hard to string a quick response together. I thought about saying something about the law is the law, but Claude would boohoo that quick enough. This was my first encounter with my neighbour, I reminded myself and let it go.

*

I woke up in my own bed amazed to find myself there. I couldn't remember how the evening ended or how I had made my way from pub to house. My head hurt, I felt queasy. I tried to retrace the evening with only partial success. I remember a few of the stories Claude told me. More unsettling, I remembered Claude's comments on the young girl. His manner was such that I could not tell if he was being serious or ironic, if he was toying with me or just fooling around. At one point, he began to sing a local song about first love - at least, that's what I thought it was about at the time. I know he mocked the project I was involved in, betting me that I would never complete it. I can't recall what we had bet. He kept mentioning a girl called Bessie, but I couldn't recall who she was in relation to him.

Above all this, my other neighbour's remarkable naked body kept coming to mind. In one day, I had been introduced to the remaining two tenants in the terrace. With Rowan, I would have welcomed a more conventional introduction, although I probably wouldn't have seen what I had seen. This image served to soften the drag of the booze, placing me temporarily into a different reality. I was determined to bump into her again as soon as possible.

As I came downstairs, I noticed a dirty white envelope on the mat. On the front in capitals:

'BRILL TIME LAST NIGHT, MATE - GOOD LUCK WITH BESSIE. SET OF KEYS AS PROMISED. P. S. AS GESTURE OF GOODWILL HAVE THROWN IN A CAN OF PETROL - SEE FRONT SEAT!'

Opening the door, a rust bucket of a car was parked on the gravel pathway outside my house. Bessie, no doubt, the last thing I wanted or needed. I would make sure he had it back by the end of the day.

I settled for tea and lots of it as my stomach couldn't handle coffee. I turned the radio on, turned it off. I turned the computer on, turned that off as well. I looked at my desk, had a vague recollection of yesterday's resolve, turned away and slumped onto the sofa. No sooner had I sat down again when there was a loud knock on the door: Claude.

'Great evening, yes or no?'

'I'm trying to remember!'

'Must have been great, hey? You like your new wagon?'

'Claude, sorry I can't accept it. Thanks, but I don't need a car. I don't want one.'

'Well, she's yours now, man - and that's what I popped round for. We agreed £200. I will settle for fifty today, the rest can follow as and when. A little short at the mo, you see. Especially after last night's beer fest!'

'Sorry Claude for messing you about. I can't call to mind buying it from you.'

'Well, a deal is a deal is a deal. We shook on it. You were more than happy last night.'

'I was drunk!'

'Well, my friend, I'm not leaving 'til I get a down payment of some kind. You can't go around deceiving people, you know. On this Island we used to tar and feather liars.' He was laughing but he side-stepped me, entered the house and walked directly into the lounge.

'Claude, I was drunk,' I said, slight desperation in my voice.

Turning about quickly, he poked me in the chest.

'We had an agreement and you owe me some cash. Don't let me down, Jack.'

'Let's not fall out about this.'

'Let's not. Give me fifty and I'll be away, and you will have a reliable mule of a car. You can get around so much easier. Think of it. You can double the pace of your research. At least, you can once you paid the car tax, that is.'

'I haven't the cash, Claude.'

'How much you got?'

'Twenty, thirty.'

'Ok, as a gesture of my goodwill and considering you are new abouts here, let's agree a first payment of thirty.'

My head was ringing, and I wanted him out of the house. As soon as I gave him the thirty quid, he was all smiles again and left the house promising another drinking session soon. I was left looking at the crock of shit outside my door. Once, I guessed, it must have been red.

*

I wasted the whole day and had to wait for the following morning for some reprieve. The headache from hell had vanished and left a calm vacancy in its wake. I was euphoric with relief that I could think once more. I dismissed the dilemma of the car outside as a misunderstanding which would soon be sorted. With something approaching elation, I spent the day reading Wellers' notes.

Tales of smugglers, witches, vermin, Vikings and shipwrecks ran randomly from page to page. There was no order or logic to them. Some stories were captured in short paragraphs, others ran on for pages. Some were interesting, some fascinating and others mundane. Collectively, they were disjointed, lacked coherence and carelessly muddled fact with fiction. What came across to me though was the depth and diversity of their content. Three severed heads were found in the foundations of a house in Underhill, their headless bodies coming out in the fog searching for their missing parts. Rituals of bloodletting started around 1200 AD perhaps in response to the plague. A mummified horse was discovered bricked up in the wall of one of the oldest houses on the Island near to the southern well. It was found in 1604 but thought to be from around 850AD. More recently, a submarine was lost off the coast in the war with all hands lost off Deadman's Bay. It was said that on windy winter nights their cries for help could be heard.

As I read through the bundle of notes, several intrusive thoughts kept invading my concentration. I tried to keep on track. You can imagine, the enduring image of Rowan kept piercing my thoughts. How could it not? I hadn't had any sex now for centuries. Putting aside a one-nighter with a friend, Rupi, who basically felt sorry for me, the last period of regular sex was with Trish two years ago. This was an outrageous record by any standards, even by my own. The drunken night itself: the jokes and laughter, the flow of the beer and, in the end, somehow ending up with a car which would have looked better at home in a scrap yard. Then there was Claude, I wasn't sure how to take the man. Friendly and accepting on the one hand, disconcerting on the other. I had no recollection of the car purchase or how we got onto the subject in the first place. I felt I had been had. Of the three tenants in my row of terraces, it was only the old woman on the end who was anything like normal.

I tried to keep myself on task, it was useless. Surrounded by a pile of notes and scribbling, I began to question what I was doing on this rock. Who was I kidding? I had messed up my chance with Trish and had effectively ran away. I ran away. Let me explain, when we met Trish and I were roughly the same in terms of what we wanted. Our expectations of the future were on a par. The way we saw the world was mutual; we shared a common understanding of our experience. Then she changed - or was it that I failed to change. She wanted to travel to Asia and after that, seriously try to start a family. She had been pregnant several times, all ending in miscarriage. Trying again would mean more heartache, IVF and all that shit. Full of doubt, I realised I was doing everything to avoid this conversation. I wanted life to continue as it was, just the two of us. When she kept raising the subject, she cottoned on that I had reservations. This resulted in another bout of arguments and conflict. Enough was enough so I left. We tried one last time and then I literally ran away, eventually ending up here on the Island. Not surprisingly, I hadn't heard a word from her. I could pick up her anger even from this distance. What was I doing? What did I know or care, for that matter, about the history of this Island anyway? Perhaps, Claude was right, the work should be carried out by a *real* local, not by someone whose grandfather was allegedly born here in the last century and yet no one has heard of.

I picked up some of the papers again and came across the whole sub-file on the phenomena of the Seventh Wave. Weller had scribbled on the margin of his own notes: *part of the Island's covenant - royal seal - this gives the meaning meaning.*

In amongst the bundle, I came across a light pamphlet by one Robert Flann entitled: *The Supremacy of the Seventh Wave.* I thought the title alone to be rather odd and foreboding. The Seventh Wave was, apparently, a local myth with global echoes. The author listed connections with Atlantic fishing, Pacific surfing and a certain relationship with the south westerly. He gave two stories which "demonstrated" this phenomenon graphically. The Seventh could bring both good and evil. One described a family holidaying in the sixties whose toddler son had been consumed by a sudden colossal seventh wave. The other one was more positive, a would-be shipwreck in the Victorian era, which had been thrown onto the beach, saving the lives of every member of the crew. I had to admit that the *idea* of the Seventh Wave aroused my curiosity more than any other story I had come upon so far.

ROWAN

Often, I do not know where I live out my life: in my head, in the world or in some strange place in between. Am I Rowan living in a house by the sea or am I living in my skull in some other place? When I hear or see stuff, to me it looks real, it acts real, it smells real enough. If you ask anyone else, I find out that they don't know what I'm on about. I don't mention the Wolf or I'm sure they would take me in and throw away the key. I keep it all to myself. The visions and the whisperings I hear, are they real or false? The message I get from the world is that these experiences are wrong and should be crushed. I ain't so confident. Either I am one messed up silly bitch or there's some other fucked up thing going on. Who knows?

Every clue to my current situation lies in the past. I dig up the ruins from the past or they force their way into view. A thousand half-remembered scenes and fucked up memories. I come to some reason why this is this and why that is that, however ridiculous. Why have I ended up here and not there? Why by the sea and not by a lake? Why on an Island and not in a valley? Why the sick feeling of being lost and never the buzz of being found? It's like torture.

I have one memory which trumps all others and is defo the source of all my shit. I was eight years of age and travelling in the back of the car, Mum and Dad in the front. I remember they were talking about something I didn't understand. I could sense they were getting angry with each other. They were raising their voices and talking over one another. I had Charlie on my lap and was talking with him about school. Charlie was my teddy, a beaten-up guy which had been my mum's teddy when she was a kid. Charlie had been patched up, refilled and stitched all over. One stitch was around his mouth and had been done in a hurry, so he wore a permanent sneer as a result. I liked that about him.

I always had this feeling that someone else was there, that something else was beside me in the car. What happened next. My mum leant over and pulled the steering wheel down with unusual force. I remember thinking that this was not normal. She never did anything like this. The car took off. It lurched powerfully to the left; we left the ground. Dad went to correct it, but this just added to the confusion. We left the earth and the car began to turn in the air. When I woke up, I was in hospital. There was my aunt and uncle beside me holding Charlie, only his body, his head was missing.

'Where's the rest of him?' I asked them.

'We have looked and looked and looked and cannot find his head. We're so sorry, Rowan. The fireman joined us looking for it. It wasn't anywhere,' my aunt's voice trailing off.

Why firemen? Had there been a fire? I couldn't remember. Had Charlie's head been burnt and yet his body had been saved without a mark on it?

'You're in hospital, Rowan. There was a terrible accident. Have you any memory of it? You were in the car. You were coming to see us. Do you remember any of it, Rowan?'

'Where's Mum and Dad?'

My aunt was beginning to cry. I could see she was trying to hold it together.

'They didn't make it, child.'

'What didn't they make?'

'They didn't make it.' She looked hopelessly to her husband.

'They died, Rowan.' It was my uncle speaking.

'They died in the car accident.'

I couldn't understand what they were saying. I heard the words but not the message.

'Give me Charlie.' She seemed afraid to give him to me. She very slowly extended her hand to me. I kissed the air where his head should have been. It became a warped fucked-up joke of mine: This was the day that we both lost our heads.

I relive this bedside scenario most days. Not every day, just most days. I will pick up Charlie and give him a cuddle. You never know, one day he may grow back his head.

*

After a terrible night's sleep, where I kept dreaming of sinking into a muddy hole, I woke up feeling nauseous and had to run to the loo to throw up all the crap I had eaten the previous evening. Sudden disruptions in my body always troubled me. I decided there and then to cleanse myself. This was hard work and necessitated a series of rituals. One was swimming in the sea. I got up at sunrise and stepped into the surf without questioning my motive or recognising its strength. I rushed in regardless and allowed the water and my fear free rein to pour over me. It was fucking cold. It was never warm. The cold was as much part of the ritual as the danger was. The sea here has its own intelligence. It is whimsical, callous and murderous. The dead lost in its belly outnumber the living by many. Stories of people diving under the waves and never surfacing again are common. It happened to one of my school teachers. He dived into a relatively calm sea. Under he went, his family whooping at his bravery. Within a minute, the whooping had become wailing. The sea offered no clues, not giving up one secret. He had been taken whole down its throat in one greedy gulp. He was a religious education teacher as well and the joke went round that he had tried to walk on water and failed.

After the swim, I starved myself for four days - only lemon juice and green tea. This gave me the wonderful kick I had been pining for. This denial of myself and the slowing of my small body and its moody obsessions were a natural high. After this, I meditated in the yard. This acts as the full stop to the whole purging process. All in the nude, of course. Every stage as naked as I was born. I need to reduce the battle between me and everything else rest by removing all barriers, as much as possible, real or imagined.

This time, right at the end, I pack my things up, salute the sky, turnabout and see that I am being spied on. I am being watched by my new neighbour. How long he has been there I have no idea? What need he is meeting? I don't have a clue, though I can imagine. I dash into the house and feel he has spoilt what I have been trying to achieve. I immediately didn't like him, this imposter. As punishment, I decided to avoid this wanker. Why is he here anyway? To record the stories of the Island, Eve says. Come on, give it a rest. I have only glimpsed him a few times in passing, to me he comes over as a lost kid. Like you can see the boy in the man. You can see the bullied idiot, kicking stones by himself alone in the deserted corner of the playground. Already I know Claude has sunk his teeth into him. I sometimes come across Claude but mostly, I ignore him. Sometimes I might speak, not often, although I notice I seem to be seeing him more regularly of late. The last time he mentioned the newcomer, it wasn't complimentary. Let's hope they have an interesting friendship.

*

Ideas are not healthy. Not for me anyway especially not if they arise in conversations with Zac. He arrived yesterday, without warning or announcement. He assumes I am in and walks straight into the house, talking away like I had seen him the day before and not weeks ago. He made no apology for the fact that he was high on *magic* and smelling of vodka. Zac knows no middle ground. He is either in the ether (*this crazy hazy life*) or down in the depths (*lower than dead - dead would be good.*) Katie's advice is that if she had her way, she would write Zac down in my care plan as someone to avoid at all costs. She reckons he's bad for my mental health. Well, I can't stop him, nor do I really want to. He may have "schizofuckingphrenia" - he refuses to say it any other way - but he has the loveliest dick I have ever seen. Though getting to it is something of a problem. There's his endless chat, his philosophising and then, sadly, there's his delusional obsessions about his phallus - or Mr P as he calls it.

'Rowan, you will never guess.'

'Zac, what is it now?' I didn't say the now.

'Guess?'

He was already in and opening my last bottle of wine. He glugged the wine into a mug, none for me, and lights a cigarette, all in one movement.

'What did I say would never happen?'

'Piss off Zac. How do I know what you said would never happen?'

'Falling in love...' he pronounced each word in slow time. He didn't like it much when I shrieked with laughter.

'That's good, Zac,' I said back to him, glugging my own wine into my own mug, lighting my own cigarette, but without Zac's zen-like skills.

'Let me describe her.' He slumped onto the chair and swung his legs over one of the arms.

'Must you?'

'Do I detect a little cynicism in your tone, Rowan. Or are you feigning indifference? Or are you to all intents and purposes jealous?'

'Get on with it, for Christ's sake!'

'Cathy - that's her name - she's a sensual, voluptuous woman, a real woman. Rowan, you hearing what I'm saying?'

'Does that mean she's fat?'

'You Rowan Clayton are a philistine. Tear out your tongue. She's how women were meant to be. Not thin and waif-like.'

'Like me, you mean?'

'She has the cutest face: blue thoughtful eyes, not the usual brown. A high intelligent forehead, with a surprising cheeky turned-up nose. Did I say she's Irish? The lilt of her accent is enough to bring life to the most lifeless of penises. Her sentences are songs, Rowan, pure music. Tits so large there must be regions so far unexplored. You could lose yourself in there for several days.'

'What happened to your lifetime obsession with *petite* ones?'

'Ha! Clever. That's how I know that it is love, the real thing!'

'So, how did you meet this Cathy?'

'Ignoring the creep of scepticism, if not spitefulness, again, I shall continue. I met her just last week - only last week!'

'But how and where?'

'Last week.' He was becoming vague.

'Yes, I know when,' I say. 'How about the how and where?'

'OK, she's working with me, part of the team.'

'You mean she's a bod, working for the Trust?'

'Who says you can't bridge the divide? Yes, ok, she is a professional.' I stared at him waiting for him to tell me more.

'My psychiatrist. Would you believe it?' he screamed at me in excitement. 'My very own new fucking psychiatrist turns out to be the love of my life!'

'Christ in heaven, Zac-twat!'

'You have a lot to learn about love, Rowan, a lot indeed!' This time he was absolutely serious.

Love didn't stop Zac coming to bed with me, but we didn't have sex, which suited at least one of us. For a start, we had gone to the pub and after, bought another two bottles of wine in the shop. I knew it was a mistake, the whole thing, inviting him in, boozing up relentlessly with a few cigarettes of skunk-plus to boot, but it happens to be a mistake I like to make. There are some things an individual gears up for; doing stuff they know is bad for them and yet they do it anyway, forever repeating the delightful pattern over and over again ad nauseam. It's the ad nauseam bit that is really the incentive, the reassuring sense that things will persist forever in its predictably fucked-up way, until the world tilts off its axis. We do what we do because we like it. We never do what we do because it's good for us. Guess what? I'm talking about me.'

We went through the well-rehearsed performance of getting pissed, having a laugh, enjoying one big row about bollocks neither of us could remember the next day and then hitting the sack, drunk, deflated, blissfully resigned to the fact that we had burnt through the cycle once again. It was fun, but when it came to intimacy, Zac began talking quietly for the first time that day, like he had instantly sobered up. This wasn't his public voice, the don't-give-a-shit voice, this was the Real Zachariah Crane speaking.

'Rowan, Rowan, you awake?'

'Of course, why are you whispering?'

'It's starting again, the thing. It's starting again.'

I knew exactly what he meant. The persistent delusion which frightened him was beginning. He believed that his prick was an alien. I don't mean metaphorically either. We can both laugh about such a belief at other times. *The alien is seeking new life, entering the black hole, warp drive and so on.* Not when it's happening, nothing to laugh about then. Zac was at his most serious and desperate. Shame, I was thinking, the alien looked wide awake to me; handsome, upstanding and curious. Unknown to Zac, I too, had to pull myself back from holding it in the flesh and instead, settle for holding it in my mind. My body was behaving strangely itself, so I couldn't land the entire blame on Zac.

Poor Zac, none of this was his own fault. The poor bastard was a fuck-up of his family's own making. His dad had been a diplomat with the Foreign Office and spent lengthy periods out of the country in places such as Egypt and Tunisia. Maybe that's where his Dad learnt what pleasures he favoured. It began when Zac was ten, right out of the blue, without warning. His father was home on leave and downstairs getting drunk with a few of his Foreign Office mates. Zac went to sleep listening to their laughter and swearing and chatting. Sometime in the night, his father came into his bedroom and basically dragged him out of bed, without saying so much as a word to him. Suddenly, Zac was standing in his pyjamas in front of his father and four other men.

'Whose first?' His father had asked.

The man who already had his prick out approached Zac and slapped him hard in the face with the back of his hand. His father had laughed out loud. Throughout the ordeal, all Zac could remember was the sight of his own prick. Despite his dread and fear, he wet himself at one point, he recalls the absolute resilience of his own body, responding magically to an unfamiliar desire and totally independent of his own self-hatred.

*

We awoke to a hammering on the door. I stumbled out of bed, half clothed, half asleep.

'You never will guess what I have been through?' It was Katie, talking as if in mid-conversation, walking into the house much as Zac had done the day before and presenting me with the same guessing game. She had seen her new boyfriend in a car on the causeway, not alone going to work as he had told her, but with another woman. She had immediately pulled over and phoned him up and he had told her he was in the office making an early start. All at the same time, Katie managed to be defiant and jealous and tearful and resentful.

'Can I never find someone? All I want is a man I can trust, just one man. That's all I ask, just one decent man. Anyone would do!'

'Trust me,' I said to her. '*Anyone* will not do. That's the mistake you are making, Katie.'

As she ranted on, I heard the back-door slam; Zac making his escape. Just the wind, I told her. She wasn't interested anyway and repeated her story all over, this time finding echoes in her former relationships.

'Have you got any of that weed left. The good stuff.'

I was beginning to despair about the quality and motive of my professional helper. Eventually, give her her due, she came around to me and abruptly looked at me for the first time that day.

'So how are you Rowan?'

'Good, ta.'

'You are looking good. What you been up to?'

'Nothing really.'

'Nothing's doing you well then. Have you put on weight? You look so healthy, fresh, kind of flushed. If I wasn't your worker and a lesbian, which I'm not by the way, I would absolutely fancy you. You look...vibrant. Yes, vibrant, I would say.'

I was doubly despairing. Is this what they teach in social work training? In sensible mode, Katie had identified issues to do with my boundaries. I didn't know where I stopped, and the rest of the world started. Hello! She said she had to leave by eleven at the latest and left at twelve. She reversed her car into the new bloke's wreck and rather than knocking on the door, she left a note under his windscreen wiper.

'Silly place to park. Won't see you next week, probs

the following one. Will text.' She shouted from the car and gave me a wave as she drove onto the road.

I went back to bed. I woke up with a start about an hour later. I looked at myself in the mirror. I did look good. Too good. Far too good, considering I had only just done the ritual. I bared my belly and stroked its slight curve.

Fucky! Fuck! Fuck! The distortion of my body, the uncertain sensations muddling through, the vomiting. I am a bloody fool; I'm fucking pregnant again. How could this be? You fucking joking? I knew exactly how it could be. Was I cursed? Was it me or this shitting Island?

I looked out of the kitchen window over to the cliffs. The rising cliff is my rising shame. When I was twenty, I had an abortion. The whole ordeal left me scarred and battered. So, when I became pregnant again four years later, I thought I would keep it to myself. I would keep away from doctors and avoid any decision. I deliberately didn't want to be given a choice. Not a soul knew I was carrying, least of all, the father. He had buggered off anyway. Not a soul knew I gave birth to a baby boy, months before he was due. Not a soul knows that he took one breath and died. Not a soul knows where my boy is buried.

Here we go again.

CLAUDE

Jesus F Christ - what is the bloody matter with the world? When did people start being so gullible and naive? It's as if the whole of England has been sheep-dipped in some sort of drug which allows compassion to filter through, often in a particularly gushing form, and yet stops dead the power to discern, the power to make sense, the power to see reality. In short, the faculty to perceive the world as it actually is appears to be a lost art. For Pity's sake. Am I to be forever surrounded by morons, literally and figuratively? They are so far up their own arses that they are blind to anything but their internal fartings and gurglings and don't stand a chance of seeing what is really happening.

When you see what you want you, take it. What in heaven above is wrong with that? Be honest, I say to others, be straight and everyone knows where you stand. This pussy footing around, not stating what you really are, feel or want, drives me to despair. Where's that going to get us? Exactly where we are now. A nation of woolly airy-fairy shitfaces who put up with all sorts of injustice and nonsense.

Take these people who I share my terrace with. What are they like? How did I end up with such a motley crew of individuals? A bunch of losers, I have no doubt of that. How I differ from this horde? I look at my situation in the cold light of day. I look at my circumstances and I think how can I make the most of this life I find myself in. I make plans and I see them through to their desired conclusion. I make sure I have objectives, targets, aims. The criteria for each project is that it must thrill me and energise me and must be guaranteed to meet with inevitable success.

To make life at least a little interesting you have to *see* what you want and then you have to see people as nothing more than entertainment. Life is chess. It is as plain and straightforward as that. I feel sorry for those of you who either can't or don't want to see that or fail to be true about the process in which we are all participants. When you have a direction and you match that direction with determination, you have motivation. I have noticed how the universe loves motivation. Recognising the persistence of a mere human being, me in this case - the universe helps, it yields, it facilitates the movement forward. The Lord, the prophets and whoever else you care to mention know this vital truth.

The other evening, I bumped into that new up-start living in number three. He's the basket-case who thinks he's going to tell me something about an Island that is almost an extension of my own cock. What's his name? Jack. Yes, Jack. As I was drinking him under the table, I saw an ideal opportunity coming. All friendly, I bought the tosser drinks all night and casually spent our time together dropping subtle messages, egging him on and delicately manoeuvring him into position. I learnt the little lech has a thing about Rowan. How dare he? If anyone is to explore that particular territory it will be yours truly. She is so obviously my game. Anyway, he is full of guilt at leaving his precious Trish. Boohoo. Is that a tear I see? Well, as you know, guilt lends itself nicely to manipulation and I could have got him to do almost anything I wished for. Add in the fact that the ale they serve in these parts has the capacity to fuse the opposing sides of your brain together and triumph upon triumph, I managed to sell him my old banger for £200. It's worth about £2.99. It hasn't worked for a year and I was wondering what to do with

the shit heap. As the Lord provides, along comes Jack.
So yesterday I woke up as early as sense allows and pushed the crate from outside my place at the back to outside his in the front. I pushed the keys through his letter box. Already he's in my debt and shitting himself. Just where I want him, thank you very much.

*

When I say Rowan is my game, I mean just that. As soon as she moved in, I knew her for what she was and decided there and then to treat her with the appropriate level of disdain. People wear the prevailing attitude of their life like clothes. In my case, resilience, courage, humour, to name a few. Fear, self-loathing and anxiety in the case of young Rowan. She is as expected, innately frightened of the world, the people in the world and particularly herself. Why not use this as an advantage? You could say, Rowan and I are a perfect match. She exudes fear and, just like the shark can smell a single drop of blood in an ocean of saltwater, I can smell fear a mile off.

With Rowan, I have been playing it cool over the last few months. I have adopted a somewhat aloof, rather philosophical stance. I carry a book under my arm as a sort of signal prop. I speak to her with wit and vigour, peering over my glasses to strike home a particular message. As predicted, I perceive the loony is slowly falling for it. The fearful are so easily impressed as they are constantly looking for a rescuer in one guise or another. They are forever scanning the horizon for a solution to their anxiety.

I play the hand the Almighty has given me, and I play

it well, even if I say so myself. I have worked on some females over the years, before attacking my prey. A master like me never puts all his eggs in one basket. Gradually, I have held my gaze, holding young Rowan in my eye. I undress her every evening and know how she would look naked. She must be about thirty but delightfully with the body of someone much younger, someone half her age maybe. How interesting is that. I kept encouraging myself, which is half the battle, telling myself, amongst other things, that God had created such a little pert ass for a little pert reason.

Now this new freak of a neighbour was planning on hitting on her, I decided to up the ante and increase my pace. I don't want that imp creeping all over her. Against me he stood not the slightest chance, but one must refrain from complacency. My moves were slow and cautious. I didn't want to scare her off. I knew she liked a smoke. Bloody Jesus, sometimes the stink of skunk emulating from her house could have constituted an environmental hazard. I managed to procure a bag of weed from some twat who came into the pub every now and then. Ganja Ginge, they called him for understandable reasons. The boy is a cretin with a shock of marmalade hair, grossly pale skin and disgusting teeth. I rightly surmised that pushing blow is probably the only way he gets to talk to people. Next time I was with Rowan, I dropped into the conversation, as naturally as a seal slipping into water, a suggestion as to whether she liked to partake. Boy, did she like to partake. We got through the £20 bag in an afternoon. I was whizzing, but she was higher than the stratosphere. A little manipulation on my part, I confess. I feigned some intakes, allowed her to hog the joint and generally kept alive an edge of consciousness for the purposes described. And before you knew it, I was sharing the sofa with her with carefully rehearsed, but amazingly artful accidental touching of her tits.

I didn't push it and left it like this, having planted my seed as it were. At this point, she was still under the impression that I was not a threat. That I knew would change in time. Not, I must add, because of my own wilful intentions, but because of her own dippy idiocy.

EVE

I keep changing me mind. I cannot decide whether if I rolled all the six husbands into a single chap, they would become the best or the worst of the species. There are so many pluses, but sadly, so many minuses as well. Two were particularly handsome, two interesting and two were as ugly as stone. Three are still living and three are with Jesus. Ben committed suicide so maybe he isn't with Jesus. I am really unclear on this particular matter. Strangely, although this was the shortest and the oddest of all me marriages, he is the one I think about the most.

My son Harry pulls me leg about the number of men in me life. I think it's his way of coping with it all. His teasing gave me an idea, which I apply myself to when I cannot find sleep. When you have been married the number of times I have been, you can look at your life in figures. Yes, you heard right. For example, the average length of a marriage is nine years and two months, for instance. October was the most favoured month to get married. Shorter husbands fared better than their taller counterparts. Their average age when I married them was thirty-eight years and four months. And so on. I should write a book about me life, a book with chapters named after each husband and dotted with graphs and tables, if I can get someone to do them for me. "Maths Meets Romance." It would be new, different and juicy and, though I know I would never write a word, if I did people would buy it, I am absolutely convinced. They may begin to see their own lives in terms of figures. They may begin seeing the patterns in their lives and in the rhythm of their days, as I do. They would begin to see how well matched their inner life is with their outer one. Thoughts turn into soap operas.

Suppose, how you feel is how it is.

As I said, Ben definitely trumped the others. I suppose I miss him the most and loved him above the rest. Poor man was plagued with a sort of twisted sadness. That's why he liked the drink, I think, because only when he was drinking, did he feel safe. He wasn't an alkie, please understand, but when he was drinking, he was at his best: jovial, warm and generous. Without it, he was a frightened animal, more timid than frightened, more shy than timid. When he was at his most defenceless, he would curl up beside me and call me Mummy. I didn't judge him for that.

I knew very little of his past really. He turned up on the Island after one of the worst storms we had had in years. He said he was from up north and when he was made redundant, he decided to up and go anywhere to make a new start. He headed for the coast and made it to us. Ben said he had been married once to an "evil mare" who chipped away at him until there was hardly anything left. A year later, the job went, and he said it made him understand the "lightness" of his life. The roots, he thought were in place, turned out to be more in his head than in his blood. Fortunately, they had had no children, so there was no stake in the future either.

He said his life started when he first stepped foot on the Island. At first, he lodged in the pub and worked there for a while. He odd-jobbed for whoever wanted him. One day, I wanted him. He plumbed in me new washing machine and never went back to the pub. For some reason, Harry loathed him, just didn't like him and would never give him a chance to prove otherwise. It may have been 'cause Ben was younger. He was far to close in age to Harry for his liking. He said Ben was a drifter and a waster and didn't need a partner so much as someone to look after him. He was right on that one, but wrong in all other ways. Ben made me happy. I liked having him around the place. I liked his silence when not drinking and his gaiety when he was. I knew he was holding a burden of sorts, which I could never figure out, whether I used craftiness, cunningness or straight talk, I could never figure it out.

'Is there anything you want to tell me?' I would say to him. '...Anything at all, it doesn't matter how bad or crazy it is? I don't care.' He smiled his thin smile but would never answer me.

On the day he died, he was quite upbeat. He was whistling in the kitchen when I got up. 'Someone's happy,' I said to him. 'Yep,' he goes 'I feel something has twigged; something has fallen into place.' He didn't tell me what. Off he went on his scooter, the one he loved, the sixties was his thing and I thought nothing more about it.

'See you later.'

'Yes, later.'

It was all caught on film. A holidaymaker was filming panoramas from the top of the Island near the lighthouse. They showed it on the local news that evening. Only once because of the number of complaints from people who said it was in poor taste. Which it was. The film is turning the full 360 degrees when it stops on a man riding a scooter across a field. You hear someone say, 'What the hell is that bloke doing?'

As the field tilts toward the sea, the scooter is speeding up until both man and bike disappear over the cliff edge.

'Did you see that?'

Whatever the secret was, it died with him. No amount of magic has revealed one iota of what was going through his head.

*

On another note and in spite of meself, I have decided to help this fellow Jack in his quest to tally up the stories and myths to do with this Island. The man is clueless and is going round in circles. I am uncertain of his enthusiasm. He wastes a lot of time and seems to worm his way to the pub when most of us are getting tea. A few hours later you see him stagger back, in no state to pull himself together, let alone pull together the puzzle of stories he's meant to be doing. A couple of things made me have a rethink. For a start, he bought Claude's car from him. Claude said he had insisted on taking it off his hands and did warn him of its condition. Claude even wrote a list of all the things which the car needed to get it road worthy. More a short volume than a list, by all accounts. Maybe he did warn Jack, but it all adds up to the picture that Jack is a hopeless mess and a lot easy to fool. The heap of junk presently sits outside his house instead of Claude's.

Then the sea caught him. This made me laugh. It appears that Jack drifted off to sleep by the shoreline. Easy to do. You can get lullabyed by the crash of those waves, constantly followed by the drag of stones being clawed back into its belly. Just as he was losing himself, the ocean threw its weight into a huge roller which reached further up the beach. It grabbed his feet and tried to pull him in and, in an instant, he was soaked from head to toe. I caught sight of him coming over the top of the pebble bank as he tottered back to the cottages. As he came closer, I could see what had happened on account of the fact that he looked like a bucket of water had been chucked over him.

'Ha. See you have been skinny dipping with your clothes on!' He told me what happened.

'I didn't see it coming.'

'That's the point, you fool, you don't!'

By this time, we were in me front room, he with a towel and with the both of us sipping a sherry tot. I couldn't stop meself from giggling at him.

'Well, Mr Scholar, this may be one of the stories you need to read about. Many lives have been lost at the demands of the Seventh Wave. Whole ships have been tossed up and taken under in one enormous guzzle.'

'Sorry Eve, forgive me, I just don't get it. Obviously, I have read about it, but still don't get it.'

'The Seventh Wave is both expected and unexpected. You know it's going to happen, but you don't know when.'

'So, it's nothing to do with it being the Seventh Wave?'

'It is and it isn't.' His face was a picture.' Tell you what, go up to the museum on Tophill. Old Flann runs it. He has made a study of the Seventh Wave as well as of many other things. He knows it all. Poor chap has very little else to think about. Go and meet Flann, he'll tell you a few things.'

'That name rings a bell. Was he the one who wrote the pamphlet.'

'The very same.'

*

All this brings me back to one place, the Book. It is at least two hundred years old and was probably copied from another, which was probably copied from another and so on and so forth, reaching back into the dark centuries before. This book is crammed with remedies as varied as a cure for toothache, an antidote for snake bite or a treatment for a broken heart. The church knew this book existed but stopped searching for it years ago. Churchmen, in any case, came to me or me mother, or her mother, for salvation or cure. I could make babies appear or disappear. It was old magic. It was the magic of the Island and outsiders feared and revered it in equal measure. It was me own son Harry who in the end made me stop consulting it, saying it was all superstition and belonged to a different age. After a few strange unexplained happenings which I will tell you about if there is time, Harry said the book should be burnt as the nonsense it contained was sinister, dangerous and, not to mention, unholy. After a lot of talking, I made a pact with him. I told him I would make sure the book was "beyond reach" and that I would no longer consult it for me or for others. I got Ben to go up to the loft, remove some bricks from the chimney and cement the Book into place. He did it without questioning me motives. I told him it was an "Island thing."

I wanted it back, I wanted it to help meself. As you would expect, I couldn't ask Harry, so I had to find a trustworthy "other" to help. It could never be a matter of asking just anyone. That book is precious and unique. In the hands of a collector, it is worth tens of thousands. To me, it is beyond price. Within its pages are the secrets of the old gods and if I recall correctly, the last chapter is dedicated to the defeat of death.

I puzzled on who to use to redeem the book. The penny dropped. Of course, we shall have to see how things progress, but I actually had two options staring me in the face. Take Jack - story collector, naive traveller. Risk: he may tell the world or use it in *his* book. Take Claude - fairly reliable neighbour, handsome trickster. Risk: he may use it over me or use it for his own good. I need help, but I do not want them to know me intention or leaning.

Here lies danger as well as remedy. The potion I want to look at requires a strange combination of words, actions and the fusion of substances. One substance I know I need is a terrible substance to attain and may cause menace in its acquisition. It is a known truth that death can be postponed only by the unknowing blood of another.

THE THIRD WAVE

Extract from the initial Proposal for Dissertation on the Phenomenon of the Seventh Wave - Russell Quirk: October 1997

In many seaside cultures throughout the world, there exist interesting notions about a phenomenon called the Seventh Wave. This phenomenon states that, for reasons unknown or yet to be proven, the Seventh Wave appears to be of greater height, volume and voracity than the six waves that precede it. This occurrence may be informative for the fisherman, fascinating for children or useful for surfers, but in terms of exploring its possible role in coastal erosion and how it may impact on the viability of certain shorelines or natural defences, it is possibly of vital importance and scientific concern.

My initial literature search, however, has proved largely unsuccessful. Certainly, there is much discussion surrounding the phenomena but very little which amounts to evidence based on methodical observation or deliberation. What supported information has been committed to paper or, more likely, to the internet, the conclusions appear to be contradictory, tenuous or unconvincing. This may be interesting in itself as it raises the question as to why an unverified phenomenon - such as the Seventh Wave in this case - should come about in the first place, be so widespread and attract such attention, despite not being based on reality or experience?

As part of this preparation I travelled to Chesil beach in Dorset, the nearest coast to my home. I studied the waves for some ninety minutes. As I did not have any equipment, I could use for the purposes of measuring height or volume, I decided to record patterns and the reach of each wave as it smashed on the shore. Ninety minutes was long enough to gain some statistical accuracy, but not too long to have to take into consideration tidal effects. Naturally, should this proposal be successful, these observations would later be conducted systematically and true to the scientific method using precision instrumentation. Firstly, I will state that there are, in fact, waves which are markedly more voracious and powerful than the rest. However, when this wave appears is either randomly determined, due to some local variation in weather, wind or terrain or pertains to a mathematical pattern to be identified at a later stage. I divided the period into two halves. From each half, the conclusion I drew was different. From the first half, I found that the eleventh wave was more powerful than the rest. From the second half, it was the eighth.

This turned my investigation into an altogether different direction. Was the significance of this phenomenon more to do with the number seven than to do with its actual nature? The number seven is deemed to be the most magical and mystical of all numbers. As such, it is famous or notorious in every corner of the globe. There are many examples: The Seven Wonders of the World; the Seven Sages of Ancient Greece; the Seven Seas; the Seven Heavens; the Seven Deadly Sins; the Seven Kings of Rome; the Seven Last Words of Christ; the Seven continents; the Seven names of God...the list would fill pages.

I am of the opinion that this subject deserves further investigation. I, therefore, submit this proposal for my dissertation.

Tutor's Comments:

Although I can well appreciate the interest in this particular and peculiar phenomenon, I am not convinced there is any scientific merit in its investigation. It seems to belong more to the study of mysticism or folklore than to coastal geology or natural ecology. As you have already indicated from your preliminary enquiries and observations, any further research is likely to prove inconclusive and possibly irrelevant. I suggest you reconsider your proposal along the lines already highlighted in your last tutorial.

Tutor's Additional Comment on a post-it:

Stop sodding about Russ and remember what you were talking about the other day. You posed a truly exciting question which was highly pertinent and worthy of your time and energy. I think you are pissing in the wind with this idea. You need to go back over your own notes and keep to your original fucking idea!

JACK

I remember so little of my childhood. It makes me question the authority of memory and, though the past obviously happened, the evidence is scant and rests on a few thin memories: a handful of pale moments, odd quirky scenes with very little context except for that of a feeling, a passing emotion.

One of these memories was of Rosie and me in a treehouse in one of the many properties we lived in. It may have been Salisbury. We were playing with our many teddies and dolls. Rosie always liked to play families. We invented one of our own: the Watson family. Like our own, the family never had a dad in it. I wanted to have one, but Rosie always stopped me. We could have uncles and cousins and a mother who could have boyfriends, but no father was allowed. One time I climbed into the tree house on my own and started playing families. As Rosie was nowhere to be seen I made sure I had a dad. I was happily playing away when suddenly Rosie emerged from under the hatch. She had obviously crept up the ladder and had been listening to my game.

'What did I tell you Jack. No dads. No dads!'

She picked up my teddy, Simon who had taken on the role of Dad and basically tore him to pieces. Off came his arms and leg. Off came his head!

'Now never, never ever do that again!'

I ran into the house sobbing.

'Oh, don't worry,' offered my mum. 'I can sew teddy back together again!'

'Can you really?'

'It's an easy job,' she said, waving her cigarette at me.

I wanted to believe her but didn't. I was right. She never put Simon back together. So early on, any word alluding to father in any shape or form became strictly taboo.

I wonder what happened to Rosie. We should be close; we should be honouring the fact that only the two of us have experienced the same things and are connected by the same history. After Mum died, we became complete strangers. I can't tell you why. We just did. We had each other's numbers, but the years went by, without contact. That's nearly twenty years, twenty wasted years. I don't know where she lives. Somewhere around Cambridge was the last place my Aunt knew about.

*

Weller wants to see me. Although he is rightly interested in how things have progressed, he will soon find out they haven't. I have been here a month - no, more like five weeks and I have done virtually nothing. I have been to his library only once and brought back a pile of books. They remain standing where I first put them down. I have spent all this time walking the shore, drinking booze, shuffling papers and dwelling on my own absurd thoughts. This is me at my worst; when I am left to my own devices I increasingly begin to live in my own head. I make an art of dumbing down. I can't leave my past alone and continually linger on thoughts of what was meant to be. My relationship with Trish is history. Or is it? Why bother to attempt resuscitation? Not sure how but I have practically lost all my university friends since my final, final split with Trish. Why bother trying to make contact? Ellis was basically a waste of space. God knows when he'll surface again.

Another distraction are these neighbours of mine I am now sharing my life with. Somehow, they fulfil my appetite for entertainment. Add in the sea and there's no time for anything else. Ever since I saw her naked in the backyard, for instance, Rowan keeps popping into my mind. Who wouldn't be distracted? She's a stunner, albeit in a unique way. Don't forget, I haven't been intimate with anyone for over a year and I so rarely see her, that my imagination takes over. I fill in the gaps and begin fantasizing about future encounters. How shall I play it? How can I get talking to her? Will I ever see her naked again?

As for Claude, he utterly baffles me. At the same time, he seems both a fiend and a friend. Always smiling and full of ideas, but underneath. Either there is no *underneath* or there is something mischievous going on. The crock of shit remains stationary outside my house; a car in name only. I have given him a hundred notes already, although I still can't recall saying yes to it. I have had a mechanic to look at it, a burly laconic guy by the name of Rob. He says it will cost a grand to get it 'seaworthy' (his words). Well, that simply isn't going to happen, is it?

Eve, however, may be an ally in my work. She thought it hilarious when I was caught by a wave the other day, but afterwards we began to talk, and she gave me a few leads and tips and helped start to reset myself (again) to the original purpose of my stay. The problem I have is that, in terms of information, I have both too much and too little. On the one hand, I have this huge pile of disordered stories, random accounts, scribblings on tatty paper, pieces of diary, a few notes I have made in passing. On the other hand, there isn't any overview or logic to the notes, no real theme, no order or sense can be made from them. They jump from myth to story, from real events to folklore, from prehistory to the current day. No coherence to it, but then, I suppose that is the essence of my job.

The only real theme, unsurprisingly enough, is the obvious fact that they are all uniquely related to this peculiar island I find myself on, an island surrounded on all sides by a sea which changes with the temperament of the wind and the moods of the sky. I am not so sure I like it here. It has charm in its stark beauty but sometimes this strikes me as repellent or inhospitable. On a warm day with a salty breeze and the sea as placid as a meadow, the Island pulls you in and endears you. In a storm the wind rips into you relentlessly and my pathetic life seems an irrelevance. Step in the water and you would be history. Hard to explain its simple indifference, the weight of nonchalance to you or to anyone for that matter, as it continues its unremitting passage from the past into the future, regardless of human worth or endeavour. As well as the tale of the seventh wave which frankly is as absurd as it is fascinating, Eve told me about the curse associated with the island, something about those that are born here will never find peace. Locals say they are 'blessed with a curse,' an oxymoron if I ever heard one. She referred to a certain animal which is associated with the curse, but when pressed she failed to elaborate.

Anyway, whatever my opinion or limited conclusions, I must prepare something for this commission lest I be thrown off the Island before I have so much as written an intelligible word. What was I going to tell Weller? Maybe I could remind him that I had to call out the water board again as another pipe had sprung a leak under the sink. He was the landlord after all, and should take a healthy interest in his own investment. I knew I wouldn't say anything about this.

*

As a distraction, I decided in my own head that Rowan's story may be what was essential in order to move on with the project. I knew this was a nonsense, but you can justify anything if you want to. And I wanted to. I found my excuse for knocking on her door. First time, no answer, although I was convinced she was at home. I tried again later, and this time I heard music (Neil Young, I think). As before, no response. I waited a whole day and made a third attempt. I was just about to turn away when the door swung open.

'What do you want?' After all that, I was lost for words, but made several shots at explaining exactly what I wanted. I babbled my way through some sort of justification as to why I was there. I tried to explain that I was talking to as many local people as possible to hear their perspective on the Island on which they lived in order to gain some sort of common understanding about its history. This was pure and total bullshit, of course.

'And what has this got to do with me?'

'Well, you're a local and I want to get your views.' She turned around and left me standing at the open door. After a moment I followed her into her lounge. My first impression was messy, a little dirty; smelt of incense and dope but cosy enough, homely, throws everywhere, a lot of colour and warmth. She rolled and lit a cigarette but said nothing as I attempted to sit down as casually as I could.

'Well, as you are still here, what is so important?'

'OK, thanks for the time, by the way. First, I would like to know if you're native to the island.'

'No, I wasn't.'

'Oh...'

'I'm a native but was born in the hospital on the mainland. Can't you tell?'

'Tell what. That you were born in a hospital. How could I?'

'Dickhead,' she said under her breathe.' No, that I am a native. There's an island "look." You see it or you don't. Going by your face, you don't.'

'What is it then?'

'It's not so much a physical thing - it's a sort of temperament, the way people carry themselves, like we're all bearing a burden but pretending we're not.'

'Is this the curse?'

'Who told you about that?' I told her.

'Eve has a big mouth sometimes. She probably told you I am nuts as well.'

'Not exactly, she said you have problems with your nerves.'

For the first time, Rowan's face lit up and she laughed.' That's brilliant. That's fucking brilliant. Yep, that's me. I have problems with my nerves!'

'Then tell me, what does she mean?'

'Then tell me, what does she mean?' she repeated mimicking me. 'Well, I will tell if you do. What brings a twerp like you to an island on the edge of the world? Are you desperate, lonely, at a loose end or are you a bit crazy yourself?'

'It's research.'

She mimicked me again. 'Oh yeah, research is it? Of all the godforsaken places, you come to this dump. Come on. Either you are demented in some way or fate has dropped you here for fucked-up reasons of its own. I question your motives and if I had anything to do with it, I would throw you off the Island and everyone like you.'

'Bit final, isn't it? I have connections here, you know. My grandfather was an islander.'

'Name?'

I told her.

'Sorry, sunshine, even your grandpapa was lying to you. There is no one here with that name. For a researcher, you're pretty crap!'

There was a knock on the door. 'That's Katie.' She said it as if I knew who Katie was. 'Before I get it, I do have a story to tell you, but I will do so in my own good time. Don't come again, I will come looking for you.' I stood up. I had been dismissed. As she was getting up, I caught a view of her small breasts in the neck of her tee-shirt. What is it with her? Must I be tormented so?

In the hallway, she opened the door to Katie.

'Hiya, here's that geek I told you about.' She let me pass. Neither returned my goodbye.

*

I was due to meet Weller later in the afternoon. With a slightly contrived interest in what I had signed up for, I decided to visit the Island's Museum beforehand. It made sense as both were on the top of the island. I had no excuse as to why I hadn't been to the museum already except as testimony to my general hopelessness. The walk took me longer than I expected. I had only done it twice. It seemed to have got steeper than the last time. I began to appreciate that despite being separated from the rest of the world, the island had, in its past, separated its little world into two even smaller pieces: Tophill and Underhill. I had read something about this already. There were decades where one would never trust the other, inter-marriages were forbidden, trade was made by sea rather than land just to avoid the pollution of contact. How wonderful humans are. The need to belong leads to the need to divide. We like the *'them and us'* scenario. Ultimately, there was a general realisation that there was only '*them*,' and the world, didn't trust either. Like two brothers who had been beating the shit out of one another for years, they eventually had to turn to confront their fears and join together against the rest.

I had to pause on the top just to catch my breath. Looking back towards England, this coastline is a celebration of sheer beauty. The curve of the beach tapering off to the cliffs in the distance. On the other side, the town giving way to a tumble of rock which bounds the sea in a white embrace. It took the breath away I was trying to catch.

I arrived at the museum and to coin a Dylan Thomas' phrase, "the museum should have been in a museum." It was two cottages running into each other, bound in the local stone and dating from Stuart times. Dingy, dark and smelling damp, it didn't greet well. Little rooms of history, pokey corners harbouring tales of crisis and mayhem, pictures of vessels with their hulls high on the beach, shards of stone used to tear fur from flesh. There didn't appear to be a soul around. I felt more like a burglar than a visitor. Old Flann was definitely not about. When I shouted for him, or anyone, in that claustrophobic place, my own voice turned in on itself and became absorbed in the stone. In the absence of human contact, I began making notes, taking a few photographs and pocketing any leaflets or postcards available. I sighed at my own capacity to consume so many facts, balanced by an equal incapacity to make sense of the stuff. As I passed from one room to another, I noticed light coming through an open back door. Without any person or obstacle restricting me, I indulged my curiosity. I entered a small walled garden with a hawthorn in the centre, edged with the usual linear herbaceous bordering. My first impression was that someone loved this place. Then I saw him. He had his back to me and was obviously mending something in the shed.

'Hello, are you Old Flann?' He jumped a mile and dropped the pot he was working on. He stood staring at the chunks of pottery before he turned to me. This time it was my turn to jump. His entire face was disfigured, so much so that his left side had drooped horribly, right to his ear. His skin was saggy, its integrity loose and pitted in places. Only his eyes appeared anything like normal.

'Shit. Oh dear!' he said in soft local tones. 'One small piece had come away from the whole... Looks like the whole has come away from the piece now!' He laughed. It plainly meant a lot to him, but he laughed a throaty croak. I found myself laughing with him. It somehow helped, taking the focus off my own shock. I thought Eve could have warned me. I helped him pick up the pieces and place them onto a modest plastic tray he had been using.

'I am so very sorry,' I said in my best so-very-sorry voice.

'Don't apologise. It was not even a couple of hundred years old.' The man was jesting with me. 'You must try not to jump on old bastards like me. Hearing's dodgy - like a radio station not quite tuned in properly.'

'Can I do anything?'

'Tea - just tea. Go to the kitchen and make some tea.' I managed the tea without further incident. When we were sitting on the bench, I explained to him my mission. Like everyone else I had met, he had heard all about me before my arrival and had expected to see me at some point.

'Poor Weller, he was promising to do this project years ago. He started it himself but kept floundering. At one point, he sent a note to the museum asking me if I wanted a shot. I had already written several pamphlets about the island, you see, but he said he wanted something altogether more expansive. He didn't only want the facts but the fiction as well. I declined, of course. I had projects of my own. So now you're doing what he couldn't and what I refused.'

'Well, I'm trying to do it, let's say.'

'Floundering too. Tut, tut. So soon and only a month in. Tut, tut!' He was laughing once more and again I was with him.

'You're wondering about my face, aren't you? Don't worry, everyone does. Why shouldn't they? I look like a cross between Quasimodo and the Elephant Man. I know, I know, I look at myself in the mirror every day and most times give myself a nasty turn. What you see before you is the result of the interaction between pure sulphuric acid and soft unsuspecting human flesh. I was out in Iraq, that's where it happened. I wasn't a soldier, just a procurer of equipment. Not even weapons, but food, car parts, furniture, really mundane crap. I was walking in a market with a colleague and a woman, dressed as you would expect there, came up to me. I thought she was going to give me something. Well, she did as a point of fact. She threw acid in my face. Why me? No reason, no idea. Could have been the chap walking with me. But it wasn't, it was me.'

As soon as I started making sympathetic noises, he hushed me and redirected me back to the nature of my commission. I told him how difficult I was finding it to organise myself. 'You're getting bogged down with what is reality and what is folk tales. From an islander's point of view there is no such distinction. It is all the same. All woven into one, stories collide and get all mixed up and then give birth to others. I may be able to help you out. Not today I'm afraid. I have a coach load of amateur historians coming my way. I must impress, you see, or the tips will be rubbish.'

We made our way to the door. In the hallway was a large framed photograph of locals having a picnic. I hadn't noticed it on the way in. Now it pulled me in and drew my attention straight away, but Old Flann was hurrying me along and I vowed to take a closer look on my second visit.

'Well, nice to meet you, Jake.'

'No, it's Jack'

'Jack what.'

I told him and immediately, without another word being uttered, he ushered me through the door and slammed it against me.

*

Weller had been drinking. He had clearly forgotten I was coming. When he realised, he had made a mistake and not me, his manner lightened, and his reception turned out to be much more convivial than my first. He came across as matey and magnanimous. He asked me what I had for him, but before I could conjure up an answer, he was asking me if I wanted a whisky with him. I could tell he wasn't expecting me to decline. Out of fresh air, he began telling me about problems he was having with his wife, Issy.

'She's a bitch, a cow and hag all in one. Have you a girlfriend, Jack?'

'Not at the moment.'

'Thought not.'

'I'm in between as they say,' I said, trying to lighten the tone.

'Whatever.'

'I'm not gay,' I said, without knowing why.

'Who cares if you are?' he said in a way which surprised me. I had put him down as a diehard right-winger.

'With my money, Jack, I could have anyone, some young nubile who would be quite happy to take down her panties for a few pounds. Issy doesn't seem to realise or appreciate this. She lives her life on some cloud. This doesn't stop her from putting all this fucking pressure on me. Doesn't she understand that she is as lucky as a lucky thing.'

He suddenly remembered me. 'So how far have you got, Jack? It has been noted that you have visited my library only once. Pursuing other lines of enquiry, are we?'

As soon as I started my apology, he began again. 'It was never love, you know, Jack. Never love. She didn't seem to mind back then. It wasn't love, no way! It was about presentation; it was about form. I was Weller the millionaire, the sole millionaire ever to live here. I knew she would look good on the arm. I suppose I too was thinking appearance. Issy was dangerously attractive - still is I guess - but no sex to her, Jack. As frigid as a statue. Wherever we go, I see men ogling her and I think if only they knew she had no sex in her. I have met some ugly cows in my time and wow have they had the sex in them. Another drink?' Relieved I hadn't been taken to task, I accepted.

It was plain to see that Weller had entered the philosophical phase of drunkenness. People with money must find it difficult to find any decent friends or trustworthy confidantes. You would never know if they were there for you, the cash or the prestige. Weller may have found it doubly difficult because he didn't come over as pleasant. Not to me anyway. The shock of ginger hair and the pale freckly skin didn't help. I could see he was winding himself up into a bout of sentiment. I was waiting for him to come out with the ubiquitous refrain by asking that open-ended question; what was it all about?

'Come with me,' he suddenly said, picking up the bottle of whisky and disappearing through the patio doors leading into the garden. The lawn led down to a small woodland which eventually led to a crumbling cliff edge. 'Everyday, the sea!' he said waving his arms wide, one hand still holding the bottle. 'Always the same, always different. Been there since the beginning of time, will be here when we are dust. What we see here, ancient man saw, and future man will see. That's why the book you're working on is so important. It helps fix us in time. How are you doing anyway?' he said, slumping into one of the garden loungers.

'It's going really well,' I lied, but again, he didn't seem that interested. 'Will have something definite to show you in a few weeks.'

'Good, good' He was on his feet again. 'Jesus Christ. A bastard on the lawn!' He ran into a nearby shed and came out with a crossbow. For the life of me I couldn't see where or what the bastard was. I was simply grateful it wasn't me. He let an arrow off before I spotted its intended target: a baby rabbit. The first arrow shot carelessly into the trees, but he got it on the second arrow. 'Boy, am I good or what? That's two in two days.' I followed him to pick up his trophy. 'Right in the eye. Bullseye, one could say!' He hung it on a barbed wire fence with several other trophies in various stages of decay.

'You have been busy, Mr Weller, but why?'

'You obviously haven't read the stories, Jack.' I am undone. 'I'm surprised at you. It's linked to the curse. I presume you know about the curse, Jack?'

'Yes, of course.' I didn't sound convincing.

'Good man. Then you have studied the story about our spiritual encounter with one of the great saints?'

I laughed affirmatively, not knowing what he was alluding to.

'You will know that against popular belief, it was the Romans who introduced these little blighters into this country. They beat the French by over a thousand years. Typical of the French to try and get the credit.'

I laughed rather dramatically in a vague hope to put him off the scent.

We returned to the loungers and sat back down. Much to my relief, he began lamenting about his failing marriage once more while tucking into the second half of the whisky. I let him have his say as I was beginning to feel a bit smashed myself. Then he told me something I didn't want to hear. Worse than this, he told me I was the only person bar one who knew the secret. A long slightly uncomfortable pause followed. He began to wonder out loud why he had told me such a truth. I was wondering the same thing. He necked another glass of whisky, stood up, picked the crossbow up lying beside him and pointed it at me.

'Our little secret, ok.'

'What secret?' I joked with him. He chuckled as well, dropping the crossbow. All very quirky and theatrical, so different from our first meeting. And my conclusion? I was working for a madman.

ROWAN

I lived with my Aunt Diane and Uncle Cliff in the county town of Dorchester for the rest of my childhood. I say lived but really, I existed. I existed in a sort of bubble of disbelief. It felt like I was pretending, it was make-believe or like I was rehearsing for something which would happen in the future. I knew that my grip on reality was weak. If the wind blew hard enough, I would take off.

They were a loveless couple, Mr and Mrs Neal. I never saw one single act of affection between them in all the years I was with them. She was one of those thin pale women who was overly interested in presenting well to the world. I still wonder if she volunteered to look after me because it would look good. She never saw eye to eye with my mother who was almost the polar opposite: round and jovial. My uncle was an even stranger fish. He was an accountant and looked like one: glasses, moustache, balding head. He had been catapulted straight from the 1930's. He would always insist on tucking me in at night and reading me a bedtime story. Cliff said this was his duty and Diane referred to this time as 'our special time.' He was tactile with me in a way I would imagine Diane would only dream about. Holding on to me too long, stroking my arm or leg. When younger he would bath and change me which even then felt weird. This creepy behaviour stopped when I asked for Diane to read stories to me. She did for a while, they took turns, then they both stopped, and I was glad they did.

At ten years old, I thought I was essentially unreal and living in a dream of some sort. I went to school. I came home from school. I made friends. I lost friends. I said hello and goodbye to Aunt and Uncle at the right time and never questioned their commitment. I put up with shit from my cousin Greg, their only son and allowed him to drop me in it when he had the mind to do so. Which was often. I didn't do particularly well at school, but I didn't do so badly either. I once won a yearly prize for "endeavour."

I played charades in the shadow of my own life right up until the day when the Wolf came. It may sound real creepy but I would say that the Wolf gave me something, a bit of a purpose. With Him, everything became both genuine and second-rate at the same time.

Afterwards, I became something I wasn't before. I somehow inherited the life I had lost in the crash. I effectively died with my Mum and Dad. When the Wolf found me, I found me.

Naturally, everybody was dismayed that I started to cut my flesh. The gratification it gave me though, tearing it precisely, genuinely mesmerised whilst watching the flow of blood brought me into life. My favourite cut was from the inside of my elbow to my wrist. A fucking tide of blood poured over the skin, like the Nile breaking its banks and flooding the plains beyond. It was *delicious*. When my arm became too scarred and withered, I discovered I could achieve almost the same effect on my thigh. Aunt and uncle began to turn from understanding to disbelief, to hostility. They felt the cuts were against them. They saw it as an affront to the love and care they had given me. I got used to mopping up my own blood.

So, I made it into adulthood. I left them at sixteen and, despite their protests, I knew everyone was secretly relieved. All but Greg who had formed a crush on me despite years of hostility. As the family gathered to say their goodbyes, it was with great pleasure I whispered in his ear something on the lines of 'Go fuck yourself, you fat shithead!' I decided to return to the family home, this little lost island. Dorchester was a dead place to me, and I haven't visited the place since and don't think I ever will. The Island was the nearest I could be to the parents I could hardly remember. They are both buried in a cemetery on the top of the island. I have never visited their grave.

This island is a fitting prison for me, and I like it. There are no walls, just the endless sea,
stretching its skin for as far as you can see. Occasionally, it too loses its cool, rages with stifled, pent-up energy and breaks its own skin with total remorseless violence. In that way, we are similar.

I haven't seen Diane and Cliff now for two years. They may live only ten miles away, but it may as well be the dark side of the moon. At first, they would try to keep in touch. I made so many excuses that by year two they gave up.

*

Boy, was I in a rage. I was fucking livid with myself. Up the gut again. Totally my mistake. Getting stoned or pissed or both was a foreplay before sex, but caution goes to the wind and before you know it this happens. I started walking the shore at night, wondering what to do. Nobody was ever about. Well, maybe the odd fisherman with his solitary lamps and flasks of coffee. The ease of the waves trashing the pebbles made that long sucking sound as it was retreating. Like it was taking breath, holding it, then breathing again. Because it was dark, all I saw was its big white lips taking a bite out of our beach. I was suspended in the blackness and loved the sensation. This was the closest I ever got to joy. I always think the same thoughts, which are endlessly boring, every thought trying to make some sense out of my twisted past. Katie said that the mind was infinite, and change was its natural way. When she said this, she would pause a bit. Excellent words but neither of us really believed them. Being pregnant, inflamed all that was wrong with me. One night, a windy but clear night, I laid out on the cold pebbles and stretched out my arms and legs. I stayed there for hours, looking up into the starry sky. Why was it so fucking beautiful and I was so fucking ugly. That thought wound itself around my skull until it ate up all the other thoughts. Was it because I was alive and all out there was dead stuff. As I began thinking about going home, I thought I felt the baby move. It was not possible, of course. It was far too early. It must have been my imagination. I was a lump of shit but there was nothing wrong with my imagination. I felt it again - impossible!

I don't know if it was the loneliness of the last pregnancy, but I was drawn to contact with other people. This would always be a scary thing for me. One fact I do know really well is that people and I just don't go. I never ever phoned up Katie, but I phoned her, and she was so shocked she had to get me to repeat my name. I asked her to visit as soon as.

'Everything alright?' she asked. I bypassed answering that one and asked her how she was. Guaranteed to put her off the scent.

Traditionally, Claude was the enemy as far as I was concerned. Lately, I have had to have a re-think as I kept bumping into him. In fact, I was beginning to think I had got him all wrong. He was friendly and interesting. Just what I needed. He was chatty and generous, bringing round bottles of wine and some dope as gifts. Not staying long so it wasn't like he wanted to get into my pants. We talked about deep crap as well. The nature of life and so on. I liked that as I rarely got it. Not from Katie, and certainly not from Zac. It felt liberating. How did I make up my mind so soon about him?

I called into Eve for a coffee and she asked me the same thing.

'Everything alright?' I told her that I had never felt better. I hadn't been in hospital now for two years. I had my routines which were keeping me healthy enough.

'Just getting on with life,' I told her. I could see she wasn't convinced.

'Here, have another slice of my dump.' As she laid it onto my plate, she sighed and then said something which took me aback.

'I think we are very similar, Rowan.' I laughed out loud. 'I know we are physically a bit different and there's the age, of course.'

'And you've been married like eighty times and I haven't even found anyone on this god-forsaken island who I can even love.' It was her turn to laugh. 'I'm the nutty dope head, don't forget, and you're a *pillar of the community*.' I said the last sentence in a silly voice.

'What I mean is that you come over as not...complete. And I often feel like that.'

'Is anyone *complete*?' I barked back at her using the silly voice once more.

'I suppose not but some of us spend all our time looking for the missing piece of us. You and me are like that.

I can see from your face you disagree. Think about it for a while. I am picking up that there is a lot going on in that pretty brain of yours.'

'So what piece are you looking for?'

'I'm getting on and there are a couple of things I need to do. You can probably guess at one of them.'

I bottled the conversation and said Katie was coming when she wasn't. 'Been great,' I told her, too quickly.

'Think about it, Rowan. There is a something about you at the moment.' I gave her a kiss and a hug to shut her up.

CLAUDE

So, this is how I set about snaring the lovely Rowan. I incrementally increased my visiting. Not too much to arouse hers or anyone else's suspicions. All the time, I became more familiar, sometimes over-familiar. Humour is, by far, the best way to trap your foe. Oh, the doors that open with the telling of a nicely timed joke. I kept it light, breezy, jovial. When Eve blew my cover and told Rowan that I was an old jail bird, I chortled out loud and told her the truth, but fashioned it with emphasis in some parts and omissions in others. I managed to portray myself as an old hippie, who had fallen short of the law because the laws of the land were essentially unfair. No big deal, Rowan, I promise you.

However, over several visits, I noticed a growing uneasiness about young Rowan. At first, being somewhat egocentric, I wondered if the unrest was about me. Then I began to guess otherwise. Something had happened. I smelt remorse. I smelt shame. I brought myself in closer, sensing an opening in which to gain the old upper hand. One particular night, a night of rain and blizzard - perfect for the exchange of confidences in front of a wood fire - I overloaded the spliffs and poured the whisky without holding back. I literally orchestrated the whole scene. In genuineness, how I do this I do not know. I fished around a bit and let out a little-known fact about myself. Just to lure her in. I intuitively knew that she was ready to spill the beans and boy were there beans to spill. In short, she told me about her lost babe, its untimely death and more positively, its burial place. This was exactly what Claude Mayfellow required. I felt there was more but let it go, murmuring sympathetic noises as appropriate. I could see she had realised that she had said far too much. Too late now, mademoiselle!

The next day I was up with the sun and searching the far reaches of the bay where the beach gives up its pebbles and reaches into the cliff. It took two hours before I found what I was looking for. The daft bitch had foolishly marked it with a lucky stone. Nobody else would have spotted this tell-tale sign, nobody but the maestro. Now the treasure is stored securely and fittingly in my cellar; a cellar, by the way, which is totally hidden from the world, which doesn't show on any plans or any blueprints. I constructed it myself: over the years. A veritable little dungeon. This gift she had given me would doubtlessly prove a cache I could use as a sort of ransom, a lever into the girl's diminutive soul and more interestingly, into her diminutive body.

Praise to the one true Lord, a few days later I went a-visiting with one goal in mind. Shall we call them 'favours of the third kind.' Everything comes to a man who waits. I play the waiting game all the time, peddling time for opportunity, anticipating chances and always on the alert for mischief or prizes to be won. That's me, I'm afraid. I am Claude, the Player of Men - and of Women, of course.

*

Once snared, one does get bored very quickly. A few visitations were enough. For men of my calibre, it is the hunt that matters. The chase is all. Once one captures what one desires, the desire begins a disproportionate plummet into the humdrum. And I admit, Rowan was more than a little disappointing in that area. I thought she would give in to my charms like most do. The hatred on her face though made me cold. She was so pathetic it made me cringe. Don't get me wrong, I loved it when she cringed. Not so when it's your masterpiece she is cringing from. So, I started looking elsewhere. Blessings come to those who are patient and grasp the way the world spins round. Within seven days, nay, not even seven, I happened to a chance encounter which made me recognise the potential for another encounter of the erotic kind. One much more in line with my traditional values.

I caught the two Stocker children, Eve's grandchildren, puffing away on a solitary fag together outside my garden wall. 'May I ask what the bloody hell is going on here?' I adopted an authoritarian tone which, as the children they were, they mistook for real. Comically, the boy hid the cigarette behind his back, the smoke drifting up over his shoulder. 'What you got there, son?' says I, in the spirit of pantomime.

'Just show him, Tom,' says his sister. It was the way she said it: with clarity, resignation and a pragmatism I immediately admired.

'Just show him.'

Tom showed it to me. I took it from him and studied it in mock solemnity. I then had a puff myself. 'Pall Mall Menthol - come in the house and I will give you a proper one - each!' I jested, accompanied by my signature wink.

Thank the Wondrous Lord, children are so easy to fool. They didn't say a word but shuffled in after me. I watched them gingerly smoke - and cough their way through a tipped Camel. At one point, Tom came over giddy and had to take a seat. Neither finished their fag.

'Of course, now we have a secret that we must not tell anyone. I won't say a word about your smoking, you won't say a word about my giving you a ciggie. Deal?'

'Deal. We agree to that, don't we, Tom?' Again, that certainty in her voice, not a trace of shyness there, the confidence underpinning her words. Much more my sort.

After they had gone, and the fresh stink of smoke still lingered, I reflected on my little prey. The boy was typical enough, about nine, clean faced, perfect teeth, annoyingly lively, but the girl, Rachel, she was a picture. She may have been twelve, thirteen. Why I had not taken her seriously before, I couldn't think. 'Am I losing it?' I said aloud, teasing myself with this untruth.

The girl was striking in her looks. I would describe her as captivating: long black hair, dark eyes, something of the Mediterranean about her. I just loved the way she carried herself. That by itself had a wonderful beauty of its own. Just the ideal age as well. The Lord provides: this was the project I had been looking for. I made my mind up there and then that Rachel was for me. Rowan was a sideshow, a dress rehearsal for the real McCoy. Jesus, Joseph and Mary, life was becoming stimulating again.

At such times, I go to think on the small bench I put under the cherry tree where sweet Anna is buried. I pose to myself the problem and I search for incentives and roadblocks. With all problems ahead, there are two core challenges: identifying what you want and then identifying how to get it. How was I to achieve the target? I can be painfully methodical about these things. There's the goal, what helps me move towards it. What obstacles stand in my way? To progress the quest, as it were, there were certain definites I was already aware of. The kids were always together, and they regularly visited Eve next door. That makes matters easier. So, I need to start flattering Eve with some extra visits on the days I know the girl will be visiting. Plus, and this may be the most testing part of the plan, I have to conjure up ways and means to separate brother from sister. At least, on a temporary basis, you understand.

I was genuinely excited about my new quarry. Rowan was the past already. She was appealing in her own way but, I'm afraid, there was no comparison to young Rachel. With Rowan, I would ensure I keep her on the hook and pop in to re-emphasis my authority. You never know when she may be useful.

EVE

After all this good feeling, I may have tempted heaven to send down a tragedy to balance the world out again. I was just beginning to think me time had come, and the period of uncertainty was finally ending. Repetitive dreams of being lost on a sea of mud didn't help. Then three extraordinary things happened over the last three extraordinary weeks, one after another. Hope should come with a government warning on the packet.

The first of the happenings was, in me own terms, the most easy to deal with. I was talking to Jack about the local wartime experience. Suddenly, there was a kerfuffle in the front of the house. A quick loud knock on the door and it burst open with Jane Bridge holding her two-year-old, Rain (these names!) Her own mother was following in her footsteps, mumbling nonsense and crying in fits and starts in chorus to her daughter's laments.

'He's dead. He's stopped breathing, he's dead!'

This was me territory. As I took Rain from her arms, I indicated to Jack to console both mother and grandmother and set them down in the lounge. Apparently, an ambulance was on its way. No sooner had she said this I could hear the distant siren as it sped onto the causeway.

'Where are you taking him?' she shouted at me. 'What are you doing?'

'You brought him here, just allow me to do me thing,' I said as quietly as possible. 'Allow me to do me thing.' I disappeared with the boy to the back room, grabbing a bottle of the precious as I passed.

Indeed, the boy was not breathing and was starting to turn blue. As I worked on him, I could hear Jane screaming her head off and trying to get in. Jack was doing a fair job at restraining her. I could hear some more neighbours swarm in aware that something had gone wrong. Over all their voices, I suddenly heard Claude trying to calm them all, eventually volunteering to flag down the ambulance when it arrived.

The terrible wail of the ambulance became almost unbearable when it pulled up outside, its blue light sending shadows into the side window. I could hear the back opening, the ramp descending, the trolley hitting the pathway. Stay away, I kept whispering. One minute, one minute.'

'Where's the child?'

They were just about to open door, when I meself opened it and stood there with Rain standing next to me as if nothing had happened to him. Everyone looked surprised. His mother barged past the ambulance crew and scooped him up for a mix of hugs and kisses.

I held up the offending crayon. 'It got stuck,' I told them simply. 'Take him in anyway. It may be more complicated. Test his heart.' It was like the old days, I thought, and allowed myself a smile.

*

The second thing was that I noticed me eyes were wandering in a certain direction. This has surprised even yours truly. Before I had put this fellow down as a low life and a jail bird. You look at him and you straight away suspect he is up to no good. He has a canny arrogance that gives you the feeling he is playing with you. Matched with this he has a sort of rugged, pinched look giving him an almost dashing Errol Flynn air. I am talking of me neighbour, Claude. Now, you say, he is considerably younger than me, maybe twenty years or more. That much is true. Yet, I challenge you back with the fact that two hubbies I had have been younger than me. Not by twenty years granted, but Ben was twelve and a half years me junior.

What has aroused me interest? Well, unusually, Claude has been coming around a great deal lately. I detect a certain curiosity about this oft-married woman who stands before you. She can still attract interest in the men of the Isle, and I remain - by reputation and in reality - active in all regions south of the equator, if you get me drift. When I allow meself to dream, I am in seventh heaven.

I can see what is happening even if the young man in question is not aware. Despite all, I have a great deal of fight about me. I have never despaired or given up. I have never ever lost hope. Even the girl I was all those years ago never gave in. I'm talking of sixty years ago, waiting in the beach hut for me Bertie, waiting for that man of mine to arrive for the treasure I had promised him. When I promise something, I promise. I will never break me word. Overhead the blasted Luftwaffe decided to deliver its deadly cargo on that day of all days. Not only that, but of all the people killed in that senseless raid, one bomb had to land on poor old Bertie. If he had lived, I should surely be with him to this day and the other men in me life would have found comfort elsewhere. Instead what happened? I embarked on a lifetime of menfolk. I'm a bit of a joke. I know, some mock me behind me back. They say, for instance, that I am the only person in history who, because they have been married so many times, has developed an allergy to confetti. I take it in me stride.

Claude is slowly but surely moving towards me. He keeps popping around on some pretext or other. One time he brought some homemade wine round. Last Friday, he brought over a dozen mackerel. He is especially good when Rachel and Tom are about. He's excellent at striking a conversation with them and getting down to their level. I think Rachel has taken a shine to him, bless her. Me son also seems to have accepted him and passes the time of day with him, talking about football or politics or the weather and the like. The other day we invited him to come for dinner. I could see he was excited and volunteered to make the soup as his contribution to the proceedings. All went so well I insisted we opened the bottle of plonk he had given me. It wasn't that good to be honest, but it most definitely hit the mark and got him singing a Frankie number. He chose *The Way You Look Tonight*, announcing it as a present for me. Towards the end of the song, he grabbed Rachel and spun her around much to our amusement and her embarrassment. When he left a couple of hours later, I gave him one of Eve's famous bear hugs. Yes, things are progressing in the right direction, but I am always one to hurry it with men, so I am having to give meself a good old lecture and take things slowly with a capital S.

This brings me back to the Book. I have decided that Claude is the man to reclaim it from its hiding place in the loft. Jack seems as hopeless as before and I wonder afresh what he is doing here. For the retrieval of the Book, he will not do I'm afraid. Again, I must wait me time because, although I desperately want to get me hands on the Book, I don't really want to tell Claude its purpose or allow him to see its contents. Such things are forbidden. It must be soonish though as I am beginning to get those symptoms once more. Me belly aches with excruciating pain. Me vision becomes dim, me hearing fades and, most worrying, the world loses its hardness and becomes soft and elastic. I fear the worse. Me mother complained of these signs just before she met Jesus. The sooner I am reunited with the Book the better.

The final thing happening was one almighty shock indeed. The day following our meal, the wind struck up from the south west and the sea reacted accordingly. The waves grew commanding and, in their enthusiasm to dash their heads on the shore, began falling over one another. Waves were blowing far too early and flowering too soon: I loved weather like this. The cockerel weathervane in me garden was shaking its tail with wild gusto.

When me son arrived with the children later that evening, he said he could see a fishing vessel bobbing up and down like a cork too near to the shore to be sensible. We all went out to have a look. From a distance, we could tell it was getting into trouble. The way the island bulges at the end of the bay has always caused a nuisance. Boulders had fallen into the sea over the centuries and what should have been easy waters were deceiving with changing depths and unseen rocks. Tom ran in for the binoculars. They confirmed the crew were getting into a mess. The boat was trying to motor around the rocks, but the wind and waves were working together to push it back towards them. We could tell they weren't from around here as no local fisherman would be where they were. A few others were beginning to gather around watching. Island folk have long memories of boating wrecks. It is said that there isn't a clear hundred yards along this beach which hasn't been the sight of some sort of seafaring calamity.

'If they had any sense, which obviously they don't, they would just stop the fight and beach the thing on the shore. Instead, they're picking a fight they're not going to win.' I hollered.

'I'm calling the coastguard, Mum,' Harry rightly said.

'I think so, son, if no one has tipped them off already.'

As if to hammer this point home, the winds multiplied its efforts and sent in a barrage of rain cloud to make matters worse. Nature is unsympathetic to the plight of men, we know that. It never makes any allowance. The minute headlight on the bow jogged about randomly and looked rather pitiful amid the strife around it. I told the children to run back and knock up Claude. The crowd moved down towards the shoreline, all of us lamenting the stupidity of foreigners.

Finally, we heard the first crunch of the hull on rock. We could hear the shouting of the men becoming more panicky and frightened as their situation worsened. From nowhere, Rowan suddenly appeared at me side.

'Where you been hiding?'

'I was up there,' she said, pointing to the steep cliffs which rose above us.

'Can you believe these silly muckers, Rowan?'

'Yes, I can actually, Eve, I really can!' she said in a peculiar way.

Another crunch and you could tell the boat was heading for driftwood. A third crack and we could see the inners starting to spill out.

'Where the hell is the lifeboat?'

The boat was now stuck on an outcrop of rock. The bow was tearing itself to pieces while its stern was prancing about like me bloody weathervane. Two of the three men jumped onto the rock. Neither made it but they were near enough to clamber onto solid ground. The third, and by the looks of him the youngest, was about to follow suit when the boat jolted violently in response to a massive wave. I wondered when the Seventh Wave would turn up. With this, the fellow flew through the air and belly-flopped into the open sea. You could see it come to pass as clear as day. Two waves, one on the rebound from the cliff, made a pincer movement on this chap in a desperate bid to make him their own. Then something occurred I would never have expected. Someone was in the water and swimming out towards him. In the old days we could use our own island dogs to do such things, entering the waves with a line between their teeth. Sadly, the last of these mutts had died when I was a girl and were declared extinct in the thirties. It took me a moment to realise that the swimmer was Rowan. Despite the urgency, and considering there was hardly anything of the girl, I was admiring the strength of her stroke. She dived under, bless her, and emerged clinging the young man under his arms.

Afterwards, I couldn't help but see Rowan in a different light. The mad so-and-so was not so mad. I had never seen Rowan move like that, with ease and with a point in mind. Maybe, there is something about her after all, something more…substantial than I had put her down for.

I called in later that evening to make sure she was alright. I told her straight how amazed I was at her performance.

'Don't worry Eve, I was just as shocked, believe me.'

I saw the little girl in the woman before me and gave her a long squeeze.

'There's something else, isn't there?'

'What do you mean by something else?'

'The small matter of a child,' I said, patting her belly.

'But how do you know? It's not showing.'

'To me it is, sweetheart.'

By the way, all three of the silly sods survived. Let's hope they stick to their own sea wherever that might be.

THE FOURTH WAVE

Dramatised Version of Events of 1824
(Given by A. Lang to Thomas Hardy 1904 - never used)

Mayfellow had an idea. Over the previous three days a gale had been blowing up from the south. Waves as large as falling houses and as frenzied as wild stallions had been pulverising the pebbled beaches with relentless violence. It was said that when you found a smashed gull on the shore, the weather would only get worse. The shore was dotted with them, random knots of feathers, broken wings waving in the squall. On the highest ridge of stones, he found a dead mullet. This was most curious. Bizarre to find such a shy fish casually tossed above the tidemark by the southern waves. This was bad. This was good. Bad for those unlucky folks stuck out in the channel. Good for the execution of Mayfellow's mean plan to make a few gains.

The good ship Hope had been spotted struggling on the horizon since midday. Hope was hopeless, pulled here and there, its sails ripped, the inevitable thrust forcing it towards the land. The odd scream could be caught trailing on the wind. Mayfellow assembled his mates. With the growing darkness, one of them manned the fires on the cove side, another on the mainland side, both showing sailors and crew where land was.

'What if the fires went out? What if our lamps were hidden? What then? What if all source of light were extinguished? What would happen come nightfall?'

Dusk came unnecessarily early, the heavy clouds sucking the light from the earth. What would come about? The border between sea and land and sky would be blurred. In the obscurity of pitch blackness, hell could have its way. The devil would spin his wheel of fortune and the result was his work, not ours. If God is in heaven, he will pilot a path through this blizzard, and all will be well. Should disaster strike, who are we to interfere with this cosmic pantomime?

Mayfellow and his mates doused some of the fires, covered others and they hid their lamps. For those watching on the beach the screams and cries for assistance became unbearable. They could hear the passengers' frantic and desperate negotiation with their predicament. The brave hearted were throwing themselves into the belligerent cauldron while the fainthearted clung to the mast or deck, mistaking solidity for safety.

The final impact of the vessel on the shore moved the earth like thunder. When it was pushed to one side by noisy but unseen waves, Mayfellow, thumping his legs with delight, knew it was time to act. He uncovered his lamp from the shelter of his cloak. Stepping over the body of a child, he ran as fast as he could towards the shipwreck. Mayfellow shouted for the others to reveal their lamps and when all the twenty did so they saw what mayhem had been caused. Some were on the boat still shouting for help or solace, some risked the water and paid a heavy price for doing so. Mayfellow was born for this moment. All manner of booty was hauled from the hull of this heartbreaking ship.

'Remember, treasure first!' he bawled above the commotion of water. 'The rest are in the hands of God so let Him do His work!'

From the surf, a survivor clambered on to the shore.

'Save my child, help me save my boy!'

'You must get another, Sir I have a different function in mind.'

The man became incensed and pulled Mayfellow around.

'Are you here for property? Can you not see the misery about? Where is your humanity, Sir?'

Mayfellow pushed past him, seeing that already stuff was being thrown onto the shore. But the survivor called out: 'I know your face; I shall be a witness to your deeds and will see your head in a noose!' Mayfellow stopped in his tracks.

'Can you not just let a man do his lawful work?' Mayfellow grabbed the man by the coat and dragged him back into the water. The man was yelling, but could not keep on his feet, which served Mayfellow's intention well. He pushed his head under and held it until he struggled no more.

The waves were merciless and striking hard. The side of the boat burst open like a pig's belly. The crowd cheered. This was the best of dreams as they watched wealth unknown to the islanders floating toward them or bobbing in the water.

A group of survivors watched helplessly in tears as the looters began hauling barrels and trinkets into a pile. The plan was working well yet Mayfellow wanted more. This may not ever happen again in his lifetime, so he wanted to make the most of it. He lifted himself into the broken vessel, pushed past a woman who thought he had come for her and went below deck. The thrill was intense: the pounding of the storm, the terrible screeching of the wood, the laments of the dying. His eyes widened with greed.

As the boat was breaking up the waves finally ripped it in two, one half was pushed with incredible force further onto the beach. The half Mayfellow was in was suddenly lighter by virtue of being released from the anchoring weight of the whole. It pushed off from the beach and vanished into the night, Mayfellow disappearing with it.

JACK

After the visit to the museum, I started an island walkabout. Considering what I was charged with doing, please don't ask why it had taken so long as I have no idea. During this walk, the raw beauty of the place grabbed me like it had done in my earlier walk up here. Its initial barrenness was being replaced by a sense of place I hadn't entertained before. Why had this island braved the elements and become the only place on the entire south coast which had departed from the shelter of the mainland in such a way. It differed dramatically from the coastline not only in nature, but in kind too, almost to the point where you questioned whether it belonged here at all. On the Island there were no rolling hills of fields and woodland. There were no cliffs sweeping in and out of the sea. It had a brutal primeval splendour, stark and robust, like one of those fortresses built by the Knights Templar around the Mediterranean. Magnificent and redundant at the same time, proud but decaying, carved by the sea and wind and yet resistant to both.

On the way back home, I entered one of the graveyards and discovered something I hadn't expected. There was a tombstone with my very own name on it. I mean, my actual whole name: Jack Robert Powys. How could this be? What is more, there was a skull and crossbones where normally you might see a cross or an angel. This chap had died of "wounds received whilst avoiding the customs" in 1767. I decided there and then to undertake my own ancestry search.

When I returned home, I sat down and read through each item Weller had given me. It took twelve hours and two bottles of wine. As I read them, I began at last to see patterns and trends in this random collection for the first time. Basically, I had five categories:

1. Academic or scholarly histories of the Island
2. Personal accounts of true historic events
3. Personal accounts of their own experience
4. Tales of Island Folklore
5. Other incidental materials such as newspaper
6. clippings, blogs, scientific and historical studies or records

Once I had established this, in chronological order, I put each into the relevant pile. The oldest story (folklore) recorded describes how the island may have been formed, but there were others. Jesus gets a mention in one of them. The most recent was a story about an escaped prisoner, who, in his desperation, met his end by throwing himself off Pulpit Rock at the southern tip of the island. Surrounded by police with dogs, he jumped, but instead of meeting the soft cushion of the water he struck the rocks just hiding below the surface. That newspaper clip was dated only three years ago.

Not surprisingly, the more recent accounts tended to be more factual than mythical. For an impoverished island basically forgotten by not only the mainland, but also by its neighbouring town, there was very little serious crime. What crime there was mainly centred around petty theft and anti-social behaviour, probably easily explained by the fact that there was nothing for youngsters to do. One story however, caught my eye. About twelve years ago, two teenage girls went missing. Neither the culprit nor the bodies of the girls were ever found. The two disappearances happened within a six-month period of each other. Nothing had happened like this before or since. The police were lambasted for their shoddy investigation and their "miserable" failure in putting the clues together, despite tremendous local support and an intensive house to house search. The press called them the Twilight Murders, as both had gone missing as the sun dipped below the horizon. I resolved to ask Old Flann about this, as it seemed in contrast to everything else, I had read.

*

Annoyingly, having found some impetus to start earning the money I was being paid to do this work, life was becoming busier and rather entertaining. I didn't need distraction, though I was always looking for it. Our row of terraced cottages had come alive with activity of one sort or another. First, there was the Bridge boy who somehow died and somehow came back to life. I was with Eve at the time, taking notes about one of her war stories. He had stopped breathing when his mother arrived on Eve's doorstep with a child in her arms. The mother was all over the place, screaming and crying as any parent would. I did what I could. Eve quietly took the boy in her arms and disappeared into the backroom. The ambulance crew arrived. Before they could do their thing, Eve emerged from the room, hand in hand with the little lad. When all had calmed and the boy was on his way for a check over, I asked Eve what she had done.

'Nothing, a little massage, that's all'

'Looked more to it than that, Eve, if you don't mind

me saying.' She hesitated. 'There is more to life than what you see.'

'Which means?'

'How do you think us islanders survived before doctors and medicine? We have been here for thousands of years; all that medical stuff is so recent. We learnt other ways to look after ourselves and how to tend to the sick.'

'You talking paganism?'

Although I thought she was about to tell me more, she bit her lip and made an excuse to leave. I made a mental note to quiz her further on another occasion.

I am sure you will not be surprised; Rowan was never far from my thoughts. One drunken night I wondered if I had fallen in love with the girl. The image of her nude burnt into my head. She was a bit younger than me, but hey ho, who cares these days. She was said to be mad, but again, who can profess sanity in this crazy fucked-up world. She was a strange girl, sort-of unusual, not worldly. Whatever it was, it tickled my fancy. Was I indeed falling in love with her? These are the first feelings of this kind since I met Trish at Uni and their abrupt arrival disturbed me.

Then Rowan herself did something which shocked and astonished me and everyone else who knew her. This latest episode only served to boost my fascination with her. A boat was caught unawares off Friar's Point, round the bay from our cottages. I'm not sure what they were doing, but the sea here can whip itself from passivity to frenzy in the blink of the eye. If the tide resonates with the wind, I have seen with my own eyes that all hell can be let loose. Two of the three on the boat managed to clamber onto the rocks. The third fell into the drink. I didn't see this part but was told the whole story later by Eve. Rowan apparently saved the third guy from drowning. I reached the shore as Rowan was dragging him in by the collar. Where had that strength come from. A few of the locals rushed into the shallows to lift the lad up onto the beach. I dashed home to fetch a couple of towels. On returning, I wrapped one over Rowan's shoulders. The look she gave me certainly wasn't gratitude, nor was it resentment so much as a direct stare of defiance.

'Thanks,' she said, but turned from me straightaway. I begrudgingly threw the other towel over the lad, who was spluttering and panting on the pebbles.

*

The next day, the postman delivered two items. One was a letter from the water board saying they were going to start work on the system later in the summer. The other, a postcard. From Trish. It was just like Trish. She does not contact me for months then she sends a postcard out of the blue, written succinctly in red ink:

Hope u ok. Must meet to discuss selling the flat - things have moved on - have something amazing to tell u. Cheers T x

Take a dagger to a man's heart. Less than twenty words could kill a man. She didn't have to speak them. Just pop it on a postcard (picture of Van Gogh's Wheatfield on the front - what was I supposed to glean from that?) She was clever. She always was clever in the relationship region of life. She knew she could run circles around me. With Trish, it was like playing a game of chess to the rules of backgammon.

I used to waste many brain cells trying to solve her conundrums. Then as soon as I thought I'd got it, I realised the game had changed again; we would be playing whist to the rules of rummy. I said this to Claude the other week and he said it just sounded like a regular relationship to him. It was my mistake anyway. Soon after I first arrived here, I had messaged her in a drunken state and told her where I was. It astounds me that you can spend such a huge amount of your life with somebody and yet it can pass like a shit down the pan in a matter of minutes. Or so it feels.

Hope u ok. Meaning, hope you're suffering and realise how much you hurt me, Jack Powys!

Must meet to discuss selling the flat. Wake up and smell the coffee. Reconciliation is impossible. Fuck the counselling you kept suggesting. That was just another way of yours to gain control!

Things have moved on. I'm fucking someone else you know and he knows how to treat me, he understands me, he's fun, new, exciting etc.

Have something amazing to tell u. What could she Mean? New career? Emigrating? Lottery? What kept popping into my head was that, for years, Trish and I tried for kids. She had five miscarriages and then a little boy was born prematurely. His name was Alex. He had to go on a life support machine in intensive care. We kept a hope alive that he would win through, despite what the doctors were saying. It was the first time I had prayed in years. I went into the local church and lit a candle. As part of my bargaining with him, I promised God this, that and the other. When I got back to the hospital Alex was already dead. They allowed us to hold him for the first time. Less than a pound in the palm of my hand. A little man called Alex, who had only breathed on his own for a couple of hours. Trish was shaking with grief and my heart went out to her. I would never leave her, I pledged to myself. I would always protect her.

Have something amazing to tell u. Could it be this then, a child on its way? Her dream answered. Our dream answered, but not in the way I had thought it would be. If it was true - and of course it may only be my tricky imagination - then this would have been the seventh child. The sort of irony that cuts you into pieces.

As usual, no contact details. Had she moved? Had her phone number changed? Would I have to go through her mum who always thought of me as a waste of space. This was her way of retaining control. Well done, Trish. What game are we playing now? Despite finishing with Trish about a million times, if truth be told, I still felt an undertone of guilt. What's up with me. I realized that my drifting from one situation to another was only possible because there had not been anything holding me down, anything real that is, like an authentic emotion. My innate state of emptiness was somehow my badge. Maybe I need counselling or therapy. Rowan showed no interest in me whatsoever and I guessed I was in for an emotional bruising. Or, was that her who keeps phoning me. When I pick up, there's nobody there. More precisely, there is someone there, I can sense them. I plead for an answer, but the line goes dead. I'm sure it wasn't Rowan's style. If not her, then who was it. Even less like Trish, she couldn't have endured the silence. I know that much about her.

This is what happens to me with Trish. Off I go into a fog of self-doubt, loathing and stupefaction. I think of Rowan. Maybe I'm playing my own game. Let's face it, Trish, even in her heyday never looked as good as she does.

ROWAN

I am unsure if I believe in human kindness, unsure if love exists or if unselfishness is a story cooked up by romantics. Dead parents aside, I have never loved, been loved or been in love. As sure as shit is shit, evil does exist. I see this every fucking where. Sometimes it invades my whole being and takes me totally over and all I crave for is punishment: hard, destructive, senseless punishment. Evil defo exists and with it, its bastard sons, Hatred and Deceit. I should have seen it coming. I suspended my usual distrust and gave permission for another to march into my territory. I am talking about Claude.

When he first presented himself as a friend, I thought, why not. He's nothing more than a quirky old git. Little did I know. Whether he had plans from day one, I have no idea, but nothing, nothing, nothing would surprise me. He coaxed me, he worked me, he played me. He said the right thing at the right time, produced the opportune bottle of vino, shared a toke in a naturally generous way, offered gentle advice when the world felt overwhelming. I put him down as an old hippie, a bit of a loose cannon but essentially straight.

It was all my fault. Of course, it was. I set myself up. I tested my own self-destruct button and guess what? It worked. Last week we both got hopelessly drunk, doubly powerful as we were enjoying some of the dope, he had bought from Ganja Ginge. This was the second time we really went for it and I was beginning to trust him. Seriously, me, trusting him. He told me about his little girl buried under the tree in his garden. He became upset. Having never seen or imagined this before, I tried to placate him. I told him about my own loss and having buried my stillborn boy over by the cliffs. At the time, he seemed to instantly perk up and I thought I had offered him some genuine comfort. I hadn't done anything of the sort. The only good thing, if good is the word, was that I said nothing about my present condition.

He visited this morning and for once, outstayed his welcome.

'OK Claude, I need to do stuff today, if you don't mind.'

'Well, there is one matter I have to discuss with you.' His manner was uncharacteristically formal? 'You see, I have made an investment and I think it's high time I collected my dues, my dividend, as it were.'

'Claude, I have not a clue what you are going on about.'

'Let me illuminate you, Rowan. You know the secret you disclosed to me the other day.'

'Let's not talk about that, shall we?' I asked, sitting down. 'I was stoned and feeling pretty desperate. I mentioned it only because of what you said. Shall we agree to let it go.'

'That's it, young Rowan. I don't want to let it go. You see, I have a little something of yours.' I was on my feet, shouting at him.'

'What the fuck are you saying? you fucking wanker!'

He told me. By the time he finished I was in a daze, staring blankly at the wall. I could feel all my defences melting, all my insides, exposed and vulnerable, ready for anyone to stamp all over them. I had done something wrong, I knew it, but hardly could have guessed the punishment would be so swift, so keen, so damning!

'So, you see...' his voice began penetrating my mind again. 'All we need to do is to come to a little arrangement.

No one need ever know.' He stood in front of me, unzipping his flies.

'You got to be fucking joking!' I said, I pulled back, but the conviction had gone from my voice. I was beaten. I was dead. How easily I fall apart. The armour on the outside is hard but thin like a shell protecting the helpless shithead inside. I wanted something to happen. To fall into a trance, be consumed in a vision, to be rescued by someone, anyone, by Katie, by Zac, by anyone.

'Remember no one need know. Naturally, what you have done is beyond forgiveness. No one would understand your actions. Nobody's ever going to know. It stays with me. The police won't drag you away. They won't chuck you in the loony bin and throw away the key. You will avoid the public humiliation, the papers, the *attention*. Let's face it Rowan, you do deserve it, you know you deserve it. That's why you are one mad fucked-up bitch. So, let us do what has to be done.'

I remained lifeless and conscious and endured it all.

*

After Claude's second visit, I seriously began falling apart. As is my way, of course, I didn't tell a soul. I could have told Katie or Eve. I said nothing. The story of my life. I sucked it into my heart, and I kept it there with all the rest of the shitty memories and forgotten crap. As far as I was concerned, this was yet another logical progression of my life. It was the curse making itself known, reminding me that I was not free and never would be. He was right - I deserved such things. Claude was merely the messenger. I swallowed my own vomit and bottled it all up. If I felt it coming to the surface, I swallowed hard, kept it in, at all costs kept it in.

The Wolf was having none of it. The first sign of Him was this crazy irritating little itch on the skin. The more I ignored it, the more persistent it became. It was like being eaten alive by mosquitoes: the hands, the wrists, the neck. My first course of action was alcohol. Drink as often as possible in the hope of relief or immunity. Then, much to his surprise, I invited Zac around and blew my skull apart smoking as much dope as I could, using the Dragon to finish the job. The Dragon made from a yard of drainpipe was the name we had christened our bong with. It killed you. Not a thought for what was in my womb. Total destruction, for me, it, both. I wanted me dead and I wanted it dead. I scrubbed my skin raw. I fasted for a day or two. All my usual crappy tricks that never work. I drank a tumbler of sea water. That really worked; I threw up the contents of my stomach with amazing accuracy. The Wolf came anyway as I knew he would. Late the other night, pulling me from sleep, grabbing my arm in my delirium, forcing it to the bedside draw and making me pick up the razor laying there in its sacred box.

When I came to, I was lying in my own blood, the duvet was soaking with the stuff. Something was different this time. Often, I feel a profound sense of peace afterwards, but I was feeling something very different this time. I could still sense the Wolf was near. Blood usually satisfies Him, and He becomes quiet, but I sensed He was still near. He was close. I could feel his breath.' You know what needs to be done.' he spoke in a whisper, but I heard him clearly.

'Kill him.'

'Kill? Who shall I kill?'

'Kill him, kill him,' He whispered more frantically.' I will help you.'

'Who shall I kill?'

'Claude, kill him.'

*

Since the command I received from the Wolf some part of me shifted. Better said, part of me feels changed. People see madness as frightening or dangerous or, if they're feeling bighearted, puzzling. I admit it can be all three. I have known people "in the system" who have done terrible things to themselves or to other people. There is always a logic to whatever they have done, be it an absurd or obscure logic. Drinking bleach to purify the body. Swallowing razor blades to spill your guts from the inside. Pouring scalding water over your head to wash away the dirt. Hearing a stranger's voice in your head or seeing things that nobody else sees; maybe these are just other ways of keeping you safe or ways of revealing a hidden part of you. Madness pushes you to limits most may not feel in a lifetime or two. Since the "command" I feel safer, I feel I have a purpose and I feel empowered in a way I have never felt before.

Three losers in a boat hit the rocks off Deadman's. It isn't unknown, boats flounder there all the time. The water goes from quite deep to a sudden wall of rock which just pokes through the surface. I went down with the other locals, as mischievous as I was curious. It's always sort of fun to see others struggle. Two of the older men made it to the rock but the younger lad didn't and became caught in the contrary waves. He couldn't swim any way without the sea foiling his efforts. I knew what to do. Nobody else was doing a thing. Everyone was dithering about waiting for the lifeboat. Eve was egging others to do something but she's too old herself. All the others were watching the scene before them as if it were a clip-on YouTube. Before I could think or give any thoughts to the baby I was carrying, I had dived into the water. Clothes still on, sandals lost somewhere. This was the first time I had swam like this for years since teenage times. When I reached him, he was spluttering and panting and trying to speak. I told him to shut the fuck up, relax and follow my lead. The words cut into his panic, because he did shut up, relax and take my lead. That way I was able to pull him to shore using a technique I had used only once aged fourteen in the swimming pool at Secondary.

When I got to shore with him, I allowed the others to take over. They wanted to fuss over me as well, but I really was alright. In fact, I was better than alright - for the first time in an age, I felt strong. I felt as powerful as shit. The place where the "command" came from was the same place which gave me the power and the will to rescue the young guy. This made me nosy - about myself. What force could push you into doing something you would never think of doing. How could my own actions shock me? How could I act outside my own nature.

*

Jack called in today. Normally, I am deliberately off with him, but I decided to act differently towards him. After the incident when he rushed to me with the towel, I thought I would give him a bit of slack. Whether he had a crush on me or not, he was hardly a threat. I broke open a bottle of wine with him. He was obviously in a talkative mood, because he launched straightaway into a rant about the project he was involved in.

'I think I may have made a breakthrough. I admit to going around in circles. I admit to not putting my all into it. I found myself reading all these stories and looking for threads and patterns. The stories merge facts and fiction, folklore arises from real events, historic events trigger myths. I have to make sense of it and now finally I am applying myself. I think.' He babbled on. 'The island is the obvious common factor but even the island doesn't feel so solid sometimes.'

'Or is it the people who are the common factor?'

'Well, again, both are intertwined. One cannot exist without the other. The people are the island in a very real sense, I suppose much the same as the pebbles are the beach. Yesterday I laid out all the stories on the floor. My whole ground floor is plastered, and I spent time looking for these trends, exploring the connections between each and every one. It was like one big family tree.'

'And did you succeed?'

'Well, I divided the lot into five groups. It's a start.'

'So why are you doing this.' I asked him.

'Do you know I'm not sure. It was meant to be filling the gap between my relationship with Trish going belly-up and whatever happens next in my life. I must confess though, as time goes on, it's feeling more like the whatever-happens-next.' He laughed at himself. 'For starters, look at what has happened since I came to the island. You can't help arriving at the idea that it is still going on, that island history is unravelling as we speak. Me, and you, all of you, are part of its unravelling!'

'What do you mean?' I said, though I knew what he meant.

As for Claude, I decided to follow the bastard about and see what he was getting up to. He had me in his power, and he knew it. Somewhere he had hidden my dead baby. Why did I tell him such a thing? Why did I trust him when I don't trust anyone? At the time, it had felt absolutely right. I see now that he was working me and pushing the right buttons and putting me into a position where he could get into my head. I feel such shame about what I did. He frightens me and I feel utterly helpless lest he tell someone what I did.

Believe it or not, I began keeping tabs of his movements. Most were totally boring and pretty mind-numbing. He was always in the pub, stirring it up one way or another. He was often calling into Eve's. Why? Eve liked her men, and I know she is looking for another husband. She makes no bones about that. She even calls herself a sixteen-year-old living in the body of an old woman. Could she be thinking of Claude as a possible? I will ask her. More to the point, what does Claude see in Eve? Why the visits? Admittedly, he is not an unhandsome man, but he is quite a bit younger than her. My curiosity was aroused. Into the notebook went the entries.

I began spying on him at night. That produced some strange results. I know he is home, it's dark, the lights are on, front and back, yet there is no sign of him. He's not in the kitchen, eating or washing up. He's not in the lounge watching TV, though I can see it's on. He may be in the hall - but for more than an hour. He may be upstairs - but in the dark. I began to wonder.

CLAUDE

In my favour, I knew the children visited Eve most weekends and sometimes during the week if their father had to work. He was no real threat, so I dismissed him out of hand. Harry, that's his name, was still reeling from his own love loss and therefore, blind to most things. It is a well-known fact of life that the police are easily fooled. Moreover, I had already broken the ice with the children with the cigarette thing. Lastly, Claude, you sly fox, they had already been in your house. That's another taboo broken and, as you know, once a taboo is broken it's hard to re-establish.

On the other hand, maintaining balance in my approach, I reminded myself that the two children always hung around together. Eve was only next door and would be on her guard most of the time. For all I knew she may already know about the smoking. At the moment, I'm not close enough to Eve to command regular access to my prize. I shall have to remedy this in some way. I have already increased my visitations, making stupid excuses to call in. So, my thoughts turned to my next big move. For me to succeed with Rachel, I first had to deal with brother Tom and Grandmother Eve.

I saw my main quarry this very morning. Rachel was climbing the bank of pebbles towards with sea. I congratulated myself on my assessment of such a beauty. Without a single doubt in my head, my original attention was more than substantiated and I knew I had selected with both shrewdness and taste. Yet again though, she was there with that annoying kid brother of hers. How to get rid of him.

As part of my master plan, I began talking to both the boy and the gran about clubs in a ruse to get the little blighter out of the way. Scouts were, for instance, a laudable experience for lads his age. I was in the choir as a boy myself and sold it to the silly bat as one of the most beneficial of all possible childhood pursuits. Look how I turned out, for example. None of these excellent ideas stuck in this family of morons. Then one night I was invited for supper which both children and their father would be attending. Seeing a unique opportunity, I argued my way into preparing the supper for them or at least helping out with a dish.

This, at least, was a chance to do mischief. Please understand I didn't want to dispose of the lad, merely to remove him temporarily from the situation. I do not profess to be an expert, but I have at my disposal a certain knowledge of common poisons. I grow rhubarb in my garden, the leaves of which contain notable quantities of oxalic acid and can be "lost" in a salad.

Possible symptoms include convulsions and coma, if you're lucky. Rosary peas are pretty and contain abrin which can cause nausea, vomiting, seizures, liver failure, and occasionally death: one single ingested seed is enough. I do not grow these anymore but keep a jar of dried seeds for emergencies. Then we have mushrooms - Amanita would blow his guts out or maybe I could use magic mushrooms and send the nuisance on his first trip. I opted to do the soup, deciding to drop a rosary pea neatly into his broth.

It didn't work. Eve was fussing about so much, guzzling back the red wine, absolutely over-excited by the occasion. She constantly hovered over me, endlessly chatting about crap. To make an error and drop the pea into the wrong bowl would have been a disaster. More so, if it ended up in the bowl of my heart's desire. At one point I thought I had the ideal opportunity and was about to deposit the pea into the correct bowl when the boy himself appeared and grabbed a different bowl entirely.

'What a helpful lad,' I said through gritted teeth.

The moment passed. When you have drive and purpose, life will always provide an opportunity of its own contrivance. I find this happens over and over again. You try to manipulate or engineer life to your own benefit, trying to play it as an elaborate game, but all that is required is patience. That's how the lion wins its prey. By biding its advance patiently and seeing what opportunities present themselves either by chance or by design. I didn't have to wait long.

*

Everything was going marvellously. Much, much better than I had hoped. The silly bitch Rowan was eating out of my hand and I was busy planning accidental encounters with the Stocker girl. All going well until the other night when an old acquaintance walked into the local. It was a wet night and they had the wood fire burning. Chivers was playing chess with me and I was about to dispense of him for the third time when, Jesu in heaven, in walked Max Hamilton. He stripped himself of his wet gear and went straight to the bar. As soon as he spotted me, he came over.

'Are you still playing?' whimpered Chivers.

'Sure,' I said, moving my castle across the board and placing him in an impossible position.' Checkmate. 'I said again, already getting up and walking over to Hamilton.' Let me get that, old man!'

'Claude. I wondered if I would bump into you, you old lech!'

'Not so loud, my friend. Come over to the corner table.' Hamilton did what he was told.

'So, how the devil are you keeping?'

'I'm keeping very well, thank you, Max. What brings you back to this fair island of ours on such a bloody awful night?'

'Well, I have had a little luck. I'm following the tail.'

This is what I feared. The last thing I wanted or needed was a jerk like Hamilton on my patch.

'You have a quarry in sight?'

'In sight and ready for plugging!' he made an inane mimic of a man shooting a gun. 'I have befriended this wonderful creature. She is perfection, dear man. You can imagine my surprise when I found out she was living on the old island. I thought get over there quickly before Claude spots her.'

The whole Hamilton family was a danger zone. They were either barmy, thick or treacherous and exasperatingly, they stuck together. A quarrel with one was a quarrel with the whole Hamilton clan. Mercifully, Hamilton Senior had set himself on fire years ago in an imaginary protest about an imaginary conspiracy involving the Hungarian secret police. His mother disappeared some time ago with a bloke half her age and his brother was in the clink for GBH or something of the sort. Max's cousin was that tosser Zac who visited Rowan. The island was peppered with other Hamilton half-breeds who emerged out of the woodwork whenever the occasion demanded. Max was the most problematic to me because he was both mad and bad and had more than the family average in brain cells. He was likewise proactive in his pursuit of yearlings.

He bought another drink and then proceeded to get some photographs out of his jacket pocket. 'Look at these and dribble!' As he handed them to me, he pulled back in a sham gesture of reprove. 'You will honour the code? Do remember Claude, this young lady is mine.'

Through clenched teeth, I reassured him and prised the photos from his hand. A pimply girl of maybe thirteen stared back at me. I turned over the back. Max had written her name on the back: Sally.

'So, this is an internet conquest?'

I detested this new breed of predator who relied on the internet to find their next victim. It was so crude and amateurish. It involved conjuring up a web of lies I frankly couldn't be bothered to construct or remember. Hamilton was a different fish. He had no finesse about him, no decorum and gave the rest of us a bad name. For example, he never fussed about stuff like understanding and consent. He didn't worry about the girl's mind and how his influence could be negative or positive, whether it could cause long term damage or not. For me, these were of the utmost concern and I pride myself that nobody I had ever been with had done so without me being first convinced that they were willing and aware of what they were saying yes to. Max had no such quibbles. To him, all were potential targets: boys (disgusting!), younger girls (appalling!), retards (please!). People like him should be taken off the streets!

'So, who does she think you are?'

'Aha, at first, I said I was a seventeen-year-old guy. Then I actually told her the truth - or a little more of it - and told her that I hadn't told her the whole story at first because I thought my age would put her off. The silly cunt fell for it. I told her I was actually twenty-two. What's a decade or so between friends, eh?' He was squealing with laughter.

'And who are these others?' I started shuffling through the six or so other photographs of girls, each with their names on the back.

'Just her mates. There could be further grazing there, Claude.'

I took a deep breath. The last photograph was of Rachel. Like the others, Hamilton had written her name on the back.

'Yes, she's quite a cracker as well, don't you think?' While I was at the bar buying another drink for this twat, I felt my world had taken a knocking. My plan was coming undone before my very eyes. Nothing grieved me more than the undoing of a plan.

'Brilliant to see you after all this time,' I said to him, overly cheerful. 'I think we need a much better catch-up than just one night in the local. And I have it. How about doing what we used to do in the old days? How about going fishing? The mackerel are practically jumping out of the water at the moment.'

'Good idea!' he yelped. Sally wasn't the only gullible shit on the island.

'Well, no time like the present. Before you go a-hunting,' I said tapping the photos. 'Let's get out on the ocean as soon as poss. All this weather will be gone by tomorrow and I can get hold of Lacey's boat. How about it? Where are you staying?'

'Gabby's Guest House'

'Perfect. Sneak out just past dawn, say six. You know the mackerel are early risers. Meet me at the far side of the cove.'

It was my turn to beam like a Cheshire cat. With my charm fully turned on to its highest setting, this sucker was being drawn in hook, line and sinker, a metaphor which was by now becoming quite literal.

'And don't tell Gabby where you're going, Max. She will love a surprise trove of mackerel for her lunch!'

*

Sometimes I amaze myself. Most of the time I am the most laid back of chaps, mooching through my life in an easy laissez faire manner, at peace with myself and the world. There is something of the Latino about me. Yet, when I'm focused, I am razor-sharp and as alert as a hare. In my usual routine, I awake from a night's sleep about eight and idle away a couple of hours, walking about in my dressing gown, drinking tea and reading the Telegraph. Not so when I'm on a mission. Take what I did to poor Rowan and her sad offspring. Now it was Hamilton's turn. The next day, I was up at five, putting everything in place for a jolly day of fishing. The rain had gone as expected but had left a sheath of grey muck which covered most of the sky. The sea was as calm as a sleeping baby. I went to the shed and found two fishing rods unearthed spare hooks and feathers, the landing net and my toolbox. I hauled this lot up to the top shore where Lacey kept his small rowing boat. I placed the gear carefully in, making sure everything was in the correct place. The boat still had its old dilapidated engine attached, rusting away, largely unused for five years or more. I decided not to bother to tell Lacey I was borrowing his boat. One, I didn't want him to know about our little trip and two, he was so steamed up these days he probably wouldn't remember if I told him anyway. I made sure all was ready in the vessel, checking everything over twice. I paid particular attention to the anchor and its accompanying rope as this was essential for our little fishing trip, especially so for this one.

Hamilton turned up fifteen minutes late which I had anticipated. My greeting was welcoming, warm and if I may say so myself, somewhat kind-hearted. We dragged the boat down the slope of pebbles and into the water. I took on the rowing and plied the waves with enthusiasm. Before you knew it, we were a few hundred yards out.

'Let's put down the lines, Max. I suggest we allow ourselves to drift for a while. Going from the tide that will keep us roughly parallel to the beach.' He aye-aye-captained me in his rather silly way and we dropped our lines.

'So how are you playing your next move? On your tail, I mean.'

'You know the score, Claude, a professional like you. I shall keep my distance for a couple of days. Do a bit of eyeing up, sussing the situ and spying on her. Getting to grips with the landscape, if you know what I mean. Whilst doing that I shall be on the chat line all the time buttering her up, telling her I'm on the way, telling her my family have kicked me out or some such rubbish. Getting her to feel sorry for me, making out I'm the wronged one, the needy one, getting her to feel that she is the answer to my problem, my little teenage saviour. All priming her for our first encounter.'

We both got a nibble at the same time. This is not unusual in mackerel fishing. You attract their attention by letting the line out until it touches the bottom and then you begin winding it in a series of swift deliberate jerks. They dart around in massive shoals and go for anything that is bright and moving. When they see twelve feathers darting through the water, six on each of our lines, they throw themselves at the feather. They expect whiting and they get a steel garb instead. Evolution is slow to teach them anything as they do this all summer, year after year, decade on decade. We landed three with ease, dropped our line and caught another four within as many minutes. Max was screeching away with sheer delight at our bounty.

'That's four to me, Claude and just two for you. Losing your knack, old fellow.' This moronic teasing was perfect, putting me exactly in the right mood for the task ahead. In a quiet spell I suggested coffee and poured out two plastic cups from the flask I had prepared earlier. We rolled a couple of cigarettes.

'Hey, let me see those photos again, the ones you showed me last night'

'You're not thinking of poaching, are you, old boy?' I laughed, by way of a response. 'And how do you know I have them with me?'

'Give me a break, Max. I know you better than you think!' He handed me the photographs. 'Oh, Max, just remembered the croissants I bought with me for breakfast. They're in the bag in the bow, be a good man and reach them.'

'It's like old times,' I said.' All those intervening years, all those wild adventures, all the new things we have learnt. But I bet you, you haven't learnt one thing yet...? 'With that I gave him an almighty kick in the butt, using the side of the boat to push against. He tipped over the side in one neat splash. 'I bet you, you haven't learnt to swim!'

He surfaced, spluttering and beating the surface in the pointless way drowning men do. He was screaming my name between alternative gulps of air and water. For a moment, just one split second, it flashed through my mind to save the poor sod. Then I thought, this man is a pest to society; he's a hyena scavenging on innocent flesh. There's not one remorseless morsel in his entire putrid filthy body!
'Help, Help! Claude, for god's sake, for god's sake!' etc.

The boat began to drift away from him, so I applied myself to the oars and manipulated myself back to my perishing colleague.

'Give us your hand. Max, give us your hand!' I extended the rope to him. 'Take the rope, take the fucking rope!'

He grabbed for it and I managed to place the loop at its end around his wrist. Instead of pulling in, I let the rope out. Hamilton began to panic afresh, with disbelief, frustration or anger, I could not really tell which. Whatever it was, he was positively beginning to irritate me. At the end of the rope naturally enough was the anchor, which I showed him with theatrical aplomb as I dropped it over the edge of the boat.

As the anchor sank at speed towards the bottom, Hamilton stopped beating the water. He became calm and motionless and looked up to me with the sweetest smile. Then he was gone. A fart of bubbles and young Hamilton was no more.

Not wanting to waste the moment, I fished for an hour more. As I rowed back later that morning, I confirmed the score to my drowned friend: Five to you, eighteen to me. Claude's the winner!

*

Thank the Holy Ghost. Now that particular situation had been resolved I could return with enthusiasm to my original purpose. Suicide is always difficult to get your head around but that is essentially what Hamilton did. Who goes on water without being able to swim? Who would be so trusting of a known competitor? This fishing trip, he really didn't think it through, did he? Suicide, plain and simple. This man just didn't want to live enough. So, I shall waste no more time on that loser. Why should I? Especially when I remind myself how, with his demise, so much harm in the world has been avoided.

I was in such a jolly mood after this, I decided to call in to see young Rowan and offer her a little mackerel of my own. Since I informed her of my investment and the need for a return, I had visited twice. This was my third time. You can imagine the conversations we used to enjoy with the friendly bottle of wine or spliff or whatever, have now disappeared. I try to invoke some response with my usual charm and merriment. She says very little. I don't mind too much. To start with I found her passivity and resignation a turn-off but since my interest in Rachel has reloaded my gun, I am finding it strangely seductive. She's full of tricks this one. As I was well aware that she was one crazy bitch, by way of an act of kindness, I kept my demands uncomplicated, straightforward and time limited. I neither want to take advantage of her situation too much nor do I want to place myself in a position where I may become vulnerable or compromised. In a prone position one is inevitably open to attack. It only happened once to me and I lost function down below for a couple of weeks. Most disconcerting as you don't know when your performance will return. Never again will I ever be in that situation.

Christos Mistos, this day was going so well, afterwards I popped into to see Jack and collected another £50 for the motor which lamentably remained in front of his house. I asked him how his enterprise was going and was both impressed and delighted to hear about his mental paralysis. He tried to dress it up, declaring he had at the very least found the right format with which to start. I could read between the lines - more of the same. It was hard to get a grasp as to what he was actually doing with his time, other than wasting it. Basically, as far as I could gather, he had done fuck all. Other than lusting over our mad filly. Little did he know I had the scent of her body on me as he chugged on. He had paid Weller a visit, which had not been particularly productive. He had been to the museum - whoopee-do! And met its resident toad, but otherwise this man was clueless. I gave him a couple of fish as a consolation prize. Leaving him, I moved closer to the main focus of my attention. I went for a cup of tea with Eve, giving her the lion's share of my haul. With much bravado I gave her a dramatic account of the catch, how I had found the ideal place, how they struggled on the line and so on.

*

'I want to ask you a favour, Claude.'

Yet again, my dear friend, the favour worked in my favour. That night I arranged to visit her to find out what was on her mind. I took my second-best bottle of scotch and insisted on ordering an Indian to save her cooking. Sadly, there was no Rachel but, in this game, one must always run on the ground you're on and forever take the long view. It didn't matter anyway, as I was about to unravel more secrets from the veritable collective of the islands subconscious. Eve sat me down and paused solemnly before telling me what was on her mind. At such times, I have infinite forbearance.

'I have wanted to tell you something for a while,' she whispered, followed by another pause. 'Have you heard of the Sisters?'

'Do you mean the old witches who kept this island in the dark ages for centuries?'

'The very same!' she confirmed and added in her specially prepared soft voice.' I'm one. I'm one of them.'

'One of what?'

'I'm one of the Sisters.'

I had to bite my tongue to stop from laughing out loud. The old she-goat was crazier than I thought.

'My aunt Flora was a Sister. She saw the gift in me and decided to take me under her wing and teach me what she knew.'

Fortunately, she began to cry, giving me an excuse to draw her closer and embrace her, all the while biting my tongue into numbness. Rowan suddenly seemed to be brain of Britain compared to this moron I was cuddling.
'Sorry, so sorry to cry. It's a relief to tell someone. I have been keeping this to myself for such a long time. You see, I stopped the practice some years ago. Harry made me do it. At the time, I thought he was right. Since then I have had other ideas. Something has happened which I think I can remedy.'

My ears pricked up; my curiosity aroused. What was this something? I knew not to push it and to remain the empathic friend, as selfless as a shadow.

'The thing is I need the Book.'

'The Book?'

'The Book. Every Sister has the Book and that's the problem. My Book is in the loft. It is not only in the loft. It's cemented into the chimney. I couldn't bin it or give it away. Harry knew I couldn't consider that. So, we compromised, and he put it up there. I can't get up there. With my wobbling pins, I can't get up that ladder anymore, but, Claude, you could.'

'Why in the devil's name did you not ask me before? For goodness sake, my dear Eve, you can totally and utterly trust me!' She nodded in silence, new tears arising in agreement.

Later that very day I was up in the loft via a wobbly metal ladder. With a torch, I easily found the place in the chimney which had so obviously been cemented in the recent past. With a claw hammer, I chipped merrily away and soon the Book, wrapped in an old towel, was revealed. Mary-in-heaven, what a Book it turned out to be. All handwritten in inks of many colours, it was like discovering the Doomsday Book, or some other volume of national treasure. In short, it was a find. Without hesitation, I began pawing my way randomly through its pages.

'Any luck, my love?' came the voice from below.

'Not quite. It's proving to be trickier than I thought. Your son did a good job up here!'

I wasn't sure what I was going to do with this until I opened the page entitled 'Bedding a Virgin.' How God-given was that? This was worth an extra read, so I took the volume and placed it between the tiles of the roof and the partition between our two houses. Later, I could climb into my own loft and pull the Book through. Simple as that.

'I'll leave it for today if that's OK? And return to the task tomorrow,' I told her, re-emerging from the loft.

'That's fine, Claude. I am so grateful to you for doing this. I suppose, I've waited so long, another day will make no difference.' Exactly!

EVE

With all this going on, I have craved for the Book more and more. Can a person really love a book? Yes, I think so. Some books are bigger than their actual physical size or the words they contain. Some are as big as the world and mine is one of these books. I not only wanted it for my own stated purposes, but I truly needed it for pure affirmation that the order of the world was still as it should be. I yearned for the old ways and the old order. I longed to hold the book, to caress it and trace me fingers along its ancient contours. When I realised, I could trust Claude, I tearfully confided in him and he agreed to release it from its stony prison. He was a pure gentleman about it, further confirming that he may well be my next hubby. I decided against Jack as he was more like a dog chasing its own tail. To me, this Jack appeared to make light on matters serious and heavy weather of the boring. I think I was right in me choice.

On the second attempt, Claude brought the Book down from its hiding place wrapped in an old towel. I asked Claude to leave me at this point, explaining that I needed a private moment with it as a decade had passed since I saw it last. He, as I thought, respected my wishes and left me. I uncovered the Book and my heart leapt into my mouth. How much I had missed it. Not only the magic captured on its pages but the very feel of it, its texture, its colours, its weight, its being. To me it was like a living thing.

I opened the first page not with the rush of hunger, but with the serenity of respect. I beheld the list of Sisters, written in differing handwriting, going back to August 1768. The first name was Esther Pearce. My name was the last on the list. I began to look through the Book, remembering the look of each sacred page, the unique and colourful script and the odd quirky language once associated with enchantment. I arrived on the page I wanted which alluded to the capturing of a new heart. I thought of Claude and smiled. I may not be needing to use this spell after all. As I was turning the pages, I stopped abruptly when I came to a white feather, stuck in the page's crease as a marker. I lifted the feather and examined it. Traditionally, it was considered unlucky to place anything between the Book's pages, lest of all a marker. It was on the page entitled 'Bedding a Virgin.' I pondered on this for a minute or two and then laid the feather to one side.

Eventually, I came to the page I wanted. This one was called *A Certain Cure against Death.* The ingredients were much as I remembered though the order and the measurements were vastly different. Among them were water from a Seventh Wave, seaweed, pepper, fur from a certain rodent and, most importantly, the essence of being; blood from a living human, who must be ignorant of the spell they were caught up in. This final element was, by far, the most difficult to source, but many a king or aristocrat in previous times had sworn by its life-giving powers.

The front door opened and in walked Harry. The draft sent the feather into the air. It drifted for a second and twirled behind the sofa. I quickly shoved the Book under my chair. Whatever happened, he must not see it as he will know that I had broken the promise, I made to him.

'Hello. In here!' I said, over-anxiously.

The good boy that he was, he came over and kissed me on the forehead. This gave me a moment to kick the Book further under my chair.

'You alright, mother? You seem a bit jumpy.'

'Son, I can honestly say I have never felt better, thank

you, but, it's true, I have been feeling a bit at odds with myself lately. Now you sit there, and I'll make you a nice cup of tea. I want to know all about what you've been up to.'

'And I want to know what's going on with you too.'

I can be a good liar at times. Including to meself. I have known people who have successfully lied to themselves all their lives. They flaunt a warped image of themselves to the world, overlooking any possible flaws despite the evidence seen by everybody else, but dreams cannot lie. They conceal to reveal. They use all manner of disguises to tell a simple truth. While waiting for the Book I have had two nights of hell dogged with two horrid nightmares. Something is terribly wrong. My childhood was punctuated with nightmares, which was probably not unexpected as they were deliberately fuelled by my spiritual relatives. The very last time I had a nightmare was when Bert failed to turn up at the beach hut, me ready for love and him anxious for it.

Like all real nightmares, they start ordinarily enough, making the horror twice as powerful when it finally shows itself. In the nightmare, I am in the lounge sitting there by myself with a coal fire in the grate, which, by the way, I do not have any more. All of a sudden, I hear whispering and turn to see who is there. Of course, nobody is. The whispering continues, it's coming from the fire. I get on all-fours and try to listen to what is being said. I can't make any sense of it despite putting me ear as close as I dare. I turn my gaze back to the fire and drop back on my butt. A baby's face is being consumed by the flame, but somehow it is mouthing words to me. It is doubly shocking because the baby is so obviously premature and has that ghastly look of a blind foetus.

The second is no better, merely a variation on the first. I am in the lounge again. I have the Book on my lap, and I am reading it lovingly. I know even in the dream that there is a possibility of the baby returning and showing its face in the fire. So, I try to concentrate on the Book, but I can't. I am drawn to it and keep glancing at it despite my resolve. I am staring at the fire, despite my intentions, thinking I am about to see the baby's helpless little face. It doesn't appear but when I turn back to the Book, the baby's face suddenly breaks through the page. I jump out of me skin and out of sheer terror I throw the Book across the room. The awful scream as the Book hits the wall is thankfully enough to wake me. So, what do these nightmares mean? I have no idea, but I know I am being told a message. Am I reading too much into this? I think not. I am a hopeless mess at the minute, but something escapes me.

I told Harry none of this, nothing of the Book, nothing of the nightmares. We passed the time chatting about his work. I asked if he had a woman on the simmer. Harry surprised me with a keen yes. About time, I tell him. He wouldn't give me any details, so I prodded him. 'She's a mainlander.'

'That's fine son, some of my best friends are mainlanders,' I reassured him. 'The only thing is that, as yet, I haven't actually spoken to her.'

'Harry, what you like? You're not Rachel's age anymore. Get up some courage and ask the poor girl out. Life is over in a twinkling of the eye.'

No sooner had he gone to collect the children from school when there was another rap on the door. With a heavy sigh, I went to the door to see who it was and there was Old Flann standing on my threshold, clasping a pile of books, papers and files. Now I have nowt against the unlucky man and have no quandary whatsoever that Flann, with his dripping face and dodgy eye, is the ugliest man on the whole of the Island, but I wasn't expecting him and could not hide my scare.

'Oh, Eve, I am so, so sorry, I didn't mean to startle or disturb you in any way. I needed to see you, please understand. I should have warned you or phoned or something. So, so sorry, Eve.' He stopped to draw breathe. 'I have come on a personal matter. I need your insight. I have stuff here for Jack.' He took a deep breath. 'I need to talk, if you get my drift, about the afore-mentioned Jack?'

The man was jabbering and making no sense. 'Excuse me for being a bit thick; shouldn't you be taking that stuff to him then?'

'Of course, of course, Eve, but, you see, that is part of the problem. So sorry.'

'I'm picking up that you're sorry, Flann. You had better come on in.'

We went into the lounge. I offered him tea or coffee. When he hesitated, I offered him whisky or beer.'

'The former please, Eve. Large may be appropriate, straight and with ice, if you have it.'

I gave him a glass and brought in the bottle. Whatever it was, this was going to take more than a double.

'How are you keeping?' he began. 'It's been a year since I last saw you. I believe it was at the village barbeque, if my memory serves me well.'

'It may have been, but let us skip the pleasantries, something is on your mind and I suggest you say what you have to say before you give yourself a stroke.'

He tried to laugh. 'Well, I am helping Jack with his project. Hence all this' he said, waving his hands over the stuff now sprawled over my coffee table. 'I must say, there is some class material here. His assignment has triggered off the old preoccupation about this island of ours and how it came to be and how it is strewn with myth and legend.'

'Please get to the point, Flann?'

'So, so sorry, Eve.'

'Stop being you're "so sorry" and tell me what it is.'

'Fair enough. I am not who you think I am.'

'What in God's name are you gibbering about, man?'

'I am a deceiver, a fraud and a charlatan.'

'Never would have guessed,' I said sarcastically.

'I am, Eve. I am all those things. You take me as an outsider, don't you? An outsider who, after my accident, chose of all the places in the world, to settle here on this island.' He points to his face, takes a deep breath and continues. 'Well, my friend, I am both an outsider and an insider.'

'You're making no sense. What you trying to say?'

'My father was born not two hundred yards from where we now sit.' He gulped back his whisky and I filled it again.' I was born a Grant, Peter Grant.'

'One of the Grants?'

'One of the Grants. You wouldn't necessarily know the story as you yourself was not born as yet. My father was an only child, unusual for those times. Much to the family's disgust, he met a mainlander when doing National Service. They married and moved to where she lived, a little village near Christchurch.'

Old Flann made a dramatic pause. He only started up again when I pulled an exasperated face.

'I was Peter who married Christine who had three children, who got divorced and who disappeared.'

'You were Peter who married Christine, had three

children, who got divorced and disappeared?'

'I am that man!' exclaimed Old Flann, enthusiastically.

'So, let me get this straight in me head, you're an Islander by blood?'

'That's me.'

I had to take a few sips of whisky meself as I processed what Old Flann was saying. I had heard this story. It was starting to have the ring of truth about it. My memory clicking in. I am pretty sure one of his cousins married one of mine.

'After parting our ways, I didn't know what to do. Ultimately, I went abroad, did whatever job came my way and there I met my fate.' He told me of his sad accident.

'When I made it through rehab after about a year, I decided to return. To cut a very long story short, I took a local name and took over the management of the museum. Nobody made the connection, nobody suspected, nobody asked any questions. Why would they? My family had gone after all. Everyone accepted that the freak had been given a token job which was within his ability and he could be trusted to do without fuss or demand.

'Wait,' I told him. 'It's coming back to me. Yes, cause we're about the same age, aren't we? I recall you visiting your dad once, perhaps a year before he died. Why Flann? Why do such a thing?'

'Appeared the right thing to do. You see, Eve, there was a certain incident I was embarrassed about. Ashamed of, may be a better way of putting it...' He left the sentence hanging in the air.

I became quieter as my brain was piecing together what Old Flann was saying. Then it dawned on me.

'Oh my God...' I muttered, standing up and walking over to the window. The beach there as ever, with the endless sea smashing against the pebbles. I turned to face Old Flann again. He realised I had got it as he was nodding in silent agreement.

THE FIFTH WAVE

Personal Account by Geoffrey M.
(A version was printed in the local Echo - July 1976)
1803

"Here Mortality with Beauty lies, Confined in Earth with kindred Cries
The Life was Short, her Death severe;
Stop Reader, Think and Shed a Tear!"

So reads the gravestone of one Mary Grant. We have two issues here: one, the means of her death - tragic, sudden, pointless - and two, her tombstone only half describes the truth about this poor lady. True, she has been confined to earth yet on diverse nights - festivals and fogs seem to be her favourites - Mary, with her terribly mutilated face, takes to the streets. For two hundred years, she has been scaring the locals near to death, approaching with arms outstretched asking for the return of her beauty.

Let me explain the manner of her passing. Oddly enough, she wasn't the only one killed on that day, but she is the only one who could never settle. Here's the story: during the Napoleonic Wars, a press gang was set ashore. Their orders were straight and simple. They were to grab some unsuspecting islanders, knock them senseless and toss them into the hull of the waiting ship, only to wake up sober, beaten and miles from shore. Fifty strong and heavily armed crew crept onto the island around dawn. On the top of the island, they were confronted by a mix of islanders who tried reasoning with them. A few in the press gang had firearms and, being both ruthless and tense, shots were fired. Mary caught a blast of shot full in her face. Her injuries were horrific, even to the point where her loved ones were afraid of her. One eye left hanging, her jaw almost completely gone, her nose displaced. The pity was that she didn't die there and then, but no, she lived for several weeks, frightened, in pain and, if we are to believe the vicar of the time, utterly alone.

I know four people who have seen Mary. For reasons unknown, she chooses nights when the island's heights are shrouded in mist. A couple of lovers were buoyant with whisky and were fooled into turning to what they thought would be the kiss of the other only to be confronted by Mary's fallen face. The woman, usually a non-stop talker, didn't speak for a week afterwards. The third chap mysteriously disappeared shortly after telling his wife. Some whispered that his wife had Mary's face without the influence of gunshot. The fourth one was me.

I was coming back up the hill from Portland's annual fair. She was standing by the church in which she was supposed to be interred. I thought it strange for a woman to be out alone at this hour. I was tipsy, I don't mind telling you, but not so tipsy as to affect my vision or gait. She stirred as I came to her, turned toward me, lifting one arm. I didn't need any further encouragement and ran down the street as fast as my legs would carry me.

You can imagine my shock. I tried to cajole myself at first. Soon I found that I was avoiding going out on foggy nights, but it is harder avoiding the place itself as I live here still. Months later, I sighted her for a second time at a distance one morning when I was off to the beach for some early fishing, I decided not to go out before sunrise and after sunset. That was one whole year ago. She plagues me still, despite my resolve. Once I fainted when her hideous face appeared at my bedroom window.

She follows me everywhere or so it feels. At first, I was terrified, but finally I have begun to imagine her former features and half see the beauty she had lost. I can understand her search.

Her search has heralded my own search. I can't settle back to my life, just as Mary can't settle into her death. I keep myself to myself these days. I suppose, I have become a sort of ghost myself. Something has changed the very way I look at life.

Note the words on the gravestone: Stop Reader, shed a tear. But one word hypnotically, slightly incongruent and dissenting, muscles in between. The singular word: Think!

JACK

You never know what to expect in a day. It began as normal - or what I now call normal. The wind had been blowing hard all night and the house felt more at sea than usual. It somehow invaded my dreams in a way in which I was unsure if I was asleep dreaming of the wind or awake actually, experiencing it. When I finally surfaced, I went for a walk along the shore. This was very much becoming part of my routine and symbolised how I was becoming more and more taken by this strange Island I found myself on. When I got back in, I put on the coffee pot and placed a croissant in the oven to warm up. With breakfast over, I began my day's work. I was slowly typing all the stories onto the computer. This was helping in many ways. The main way was that it was contributing to my increasing fascination with the Island's weird history. Don't faint, it had taken a century or two, but my interest was clicking in at last.

Late morning there was a knock on the door. This happened so rarely that it startled me. I suspected the postman. It turned out to be Eve and, huddled behind her, Old Flann, the museum chap with the face.

I stood there blankly for a moment before Eve said, 'Well, can we come in.'

I left them in the lounge to top up the coffee pot, whilst wondering why they were here.

'I've bought some papers for you, Jack,' started Flann, rather self-consciously. 'Some original accounts of some of the shipwrecks, a couple of autobiographies by local men and a rare book, long out of print, on the history of witchcraft once practiced on the island.' Eve coughed at this point but indicated that the conversation should continue.

'Oh, yes and I have a couple of tales from the last war, tales of a supernatural nature, no less.'

'Do progress, Flann,' Eve suddenly snapped before I could thank him for his trouble. I was at a loss as to why she was here.

'Yes, yes, quite!' Taking a deep breath before adding, 'I also have another story to tell you, one which involves the people in this very room.'

Eve rolled her eyes theatrically.

'I was born in 1929 in Christchurch. My father, however, was born here on this very Island, indeed in this very village. He moved to the East of the County when he met my mother after the first War. The family home here was blown to smithereens in 1942. The house was destroyed by a stray bomb. Where the house was there's nothing there now except an open space. That space in the road behind the pub. Fortunately, everyone was out except for my grandmother. My aunts and uncles were all at school or work. There was a lot of them. Nine, I think. His dad, my granddad, was at work. He was a fisherman, you know. My grandmother unfortunately passed away from her injuries. A real blow to the family, as you can imagine.'

'Please, not a blow by blow account. Cut to the chase, man!' Eve barked at him.

'Yes, I will cut to the nub of the story, I was brought up in Christchurch. We used to come to the island every now and then to visit family. I married a mainlander, much to the disgust of the extended family. It wasn't a particularly good marriage. Much to the family's delight, we turned out to be somewhat incompatible. I loved her to bits. I'm sure you know though that love has two components, joy and trust. There was much joy but not so much trust, I'm afraid.

Anyway, we made a go of it. We came back again to the island a few times. Not to settle, just to visit, you understand. We realised that it was ending, the marriage. We stopped communicating, that much is a fact. Then it all came to a head one afternoon.' Old Flann was becoming tearful.

'When we decided to call it a day, we both went on walkabout, as it were. This time separately. She dashed around the country, trying to settle here, there and everywhere. I did several meaningless jobs. Eventually, I travelled abroad, throwing myself into whatever came my way. It led me to this.' He pointed to his face. 'After, I decided to come back here, my new mask meant I could reinvent myself. You see, nobody recognised me. I felt wonderfully invisible. I will tell you how it happened. I went to the post office in Christchurch to send a parcel. It so happened I was served by an old neighbour of mine. It was obvious he didn't know who I was. When he asked my name, without thinking, I found myself saying Robert Flann. Having got away with it, so to speak, I decided to return home, to come back to the island under my new name and in my new guise.'

'This is genuinely fascinating,' I Interjected. 'I should be writing this down. That is, if you want me to, if you don't mind that is.' Eve rolled her eyes again. Old Flann patted the air with his hand, gesturing for him to be allowed to finish.

'The day I left her standing, waiting with the kids on the station platform, that was the last time I ever saw her…I never saw Christine again.'

'Christine. There's a coincidence. My mother's name was Christine.'

'And we had a boy called Jack.'

'Wow. Another coincidence'

'And he had a sister. Rosie.'

Then silence.

The next thing I can recollect was me running along the beach road with not a thought in my head. I couldn't stop, didn't want to. I wanted to run to the edge of the world and jump off. I ran over the bridge and onto the coastal path. Soon enough I was in the open fields which trace the fleet lagoon. I kept running with remarkable prowess for me. As long as I was running, I wasn't thinking so I just kept going. I split from the path and entered the Old Village and finally came to rest in the churchyard.

My father!

I cried. More like a sob than a cry. More like a child's wail than a sob. There are some moments when you know that life will never be the same again. Suddenly, there is a before and after. Suddenly, there is a BC and an AD. You can't go back; you can never go back. Life is on a new footing, a new level. New rules apply. Your perception of your life hasn't so much been revised, it's been transformed. Nothing before prepares you for this moment. And it hasn't come from within; the world has slapped you round the face. This was such a moment.

At such times, the heart beats the head hands down. The mind shows you its limits and can't keep up with the torrent of random thoughts floating on the river of emotion. I know I am mixing metaphors here. This is an honest reflection of my bewilderment. To my own surprise, I start laughing hysterically. Just my luck to have Quasimodo as a saviour. Searching all my days for Papa and I end up with a gargoyle. I knew this was a cruel and callous thought, but it left me rocking with the comedy of it all.

I went for a drink. Five double whiskies later, I thought I would return to the island. This time at a much slower rate. All the power that had pushed me north had been spent for the way back south. It was the longest walk I had ever undertaken. When I got back, I went into Eve's house.

'You OK, Jack? Must have been a bit of a shock for you.'

'Just a bit.'

'I didn't see it myself. You were told the wrong name, that's why I never did recognise it. She gave you her maiden name, Flann said.'

'Thanks Mum!'

'What are you going to do.'

'Eve, I truly don't know. I always knew my life was a fuck-up. I always thought it was my fault. Not so sure now.'

When I got home, I slammed the door behind me and fell back against it. What now? After an age, I got back onto my feet with a sigh. I went into the kitchen and found the old packet of cigarettes I had stashed when I last gave up. Why is it that when emotions are overwhelming, we reach for anything and everything to somehow soothe or defuse their impact? I took them into the lounge and stopped dead when I found Old Flann sitting there just as I had left him hours before. He didn't say a word. He was clearly hurting. I went to leave but he reacted with such alarm, abruptly rising in his chair, that I stood my ground. He then fell on his knees and grabbed my legs. After a moment's hesitation. I knelt down with him and gave him a hug.

'I can understand why you and Mum separated - I know what she could be like. What I am struggling with is why you chose to stop contacting us, Rosie and me. We were kids.' I could immediately see I had touched a nerve.

'Shame, Jack. It was shame, which prevented me. To the very core of me, I was ashamed. I had acted selfishly. I yearned to get in touch. The more I tried the harder it became to do anything. In the end, I couldn't bear to think of you. I became paralysed. When this happened,' he said, pointing to his face.' I saw it as punishment and release at the same time. To me, it was the final solution. It made sure I didn't have to contact you.'

Gradually, tentatively, the silence turned to clamour as we exchanged stories and began asking each other questions about those missing years. We kept it up until about two in the morning when we both had to admit that we were exhausted, both mentally and emotionally from the revelation of father finding son. During our endless ramble, we actually made up our minds to work on the project together. Why not? He had access to a wealth of local material, and I had the commission to put it into some order. Old Flann - I could not bring myself to call him Dad yet - didn't want Weller to know he was involved, saying that it was me who won the commission and I should accept the accolade when it would surely come. This was the only thing he said all that night which seemed disingenuous and I resolved to find out why. At the time, the excitement of all that had passed trumped my curiosity.

'We need to access to his library, Jack. You will have to go alone, I'm afraid.'

Old Flann slept on the sofa despite my protests. As we were sorting the sleeping arrangements out and manoeuvring around one another, there were a few moments of self-consciousness, which was probably to be expected, a more honest reflection of our relationship. Basically, we didn't know one another.

When I woke in the morning, I literally had to pinch myself. To think that downstairs sleeping on my sofa was my father, dismissed from my mind over years of denial, confusion and resentment. At breakfast too, it was awkward, both of us tongue-tied and polite. We made attempts to resume the rapport we had enjoyed on the night before, never quite managing it. To continue the incongruence of the situation, we decided breakfast would be boiled eggs with dippy-in soldiers. All I needed was mum to enter the kitchen in her dressing gown and I could have easily imagined throwing away thirty odd years into the sea, making out I was back in the family home in some murky part of the last century.

'Odd images keep coming back,' I told him. 'But there are huge gaps. I can't remember you splitting or anything about that time. I can hardly remember you. It's all so vague. My mind seems to jump to when Rosie and I moved into the bungalow in Warminster. There are so many missing chunks'

Having said this, the more I stared at him, the more I began to see him, my father, hidden in the folds of his broken face. Naturally, before I hadn't been looking and just put him down as an unfortunate and lonely old man. When we first met, I had avoided ogling him on account of his face. Now I couldn't take my eyes off him. The more I looked the more I saw, and the more I saw, the clearer his face became; his original face.

'So why did you and mum split.' I dropped the question as if I had asked him to pass the salt.

'Ah, Jack,' he replied after a while. 'There's the rub!'

'Excuse me.' I asked, realising I had stumbled on the shadow I had seen the night before. 'There were many reasons. Soon we shall talk about them all I am absolutely certain of that.' I already knew he was a reflective, laconic chap who needed time to relay his thoughts. I was desperate for him to tell me all. 'Yes, there were many, many reasons. One I think you picked up on last night. We didn't get off to a good start. In the early days before we got married, I had a relationship of sorts. Despite being over way before, once Christine knew about it, she wouldn't let it go. It always came up in arguments.'

'You mean you had a fling. Why was that such a big deal.'

'That may be one way to describe it. It only happened three times. Think when it was, Jack. Early Sixties in a rural county. It identified more with the past than present. Much more. The future was so far away. Around here, it was a backwater where everyone knew the other man's business and to break the rules was a considerable thing to do. Now it is almost an expectation. In those days anything unusual or different was considered a faux pas and could find its way onto the front page of the local paper.' He allowed himself a chuckle. 'But people must have had affairs in those days.'

'Yes, yes, they did of course, but certain relationships were seen as, well, near as damn it, demonic.'

This time I was ahead of the game. When I visited Weller that time when he was drunk, he had told me something in confidence about a relationship he had had in his late teens with an older man.

'Weller.'

'Weller,' he said with a sigh, slumping back in his chair, visibly relieved to have said his name. 'We had a summer. I was staying with the family here. How, in heaven's name, did you know.' So, I told him.

'Yes, that rather obnoxious fellow who ironically bought you back to this island of ours. I am obliged to add, Jack that he is the only person I have ever loved in that way. It was a great love.'

'And that's what he said.'

'He doesn't know it's me. I mean, he doesn't know I am the person I was. The nearest I have been to him is at an island fete. As soon as he saw me, he turned away. A mutual friend told me he was heard making jokes about me in the pub. I can't blame him. I don't blame him. All he is seeing is my ugliness. Little did he know...I wonder what he would do if he found out.'

'That is something we shall never know, Jack. Look, there's more to tell. Not for now. We have time,' he said, taking my hand. 'I think we have already had a rather large belly full of surprises to process!'

'And how have you two fared since I last saw you.'

We bumped into Eve as Old Flann was saying his goodbyes. We told her our story and how we had agreed to work on the project together. 'Sounds a very good idea, gentleman.' We could tell she was still distracted, but she immediately came to life when she heard the phone ring. Without saying anything, she turned and disappeared into her house.

'So, when shall we plan to meet again.'

'How about tonight. Come down to the pub and we can start planning.'

'Excellent!' We went to shake hands and then realised a hug, be it uncomfortable, would be more appropriate.

'Can't wait to give you the whole story of our family. See you later, Jack.'

'Can't wait for the next instalment!' I couldn't bring myself to call him anything.

I watched him walk down the path to the road. Before disappearing, he turned and waved. I waved back, appreciating that he was probably as tearful as I was. I thought I would share my good news about Old Flann and knocked on Claude's door. No response. So, I knocked on Rowan's door and again no response. What were they up to this time of day. I had a flash of Claude and Rowan together, writhing around each other and I flushed with a bizarre mix of desire and jealousy. I walked over the bank to the sea. It was time to think and reflect on what had happened over this last day. A breeze was picking up from the southwest and I took, long deep gulps which tasted as delicious as fresh water when you're thirsty.

Then I saw it. At first, I couldn't believe my eyes, but, scrutinising the waves, it was clear that a summer visitor had come to the island. It was truly an amazing sight and, looking about and seeing nobody else around, I thought that this was for my eyes only. About half a mile out was a whale - later I identified it as a fin whale - frolicking in our bay. I knew from the tales I had read that this was a rare event for this coast especially at this time of the year. Call me silly, but I took this as a good omen, a special sighting, the dance of a solitary whale and just for me. Just for Jack Powys...If that is indeed my name.

I began to laugh at the turn of events but, as soon as I did, a cloud literally blocked out the sun and a sudden change happened. When I glanced again, the whale was nowhere to be seen.

ROWAN

Katie visited, I guess in response to my plea for some help. I hadn't seen her for a few weeks. It took her only a few moments to explain why.

'I'm so much busier than I want to be. I don't do busy well. Here I am trying to help people with screwed-up minds, no disrespect intended, and hello I'm the one going mad myself. Have you any dope, Rowan. I need to get off my face for an hour, would you mind. I think I owe myself that much.'

I didn't mind. I thought it strange that my key worker was as bonkers as me but hello. This is the game we appear to be playing. As always, she liked talking about herself, which was fine because I didn't like talking about myself.

'And how is that neighbour of yours?' My stomach turned as I thought she was referring to Claude.

'Which one?'

'Next door, what's his name?'

'Oh, you mean Jack. He is what he was before, a bit of a twat I think.'

'But sort-of cute?'

'Not at all, more like sort-of weird.'

The dope went straight to her head. There's no doubt that, when under pressure, you are often more susceptible to its influence. Katie had forty-five people on her caseload and had to make at least seven contacts a day or the shit would hit the fan.

'Going from how I am,' she said looking me up and down, 'I can only conclude that the shit is going to hit the fan.' She started laughing at her own joke which heralded in a spray of tears. Over she came onto the sofa with me and threw her arms around me. I hugged her back and wondered if she would ask me how I had been.

'You know, Rowan that you are the only person who I can just be myself with.' I found this difficult to believe. 'You have a special something about you.' I wondered if she could sense the new side of me.

'That dope is strong, isn't it.' she said in a weak voice, breaking the short silence. 'Rowan, I didn't mean to be so…' I hushed her with a kiss.

'Don't worry. We've become friends, haven't we?'

She smiled broadly, and I could see how she liked me saying that.

'How have you been anyway?'

*

When Jack left after his last visit, he gave me an idea. I too hauled all my notes out about Claude's comings and goings and spread them over the floor. I too needed to find a pattern. This man was up to something shady and I was determined to find out what it is. I opened some wine, smoked myself through a handful of fags. I moved some notes around, pondered on this and that, willing it to fall into place. And it did. Claude's visits to Eve more or less coincided with the times when Rachel and Tom were visiting or staying over. A piece of the jigsaw had fallen into place. It made complete and total sense. Claude wasn't interested in Eve; his target was elsewhere. Funny enough, he wasn't really interested in me. Seeing it felt obvious and I began questioning why I hadn't seen it before. This light bulb moment led me to think:

I needed to up my ante. I needed to get into his place and try and find some juice on the wanker.

Claude walks to the pub. I watch him from behind the curtains in the bedroom window. He idles down his usual customary short-cut down the hill. He meets the path and waves to someone I cannot see. He chooses a pebble and throws it into the sea, a habit of his I have noticed before. Typically, he is there for two hours, sometimes three. On a Saturday, he's there all night. I take my chance. I whizz downstairs and leave the house through the back door. The small top window in his kitchen is open as usual. This is no obstacle to me. I am small and pretty flexible. I jump on his bin and ease myself through. I had never been in Claude's place and had never wanted to. He had always come to me. The place reeks of years of bachelor living. Stuffy, unloved and smelly. His kitchen was untidy with a basin full of dirty plates.

I hadn't realised how thrilling it could be breaking into someone's house. As I made my way upstairs, I really got the excitement of voyeurism. The spare room was empty save for a few boxes. I flip open the first one and wasn't at all surprised to find it crammed full of dodgy porn DVDs and a few old video tapes. Some appear to be handmade. The bedroom was pretty bland as well. An unmade bed, a chest of drawers and a wardrobe. He obviously took pride in his appearance because, in contrast to the rest of the place, his clothes were either hung neatly or meticulously piled on the shelves. I noted a huge wet patch in the corner of the room, doubtless evidence of our last big leak after the horrendous rainfall last week.

The lounge provided more evidence typical of a bloke living alone. Unemptied ashtrays, a few dirty cups and bowls on the floor, a huge TV above a DVD and video player. What dumbfounded me was a bookcase full of classics such as 'The Heart of Darkness,' 'The Four Quartets,' Shakespeare, and, more in line with who I thought Claude was: De Sade, Henry Miller and volumes by Eric Gill.

I slumped into his chair, disappointed that I couldn't find anything incriminating or revealing. I am fairly sure, some of the video's upstairs were suspect, if not illegal, but wonder if this would be enough to snare the bastard. Maybe there is something in the attic. I dashed up the stairs, came down disillusioned. A small hatch, no ladder. I was about to give up hope, making the decision to leave, when, passing the lounge on my way out, I happened to notice that a rug near the bookcase was slightly off centre. I pulled it aside and there was what appeared to be a trapdoor. I placed my fingers along the rim and teased it open. It was dark but I could clearly see the steps of the wooden ladder descending. "Aha at last!" This was exactly what I had been searching for. I was on the point of entering, when I heard the latch go on the door. I moved as quickly and silently as I dared. I was still in the kitchen when Claude entered the house. Fortunately, he went straight into the lounge. I jumped onto the sink and practically fell out of the window head-first, knocking the bin over as I did so. Claude was there like a shot. From the other side of the garden wall, I listened to him putting the bin back up. If he had walked through the garden gate, he would have discovered me. I steadied my breathing, crept away hearing him snapping the open window shut.

I now had an explanation as to how that pervo Claude seemed to disappear in his own house. All his secrets were down in the cellar. I had been given one hell of a clue and needed to get down there as soon as I could. What was essential was a plan in which I had plenty of time to explore the contents of that basement. It intrigued me. None of the other terraces had a cellar as far as I knew. Did the man build it himself. How and when. He must have done it way before I returned to the Island. I will quiz Eve about it.

I kept waking up with another new thought prodding my mind. Claude was no fool. Bet you, he already smelled a whiff of something not being quite right. He was smarter than me, by far. Look what he is doing to me? How clever is that? Taking the long view and then pouncing and now destroying me piece by piece. Every contact with him filled me with plain and pure hatred. If I was right about his gaze turning on Rachel, what should I be doing. Am I over-reacting? Should I warn Eve, or Rachel, or both? What was I to say...it was all in my head at the moment. Go to the police? With what, Rowan, with what?
What were they supposed to do? What if I were wrong?
But I wasn't wrong.

CLAUDE

Well, I was moving closer to the old maid Eve with methodical diligence. I called in several times a week, getting to know her and her routines, getting a robust understanding of her life from the inside and getting foreknowledge of when the grandchildren were most likely to visit. I allowed myself to play on the woman's affections, flirting gently, touching her arm or her hand lightly while we spoke. I tried anything which indicated to the old battle-axe a closer relationship than actually was the case. I began to note her eyes lighting up when I came calling. What astonished me more than anything was that previously she had shunned or even trashed me. This is testimony to my artistic skills. I had obviously stumbled on a need of hers. That need was the key to open another door for yours sincerely.

The club ideas for getting Tom out of the picture hadn't worked. The small matter of trying to poison the little runt was a great dissatisfaction. I was reliant on the wheel of fortune and vigilantly scrutinising the horizon for some new opportunity. One followed just a few days later.

As I was flavour of the month, they invited me for an afternoon stroll along the promenade that had been built on the high shore. The pub was to be our final destination for a meal and a few beverages. Always the speculator, I agreed wholeheartedly. I was able to enjoy my first "free" conversation with Rachel. Stuff about school, favourite subjects, good and bad teachers; the usual rubbish but, within its flow, I dropped in several anecdotes. I could see she found this interesting, demonstrating that I was engaging her in a "grown-up" way. I dovetailed in a few jokes - one specifically about her brother being a pain, though I cautiously didn't use that particular word. When she found something amusing, she would flush with an endearing almost silent laugh, concealing her mouth with her hand.

Later, we heard the ice cream van on the street below, piping the inexplicable *Somewhere Over the Rainbow* tune I insisted that it would be my treat and Rachel and Tom ran off with my fiver. In my best benevolent uncle guise, I followed at a distance and waited on the other side of the road for them to return. My chance materialised. I will tell you straight, the fates willed this to happen. Tom emerged from the back of the van, holding his ice cream. Rachel was still being served. I could see a truck hurtling down the street, but I indicated to Tom that the road was clear. He stepped out.

I know my business and started on Rachel without delay. She was upset and tearful, as you would expect. I was deliberately comforting and as tactile as was appropriate, taking liberties with the discretion of a butler. The girl was stunning. In all my days, over all my liaisons, I have never come across such a radiant beauty as this young Rachel. Jesu made you on a Sunday, girl. No wonder the family speculate about a historic Spanish connection. Even upset, her face was transformed by a subtle vulnerability which added to her magnificence. I convinced her that wine would do her good in this situation. It would soften the blow of the accident. By the second glass, she was already showing signs of self-conscious drowsiness. I suggested lying down upstairs and off she went without further encouragement. I followed her up with a third glass of wine. You must be too hot, says me - and I help her out of her pullover, a quick flash of flesh revealing itself like a promise. I patted her head and managed to cup one of her breasts without the lass twigging what was going on. My treasure was about to be delivered. Then there was a bang on the door. It turned out to be that shithead, Jack.

'Just heard what happened, Claude. Anything I can do?'

I felt like saying that the best thing he could do was to go and fuck himself. I thought better of it as that may have aroused suspicion. I informed him I was looking after Rachel. 'She's not doing well as you can imagine,' I added.

Having got rid of the joker, I bolted upstairs to my true love. No sooner had I got up to the top of the stairs and there was another bang on the door. Jack again. This time I could have pierced his stupid fucking brain with a poker. What he was blabbering about, God knows. I told him the same story. I pounded up the stairs once more, jumping two stairs at a time. Rachel was standing by the window, so I encouraged her to return to the bed, muttering all sorts of nonsensical platitudes. Would you believe, a third bang on the door. I was ready to annihilate the shit and return to take Rachel by storm. I did neither, as it happened. That bloody old banger of a car was mysteriously alight, the whole thing ablaze. Popping and crackling, it wouldn't be long before the whole thing exploded, making a massive dent in our terrace.

Between us, we put the blaze out; more or less. I had the fire extinguisher which had originally been in the car and Jack poured buckets of water in places where he thought it would make a difference. The fire brigade turned up to douse down the rest.

'Now if you had that insured,' I sneered to Jack, 'You would have got your money back. As it is my friend, don't think I'm letting you off the final fifty smackers!' I was about to ask him how it happened when the fire officer came over with a notebook, probably to ask the same thing. As I had other fish to fry, I left them to it. Holy Christ, when I got upstairs again, Rachel had disappeared. I smashed a few glasses with sheer, untainted rage at my loss.

*

I decided that the sheer pathos of my frustration warranted a justifiable deviation from my principles. Not something I will do lightly, I assure you, but after the debacle of my attempted seduction, I was absolutely livid. I almost wanted to murder someone, anyone, especially that wanker Jack, who must have the brain power of an amoeba. His story goes like this: he decided to take the car to the hospital (what immediately after knocking on my door.) and was filling up the tank when his lit cigarette (does the fucker even smoke?) and whoosh!

What a pile of crap. Whatever he was doing, this indubitably cannot be the truth, but he's sticking to his fairy-tale. Whatever the facts of the matter are, I was furious and, more to the point, I was beyond irritation. Not a healthy combination. I was about to go to heaven with the young lady and I had fallen down to earth with a crash. I was as pent up as a volcano about to let rip. I began thinking revenge. So, I took time out and instead of going to the pub, I walked up the hill and laid low until it grew dark.

I knew where the local kids hung out. It would be one of two places. In the scrub land by the cemetery or one of the old quarries near the prison. It turned out to be the latter. I secured myself a viewing position and waited for my time, comforting myself with whisky from my flask. Bloody kids do the most stupid things and talk the most stupid twaddle.

This was no exception and I had to endure this crap ad nauseam. Around about twelve midnight, the group started breaking up. I followed three of the main group at a distance, one boy and two girls. At the turning into the estate, two of them went off one way and the remaining girl, maybe fifteen years old, went the other. I followed, progressively moving closer. I took a supportive gulp of the golden stuff and pulled my balaclava over my face.

'Hey!' I shouted. 'Wait up!'

She stopped and looked up and down the road to check if I was indeed talking to her. You could see that she was on the point of making a run for it, so I hurriedly asked her for a light. This seemed to slow her down a tad. Yes, she had.

'Why not have one of mine?' She took one.

'So,' I said casually. 'How do you want to do this?'

'How do I want to do what?' she replied, defiantly.

'Well, I can offer you money, if you wish it. I have £200 on me which is probably more than you're worth. I will give you the two hundred if you just lie down and let me do my business. Deal or no deal?' I thought this was more than generous and, frankly, gave myself an invisible pat on the back. Despite my exasperated self, I was at least trying to get the bitch on board by offering her a choice.

'Fuck off, you wanker!'

'No deal then?'

She was on the ground before she could draw a second breath, as I can rely on superhuman strength at times as these. Annoyingly squirming about, she was calling me all sorts.

'Wash your mouth out and shut the fuck up,' I commanded her. To remind the little whore of my good intentions, I flicked open my all-purpose knife. Its appearance seemed to pacify her somewhat. In my humble well-informed opinion, this sudden compliance was further evidence that I was doing nothing dishonest here. The circumstances were not ideal or even desirable, but the inevitability of it all strikes one as fortuitous. She had probably hoped to get laid anyway. She had probably fantasised about her mate's boyfriend. She may have been desperate for anything which amounted to attention and here I was giving her a share of my subsistence. Usually, of course, I welcome the foreplay, the hunt, the chase. As you are aware, I usually seek the woman's blessing or compliance or, at a minimum, her wilful submission. This one wasn't having any of this, so I left her with a neat cut on her left cheek. When she would view the scar in years to come, she would remember and hopefully draw a powerful meaning from her experience.

EVE

The first thing I saw was the ice cream lying in the road, wrong side up, on a slant, looking like a tilted party hat. By the time I got to the back of the van, I could see our poor Tom. He wasn't moving. One leg was twisted crookedly about the other. His face was pressed to the ground and a ribbon of blood was running into the gutter. How quickly blood comes. I have only screamed three times in me life. Once when I heard about Bert. Once when Ben died. This was the third.

We had been having an amazing day up until then. We were walking the cove, working up an appetite for lunch in the pub. All the family were there, complete with our newest member, Claude. He was excellent, by the way. First on the scene, he phoned the emergency folk before Tom had barely hit the ground. By the time I had waddled over, he was with Tom doing what he could. The ambulance arrived, believe it or not, with the same crew from the other day. I was adamant about going to the hospital with Harry and me grandson. I was more than happy to leave Rachel with Claude to look after. He could see the extent of Rachel's grief. She was absolutely distraught, poor lass. Tom was everything to her.

It turned out that Tom was lucky although it didn't seem so there and then. Apparently, the lorry which hit him did so at an angle which sent Tom flying rather than falling. It was like the vehicle had simply budged him out of the way. It was not so much the impact of truck on boy, as boy on ground. He was pushed to the side rather than pulled under. Not sure if it was to calm us down, but the doctor in casualty said that this was always the most likely outcome in these circumstances. This is what saved him. His right leg was broken in three places, his spleen popped, and he may have a scar from ear to chin, but so what? Tom was alive and all the talk of him walking through his life with a limp was missing the bloody point. It would take a long time to heal, months. That didn't matter. What mattered was that, praise heaven, he was alive.

*

Life had taken another strange twist. It was giving me a right old mix of signals. I didn't realise it then and I still don't get now, but it was just the beginning. I had survived a war, six marriages, twenty affairs, a near drowning, bankruptcy, a tragic bereavement, a heart attack and the loss of the family fortune, but nothing, but nothing could prepare me for what happened next.

I don't know if I'm coming or going, whether things are heading in the right direction or in the wrong direction. The worry about Tom and his injury has been our main concern. Harry has been excellent, as you may have predicted. He is up to the county hospital every day, joking with the lad, reading to him, talking to him and generally jollying him along. I wish his mother was here, but apparently, she is on a pilgrimage in Spain - foolish minx. Rachel goes with her father most days, bless her. Since the accident, she really hasn't been herself. She seems in a constant worried state. When we returned from the hospital immediately after the calamity, she was terribly edgy and said that Claude had frightened her. This just added to my misery.

'One thing, Claude, if you don't mind me saying.'

'What is it, honey?'

'It's Rachel, she said you got her drunk and made her lay down. She said she didn't like it. What do you make of that?'

'Oh, Eve, I'm so sorry to hear that. After the accident I must concede I was in a tizzy myself and needed a glass of vino to steady my nerves. I mistakenly gave some to Rachel. I wasn't thinking straight, you know? I realised what I had done when she began to feel drowsy. I thought she had better lie down, poor little thing. I tried to make her feel comfortable. Apologies for upsetting the young lady. I think all of us were all over the place that day. In retrospect I can see it was foolish of me.'

You could see how sorry the man was. I reminded myself that he had never had children of his own and may not have the insight us parents have. His explanation reassured me. It was possibly his overbearing nature coupled with a bit too much wine, coupled with the sheer stress of it all. Sometimes I have found a strong headedness about the man and a sort of wild liveliness gets hold of him. These are all forgivable traits though. Desirable traits in another situation. Despite the age difference, it is abundantly clear now that Claude does find me attractive. He comes over often. He is upping his game and the level of affection to me makes me quite queasy. He is friendly, warm and charming. He brings flowers and holds doors open. On the other hand, he could be selective in his attentions. Sometimes he is here, day and night. He loves the children no doubt whatsoever because he is hardly absent if they happen to visit. Then I will have days of either not seeing him or seeing him only in passing.

What am I saying? Being truthful, he is me number seven, I know it as firmly as I know the sun will rise tomorrow. With anyone, there are bound to be reservations. We remain caught up in this play of love, both a shake afraid to either overstep the mark or be too timid. When all this fuss has gone quiet, I aim to show me true colours soon and tell him what his heart already knows. I am a woman of needs, you might say, and I have had enough of kisses and squeezes and am hoping for more. I briefly wondered if he may be frigid or impotent, whichever word is correct for a man. That's OK by me, as long as I know. There's a recipe for that as well.

This will have to wait. There was far too much going on. My worries were breeding. Adding to Tom, there were other omens afoot. The Hamilton fellow has gone missing. I had seen him briefly the days before and we had passed the time of day. I recall it as it was the day the storm came at teatime. He was pleased to be back on island soil and told me his plans were to stay around, possibly for the summer. That's what I told the police anyways. They agreed with me that it made his unexplained vanishing most peculiar. Then, heaven help us, there was a sex attack on Tophill. The papers couldn't tell us who she was, yet all us islanders knew. It was the youngster Karen Moore, barely fifteen and in the last year of school. I have spoken to her parents since and the lost soul can't face going outside. She stays in her room for hours at a time. Her parents said that what concerns them more than anything is her silence. Her lack of reaction distresses them greatly. She doesn't cry or shake or show any other signs of the agony she must be suffering. He left her with a scar on a cheek as well. Why do that? He had got what he wanted. Why did he have to give her a reminder? And one she would see every day for the rest of her years. I can only think of what I would feel if our Rachel had suffered like this. I wouldn't be able to sleep until I had separated the man from his balls by magic or knife, or whatever it took.

*

With the kids not around so much, I found myself often daydreaming in the kitchen staring at the Book and thinking about my life. On top of everything else, I feel this illness I have is advancing. My health is failing. I am dying. Nobody knows yet. I thought I would use my old knowledge to bring me back to life, before anyone cottons on. I read and re-read the spell I hope to use to save myself. I looked through the recipe. My gaze keeps returning to the final ingredient; blood from a living human, who must be ignorant of the spell they are caught up in. The whole thing sounded a bit theatrical and, despite my calling, a tiny far-fetched. I knew how rarely this particular spell had been used. The last time I can recall is by my other Sister during the last months of the first war. Blood was more a-plenty then.

The nightmares increase and I can't seem to stop them. I see the baby's face everywhere. What does this mean. Whose face do I see? Simone, is it you? Are you trying to say something to me? I am feeling odd, distant and losing touch. I thought the Book would bring a transformation in my world, but I am consumed with self-doubt and question its power. The concoction for nightmares simply didn't work. Is it my belief that is in question? They only work anyway if you are a member of the Sisterhood. Like I am. You can't merely steal the Book and think you can perform magic. You need to be part of the tradition. You also need to believe, and I am wondering if the woman who recovered the Book is the same woman who hid it?

THE SIXTH WAVE

The First Invasion of England by Vikings AD 789
From the Island Chronicles Volume Two: AD 501 - 1051
(By Sir C. Freeman - only volume to survive house fire)

Before they came, there were omens in great numbers. Winds blew from the South with the stench of the underworld. Folk saw double rainbows, one inside another. Two fellows, both honest enough, were fishing near the point of the island and testified in front of the elders, that they had seen dragons fornicating in the heavens above. It was my task to heal these transgressions of perception and gently wrestle with these fears in a way which cooled, not heated them. I am the island's answer to a priest and, though my feet are buried in the myths of our Pagan roots from my torso to the tip of my head, the heart belongs to the New Faith, to the true Son of David, rod of Jesse.

That spring was indeed unnatural. I kept my reservations to myself and notioned that, like most worries, concerns and wrongings, they would be gone in the light of summer. Then, a whole flock of sheep got it into their head to work themselves into a fuss and hurtled blindly over the cliffs into Freshwater Bay. When the sun winked, the islanders, depending on the bent of their temperament, ran from house to house either whispering or shouting catastrophe. It lasted but a moment or two and, maybe in happier times, may have been taken as a celestial waggery. My work was to bolt here and there, hushing air, patting hands, spouting prayers and asking folk to trust me and the Lord I served.

Yet, they were right and I, alas, wrong. Three ships broke the horizon one May morning in three places. Those that saw them brought others to witness their arrival. When I, a pious advisor was called, a few hundred had gathered, all of them spellbound into some form of stupor. I wanted to use any one of my Pagan expletives, but, with the Saviour's help, I desisted. I tell them that we should make preparations, call the reeve at once and his deputies. Tell them to bring sword and dagger in case our visitors misread the hospitality of these shores.

All too bloody late!

By the time the reeve and his pack arrived, all sweaty from their exertion and as dishevelled as drunkards, the ships were anchoring up and burly men with axe and shield were wading into shore. I could tell from a distance that they were not here to preach the good gospel but to spill some blood. Finally, the folks woke up from their sleep and saw what I saw. They started their running around. 'This is what the omens were doing. This is what we were warned against!' 'This is the end of our dear life!' 'This is the curse of the island revisited' and the like. Aware of my status, I was torn between fleeing with some vigour and trying to pacify them with a gift of Jesus and reason.

Too bloody late for that. Already blades were being sliced into flesh. Young Dag lost his head and, before his heart stopped, his body looked for all purposes to search for it. The reeve charged with tremendous bravery until some odd inner organ was skewered out of him on the point of a spear. Some of the invaders went straight for the women. For these, on the waves for a season, the spilling of seed was clearly more important than that of blood.

I found myself somehow in the middle of this mayhem and wished I had my large wooden cross with me so I could wave it ominously about or, at least, defend myself with it. One of their number ran towards me, all beard and helmet, hollering in a tongue which should have never been heard on these shores. stood my ground or froze; I cannot recall which. Coming up to me, he suddenly stopped, puzzled by my reaction.

'I am the Gon, the goodly and godly man of God!' It sounded nonsense and he imitated me (all those g's) then swung his sword to his right, my left. My arm fell to the ground. The fact that I stood back in awe at his precision, I think saved me for the second stroke ploughed a furrow from my forehead to my chin. Blood was everywhere and he left me for other prey.

They killed many over those few days and left with some of us as quietly as they had arrived. It was after this sad story that many of the Islanders said farewell to the one and true Lord. Some went back to the old ways. The Sisters, witches for the best part started all over, openly showing their wrongful trade.

Maybe I should have been one who was also smite for after this nobody believed a word that I uttered. The scar crossing my rugged face was taken as a bad sign, not a good one. I lived long but alone in a cave in the Ope, living off any scraps the sea or the humble offered me.

JACK

I had already downed four pints in the pub to celebrate, somewhat prematurely, my new-found energy, when Lockie burst in, shouting at no one in particular, that Tom, Eve's grandson, had been knocked down. Lockie said he was whipped into the air by a truck and landed badly. "Near as death as you could get," was Lockie's conclusion. We gathered around him, asking the usual where, whys and how's.

'No' he responded to my question.' He was the only one hurt. They've all gone off to casualty with him. Except Rachel, she's with Claude.'

I was halfway through my next pint when I thought I should be doing something. Eve had been kind to me, more or less, since I arrived. I staggered over to Claude's and hammered on the door with the force I felt was necessary on this occasion. It still took three hammerings before the door swung open.

'Just heard what happened, Claude? Anything I can do?'

'Go back to the bar, if I was you,' looking almost disgusted to see me. 'All is being done now, so don't you worry.'

'Rachel alright?'

'Her brother's just been flattened by a truck, so she could be better, but she's got me, hasn't she? Go now, I will keep you in the loop.'

The door slammed shut, but, as I turned, I saw Rachel standing in the front upstairs window. She was waving at me frantically. I waved back to her as reassuringly as I could.

Then she mouthed something to me and, even in my drunken haze, I could detect that it wasn't worry on her face. It was panic.

I knocked on the door again and could hear Claude thumping down the stairs.

'Are you sure Rachel is alright? I've plenty of time on my hands if you need another pair of hands.'

'Your intentions are in the right place, I'm sure,' he said slowly. 'But all is as fine as it can be, so please piss off, there's a good fellow.' I looked up to the window and he followed my gaze. Rachel wasn't there. He smiled broadly and slammed the door once more. I walked back to my place, glancing up every now and again. I stopped by my dilapidated car. I kept thinking over what had just happened. What had Rachel said. Two words only. I mouthed them myself; 'Help me.' Was that really what she had said? Could I be so sure? Well, I wasn't in the least. I couldn't bang on the door again. No, no, it was nothing. It was fine. She's upset about Tom. Of course, she is, but what if she had mouthed those words? What if she did need my help and I was ignoring her?

It was my turn to panic. I went through this internal dialogue about thirty times in as many seconds. Then I became convinced that I was picking up something, something was not right. She had said 'Help me!' So now what? It was then I saw the can of petrol on the front seat of the car. I opened the door, for the first time since owning it, I may add and poured the stuff all over the seats. I lit a match and threw it in and as soon as I did, I ran back to Claude's, this time hollering as well as hammering. When the door opened, I literally thought he was going to swing for me, and

he probably would have if the car hadn't exploded at that point into a fuss of fire.
'Jesus fucking Christ!' He swore and came rushing after me.

*

'Hello, is that Jack Powys?'

The following day, still shaken by this turn of events, I awoke to a telephone call.

'Yes, this is he. Who am I speaking to?'

'It's me.'

'Could you be more specific?'

Silence, but in the silence, some intuitive spark ignited. I knew who it was. I hadn't heard her voice for so long.

'Rosie.'

More silence.

'Sorry I have been out of touch.'

'Sorry you've been out of touch. It's been nearly twenty years, Rosie.' I was mostly angry. This was being quickly overtaken by pangs of sadness. 'Where have you been?'

'I could ask the same question, Jack?'

'Why now? Of all days to phone, why today?'

'Hard to say, Brother,' she was attempting to be light. 'This call could have been any time in the last ten years. I ummed and ahhed for a millennium and sat on it until I got piles. That is until this morning. I had a dream about you last night and I thought why not? If not now, when?'

I could feel the sharp spikes of tears rising up through my body, like the first heavy drops of rain before a thunderstorm. I realised she was telling me about her dream.

'...We were younger, all the family were together, and we were running down a hill. I thought we were running too fast and, as soon as I thought this, we started falling and then rolling like we were stones. I shouted to you to stop, but none of us could.'

'Rosie, what are you talking about?'

I could hear her take a breath and clear her throat.

'We must meet up, Jack. I need to tell you the story, the whole bloody thing. I need to tell you everything.'

'What story?'

I could hear her words. The real communication an undercurrent of emotion. Emotions cannot lie. On some level, I was picking up exactly what she meant. Just because I couldn't articulate it or make any sense of it made it no less real. I felt like I was about to blubber.

'The story of us, Jack. The story of us.' After a pause, she added, 'I'm coming down to see you.'

'If you mean the stuff about our father,' I said cockily.' I know it already. He's here on this island. He calls himself Old Flann and he's lived here incognito for years. So, I know all the dirt, Rosie. I probably know more than you.'

'Yes, there's Dad, Jack. I have guessed he was there for the last couple of years. I received an unsigned birthday card with a Dorset postmark on it. What has he told you?'

'About the missing years. What happened to him about leaving us? How it was a mistake he had always regretted. That sort of thing.'

'There's much more, Jack.'

'How much more could there be?'

'There's more.'

The telephone call from Rosie left me exhausted. I

slumped on the sofa and stared into space for hours. Was there no end to these surprises? I think in my mind, I written Dad off as a waste of space when still a teenager. I gave up hope for him ages ago and, if Mum hadn't burnt his photograph and all my momentums of him, I would have done it myself someday. Rosie had likewise died with Mum. When we buried her, Rosie and I buried our relationship. When she kissed me on the cheek after the service, I could see she was in pain. When she said that she loved me and told me to take care, I hadn't realised that was a farewell which would last until today.

I sat there thinking all sorts of rubbish, some things making me heated, some unsettling, some upsetting. The re-emergence of my dad, my sister calling me, what next? Was Mum going to rise from the dead? My brain had become over-busy trying to re-construct a dodgy past with large pieces of the jigsaw still missing. I may have completed an edge or two, some images were clearer, but the overall picture had yet to reveal itself. I could sense myself bulking at the prospect of having to re-examine my life.

I had got used to thinking of myself as a bit of a waster. I think I had got used to this perpetual feeling of wandering around the earth like some sad mythical being looking for his soul. To be honest, I thought this was normal.

Old Flann appeared again later that day. He entered the house, beaming from ear to ear, holding another armful of books and pamphlets.

'Jack, we have so much work to do. I haven't been as excited as this for years!'

'Before we do,' I was struggling to know what to call him. Dad seemed too much too soon, and I wasn't sure I could even say the word. Whereas calling him Old Flann seemed a piss take considering all we had been through. I cleared my throat. 'I need some more details; you know about the past.' This stopped him in his tracks as he let out a slow sigh.

'OK...Take a seat. I'll get the coffee.'

In the kitchen, I found that I was making the coffee as slowly as possible. I had no idea what I was trying to avoid. I needed a few answers, that much was obvious. We had rediscovered each other after a lifetime and there were numerous gaps to fill in.

'I had a phone call this morning.' I could tell Old Flann was on edge, sitting upright and looking straight at me.

'Guess who it was?' He didn't respond. 'No guesses? Rosie. It was Rosie.' He remained silent. I could see he was trying to keep control of his emotions. 'That was the first time I have had contact with her since Mum's funeral.' Saying those words prompted an unexpected tearfulness. 'That's a lifetime ago. She says there is so much I need to know. What does she mean by that? What does she mean that there is so much I need to know?' Old Flann was staying silent. 'Well?' I said forcefully. With that he seemed to come to. He cleared his throat.

'That is excellent, Jack!' He was trying to be upbeat. 'I would love to see Rosie again. There is a real opportunity here for a family reunion. Wouldn't that be the most wonderful thing, Jack?'

'I had given up any hope of that years ago. Maybe, it is possible now. She seemed to be talking about something specific, something I need to know. I am younger than her by three years. I struggle to remember one thing from those early years. It's like my memory was completely wiped clean. She obviously remembers much more than I do.'

'I'm not so sure she means any one thing. I think she must be referring to the conflicts I had with your mother before we finally split. There was one occasion. I hadn't meant to, but she was driving me mad, saying I was having an affair and nonsense of that sort. I pushed her, not that hard in fact and she fell down the stairs. Rosie came onto the landing, right at the wrong time and saw the whole thing. With her mother at the bottom of the stairs, bleeding from her nose, Rosie hissed at me that I was a murderer and she was calling the police. She was six and she would have phoned the police as well if your mother herself hadn't stopped her. Needless to add, there were more incidents of that nature.'

'Not sure why would she want to tell me that. Phoning me up out of the blue like that. Doesn't make any sense to me. Does that make sense to you?'

There was an awkwardness developing. I could see Old Flann was squirming on his chair.

'She would have her own reasons for calling you, Jack. You told her about us meeting up again? Is she coming down here?' He was trying to change the subject.

'What was she talking about? Just tell me.'

'Give me a little time to think, Jack.'

'No problem,' I said, standing up and taking the coffee cup from his hand. 'You go away and have a little think. Come back when you have something to say.' I knew he was lying or concealing the truth from me. He knew exactly what Rosie wanted to say, but he was refusing to tell me.

ROWAN

Literally, not an hour passed after stealing into Claude's house when there was a knock on the door. I automatically thought it was Claude, but, in my heart, I knew differently. I opened the door to Rachel.

'Don't worry, I know why you're here,' I said, pulling her gently towards me. As Rachel was talking, I could not stop myself from comparing her with a younger me. I had spoken to her before. During the summer holidays I saw her practically every day, but the chatter was always in passing, limited and brief. This was the first opportunity I had to really have a conversation with her, and yet all I could think about was me. This was a different, better version of me standing there before me, a me who had been brought up well, who had never had to fight with anything major.

By the time, I was Rachel's age I was already damaged goods. I was so caught up in the mess of "my uncles and aunts" heads that I was punishing myself continually for a crime I believed I had committed. The crime was the loss of my parents. Not one but both, mother and father gone in one hit. Why did I feel guilt for something I had no control over whatsoever? Cutting myself helped. Starving myself and making myself throw up helped. Sometimes, I used a lit cigarette to the flesh; particularly satisfying. The ritual of stealing a fag and taking myself to my room, lighting it and applying its hot glow to my pale skin was fascinating. It's how I started smoking.

'Go on.'

'Well I began to be suspicious of him, of Claude, a few weeks ago. He kept hanging about, puking praise on Gran, doing this and that for her, but in a way, which wasn't like…

Well, it didn't seem right to me. He was always there when Tom and I were visiting Gran and was sort-of all over me in a way I didn't like. At first, I thought he was just being a nice guy. After a while, I thought he's what, a hundred years old. Why would he want to talk to me? Then Tom had his accident.'

'Tell me about that.'

She told me and I pointed out to her that wasn't it strange that Claude had also been around that day. He had never been on a family walk before nor since and the day he did Tom was hurt.

'Yes, it was odd, you're right. When they all took off to hospital, I was left alone with Claude. As soon as they disappeared, he was onto me, Rowan. I was in a state. He gave me wine and I felt worse. Somehow, he got me to lie down. I was frightened, I didn't know why or what may happen, so I did what he told me to do. It was only Jack who saved me by knocking on the door.'

'The car fire.'

'I'm positive, Jack did that for me.'

'So why come to me and not your gran?'

'I did try to tell her, but it didn't make any sense and he hadn't actually done anything to me. It all sounded made-up and silly. She said she would have a word with him, but that was the last she mentioned about it. Don't forget, she likes him, and she has always had a blind spot as far as men are concerned.'

'OK, Rachel, let me tell you my story. I've decided to give you every warped detail.'

I didn't pull any punches. I told it all to her; about my so-called friendship with Claude and how he manipulated me. I told her about the baby and how he had used that to abuse me. By the time, I had finished she was sitting there silent and wide-mouthed. I wondered if I had overdone it with her. She was only twelve after all.

I made a cup of tea for the poor girl and, coming back into the room, I announced more emphatically than I had intended: 'So here's the plan.' I lit up cigarettes for the both of us. 'But, before I start, are you sure you want to be part of this?'

She paused after taking her first drag. She looked at me with her dark eyes and I could clearly see the woman in the girl. Then she took me aback by saying. 'Too fucking right I do!' I laughed at the irony of it all, let alone those words coming from that young mouth. She joined in. I'm not sure if it was relief or anxiety, but soon we became almost hysterical. I knew I had found a kindred spirit.

'So, what are you thinking?' I asked Rachel.

She didn't respond right away, but then said: 'It's not so much what I am thinking; it's what I have been feeling.'

I must admit that I was taken by surprise at the maturity of her response. I knew that Rachel was going to be part of the plan I had in mind.

From this first chat, Rachel and I kept meeting up. I looked forward to her visits. She liked them too. I think it was the secrecy and scheming. For Rachel, it was like a crude introduction into the adult world of chaos and pandemonium. I should have brought Eve into the plot, but Rachel didn't want this. She said her grandmother would either stop it in its tracks, take over the plan or get her dad involved and call in the law. We agreed to take matters in hand ourselves. It fell on us to do something. From an outsider's point of view, Claude hadn't done that much, probably nothing at all which would amount to breaking the law. It crucified me that he had me firmly under his control. Don't forget, I had only my mad self to blame. Telling him stuff, getting too close. I had given him the power, no one else. As for Rachel, he had made a move on her, but so what. In terms of evidence, there was none. Eve may have confronted him, but if she had, he was still hanging around so he must have hoodwinked her in his usual evil way. No, it was our job, nobody else's. If we didn't do anything, who would?

Rachel would sneak around to my place, always coming to the backdoor. I became familiar with her quiet tap on the glass. I told her she could just come in, everyone else did. I never locked it. What was the point? I had bugger all to steal. She always knocked though.

We spent our time, drinking coffee and smoking. I did most of the smoking, I will come clean, but I allowed her the odd one. It was a pleasure to be free to talk to someone openly like I could talk to this twelve-year-old. Laughable really, but I found a buddy in her. Several visits later, I became conscious that we were putting off the task. It was easier to talk about stuff than actually do anything about it. We could have a bash at Claude. We could chew the fat about dishing out all sorts of punishment to the old pervert. We had a hoot talking about cutting off his balls. We knew we were joking, but it was good fun imagining ways to humiliate the tosser.

'I think we're ready, Rachel,' I eventually suggested. 'Let's go for next Tuesday, his town day. He's usually out of the way all day. There's no school for you. If we spy on him when he leaves, we can get straight in there. Into the lounge, open the hatch and see what's in that hideout of his.'

'What if someone sees us? Or if we get caught?'

'That's not going to happen, is it? Claude's routine is

pretty much watertight. If anyone sees us, well, we can make it up as we go along. Anyway, that's not going to be happening. Hardly anyone comes up this far.'

'Next Tuesday?'

'Next Tuesday. Don't think too much about it.'

'Next Tuesday it is!' she beamed after a pause. The plan was set. To celebrate the decision, I made more coffee and rolled a joint. I allowed Rachel one puff only, but that was enough to give her the giggles for the next hour.

CLAUDE

In the morning, I was awoken from a deep dreamless sleep, by an abrupt knock on the door. It was the police. My very first thought was "How efficient." They put two and two together for a change and they came to the right solution." Somehow, they had tracked me down. The girl had squealed, managing to give them a few drops of information which lead them to my door. But no. They were investigating the sudden and unexplained disappearance of one Max Hamilton. Why they were wasting their time with the likes of him, I have no idea. He was a known pest and now he was dancing his marionette's dance to the tune of the oceans. His vanishing had done everybody a favour. How many young innocent girls had been saved as a consequence?

There were two of them, a man and woman both in uniform. I admitted knowing Hamilton as there was little point in denying it. Most locals would have known him, or of him.

'But,' I said in more helpful-citizen mode, 'he is from a family of misfits, knaves and ne'er-do-wells. Hamilton has a reputation for flitting from one thing to another. You must know from your records what he was like.'

'You said *was*,' pointed out the female.

Oops!

'Manner of speaking, love.'

'So, when did you see him last?'

'I had a drink with him at the pub only last week. We bumped into one another there. I hadn't seen him for years, he bought me a drink, so I thought why not. Getting drunk with one fellow was as good as getting drunk with another. Not seen the beggar since.'

'How would you describe your relationship with him?'

'Non-existent. Just someone who I knew from the past, a man I hadn't thought of in years and probably wouldn't again if it wasn't for you mentioning him.'

'Did he say what his plans were? Did he say what he was up to? Where he was going, anything like that?' It was the female bobby again. Why do they let youngsters like her with no experience of life loose on the public? Who does she think she is?

'Not really. Hamilton was always an empty vessel, a lot of noise and no substance. I think he alluded to looking for work or some such thing. By then I had turned off, to be frank.'

I followed them to the front door and nonchalantly lit a fag while they knocked on Jack's door. Eventually, he answered and, even when they explained their purpose, he looked muddled and confused and unable to string two sensible words together. As I stood there along came the paperboy and thrust the local rag into my hand. The sex attack covered the entire front page. The hyperbole was fascinating. Reporter Darren Carlton had swallowed a copy of Roget's Thesaurus. Malicious, demonic, callous, brutal and my favourite, "horrendously sickening." Jesus, Darren, she's still alive, is she not? One little cut hardly amounts to a "terrible disfigurement."

Eve joined me on the doorstep. I gave her a kiss, this time on the lips to detract from anything else which may be going on her mind.

'How's the boy, dearest? How's Tom?'

'Going to be a few more weeks in hospital, I fear. He's alright in himself but will have more steel in him than the Eiffel Tower by the time they've finished with him. One leg is shattered completely, but they think he will walk again, albeit with a limp.' I tutted and nodded in all the appropriate places. 'Claude, do you think we can have a chat?'

'Naturally, sweetheart. What do you want to talk about?'

'Us. I want to talk about us.'

My first thought was that there was no "us" and as long as the waves keep beating on the shore, there never would be an "us." It did give me the confidence to realise that "Plan Rachel" was working well. Tom was in hospital, Rachel was being warmed up, not as fast I had wanted, but warmed up nonetheless and Eve was swallowing the whole thing lock, stock and barrel. We started to walk towards the beach.

'I am aware that you have designs.' Yes, I have madam, but not on your fat ass.

'Don't think for a second that I haven't noticed your calling around, giving me a lot of attention. You rescuing the Book from the attic for me. That was a sheer act of kindness.'

'My pleasure,' I replied. 'It is an excellent tome. Must be worth a fortune to a collector.'

'It's priceless, no doubt on that. All your comings and goings and your help with the kids and all has led me to believe that you wish to get closer. I have long made it my ambition to find a partner for this sweet time in my life, shall we say, the final chapter. I know my reputation around these parts on account of my serial husbanding.' This was meant to be a joke, so I followed her lead and guffawed with the fat hag. 'Whatever the reputation, Claude, the reality is very different. I simply married the men in my life. I was always the romantic fool and still believe in marriage and all that it entails.'

'It's that commitment to basic values which is definitely missing these days,' I volunteered, Eve completely overlooking the sarcasm.

'Can I be frank, Claude?'

'Please do, my love.'

'I am wondering if we could move on to the next stage?'

Jesus, light-of-the-world, the woman is more delusional than the mad bitch next door. Yet, I quickly corrected myself, think Claude Mayfellow of the longer term. Keeping Eve happy is keeping Rachel within arm's reach.

'You have read my mind, Eve. How did you do that? Must be the magic you have in your blood. Whatever gift you have, it truly is blessed. Let us proceed to the next stage.'

Her face beamed with a light I hadn't seen before. I nearly felt sorry for the old witch because I had told her exactly what she wanted to hear. Poor cow, sometime sooner or later, she was in for a shock or two. For now, though, keep the fires burning, Claude, and don't blame yourself for the stupidity of others.

EVE

Claude is willing. I'd plucked up the courage to ask him about our relationship. He was so enthusiastic about it, I wish I had asked him sooner. So, heavens bless me, I am moving forward to meeting my two goals. Hubby number seven may well be on his way and with the Book once again in my possession, I could start on curing myself of this disease that is trying to kill me. Now it has come to it, I am more than a bit afraid to use the magic again, to summon up the old powers and bring forth the healthy years I need. I could have twenty more if I am lucky. I keep drifting into a picture of future happiness with Claude. Watching the kids grow up. Seeing Harry settled again. I was determined not to get too carried away. It was hard not to though as I had longed for this for ten years. I wasn't so loopy as to think that all life would be perfect, but certainly it could be much better with a sprinkling of love!

Tom was discharged today and is out of hospital and Harry has taken more time off work to look after him. I have missed Tom's regular visits. As for Rachel, not sure what's got into her. She still calls in but not as much as before. She is always busy these days with something or other and has started disappearing at odd times. When I ask her where she's been, the answers I get seem to my ears, like I am being fobbed off. She appears to be keeping stuff away from me. I feel she is slipping away from me. I guess it is her age, it is normal enough. Six months ago, she told me absolutely everything. Including, may I put in, her crush on her science teacher. As a reaction to this, I am having to be firmer than I am used to. I keep reminding her that a sex attacker is on the loose and still hasn't been caught. She quickly replies that the attack was on Tophill, not down there. I quickly reply that it is only a short walk away and that the attack only happened a mile from Mandy's house, a girl I had never trusted. I couldn't understand why Rachel had started up with her again. Is this the beginning of her teenage rebellion?

Again, I had that overwhelming feeling that the world was changing in a way I could never have predicted. I thought that maybe I should consult the other Sister, Clara, on Tophill. We haven't spoken for ten or more years. When I turned my back on it all and sealed the Book in my chimney, Clara said it was like sealing her up there. I had heard through the Island grapevine that she rarely leaves the house now. She must be nearing a hundred years old, I suppose, so maybe it's not that shocking.

I am finding myself drifting, sitting around, absentmindedly stroking the Book. I keep touching this huge lump on my side and feeling rather disgusted by it. Yet there was no denying that it was a part of me.

It was such a beautiful book, no doubt there. It was as if it were alive, breathing the magic and wisdom of this little isle, sparkling in its vivid colours. Maybe the magic hasn't left it, maybe the magic has left me. This morning, I gave myself a big talking to. 'Get your act together Eve. You have much to be grateful for and more to look forward to.' I forced myself to come back to my senses. I marched into the kitchen and started brewing a pick-me-up potion. Come on Eve Hill, wake up and come back to life. I was stirring the potion gently, when I happened to glance up. Over the stove I spotted a crack on the wall I shared with Claude. For a member of the Sisterhood, I am so unobservant. I wondered how long that had been there and why I hadn't noticed it before. A good excuse to employ Claude's good services.

THE SEVENTH WAVE

Witness Account by Greg Neal
(used in part in a BBC 4 Production of 'Of Sea Gods and Monster' 2003)

Like the murderer who will make himself known in a nightmare, sea monsters will occasionally break through their salty prison and make themselves known to the rest of the world. I personally wish they wouldn't, but they do and there's the fact. I also wish I was not the fellow they revealed themselves to, but sadly, I was. I hadn't been drinking either. I hadn't been smoking herbs or swallowing acid. Though they may have helped. Though I lived in London, as a child my home was in Dorchester. I was visiting the island with a vague notion of looking for someone I had once loved. Approaching it, I was a little suspicious of its geography. A grey lump of rock, void of trees and tethered to the mainland via a monotonous chain of pebbles. Moulded and moving constantly by wind and wave, this was a landscape you couldn't trust.

I decided to walk the beach later that evening. This wasn't the famous pebble shore which stretches all the way to Devon, but the bay on the east side. The other shore scared me, to be frank, but this bay was as quiet and submissive as the other was noisy and aggressive. Little did I know. I walked the hundred steps down to the shore, past a broken church whose graveyard is said to be full of pirates. At the bottom I sat on a rock and lit up a cigarette. Nobody was about and I was settling into my thoughts when the sea right in front of me began to stir. I thought seal or dolphin or shark. You would have thought the sightings of sea monsters would usually occur during storms, in fog or at night, wouldn't you. To my amazement, a monster emerged from the commotion of water. It may have been the length of two men and, I can only describe it as half bird, half sea horse. I stood up, dropping my cigarette, ready to run for it but unable to move. He/she/it looked at me and disappeared as quick as it had arrived, the stirring surface quickly covering over. I looked around to double check if anyone else had witnessed what I just seen. Not a soul. Just my luck.

Afterwards I found out that this beast was a familiar visitor to this Island. Why there were no warning signs up I have no idea. The chronicler Raphael Holinshed first identified the monster and named him Veasta. He claims that in 1457 the Veasta arose from the waves. He described it as being more like a cockerel, crowing like one and wearing the wattles and comb of one. There were definite sightings in 1757 when both a live specimen was seen and the corpse of one was washed up on the beach. More sightings followed in 1965, 1995 and now this very year by me.

It wasn't long before I wished I had kept my sightings a secret. The local papers had a field day with me. They took photographs of me pointing to the spot where the creature emerged. An artist drew a portrait of the creature based on my description. 'Was I frightened? Did you think you were going mad? Why do you think no one else saw it?' You can imagine the questioning. I felt such a loser especially when I made the front page - obviously not much happens on Tuesdays in November. What I didn't tell the press was what I am about to tell you. When I saw the Veasta the overwhelming feeling was erotic, and I had a strong urge to enter the water and join it in its watery bed. Imagine the headline if I had told them: 'Shock horror. Local monster gives tourist a hard-on!' Imagine there's this picture of me: One hand pointing to the water, the other to the unmistakeable bulge in my jeans.

I kept that bit to myself.

JACK

Great at blanking out anything I couldn't handle, I spent a marvellous time on the beach with Henry, pulling in the mackerel with tremendous ease. After last night's storm, the sea was as meek as a lamb. The terraces had been creaking violently and it felt as if we were all about to sink under the waves. The thought of cracked, bent or buggered pipes kept coming to mind, but nothing happened. One of the old boys around here, Henry, was teaching me to fish mackerel properly from the beach. 'Fishing from a boat is for pussies!' He demonstrated how to cast: by bringing the rod swiftly overhead and then just at the right time, he released the catch, allowing the weight to carry its cargo of hooks and feathers through the air and land a hundred metres offshore. Once there, he started winding the line in, whipping the rod in a rhythm of quick pulls. This apparently fools the fish into believing the feathers are live whiting rushing at speed through the water. They must be easily fooled because Henry was landing them three, four, five at a time.

'We have a shoal,' he told me solemnly.

When I had my first go, I got out less than half the distance Henry did, and the returning line didn't have a single mackerel on it. I repeated this several times. He demonstrated the procedure to me a second time. When I tried again, the line bent almost at once and I felt the magnificent wrestle of fish, trying to free themselves from their bait. I landed two. By the afternoon however, I was reeling the blighters in and feeling quite pleased with myself. So was Henry until I reeled in six on one line, something he hadn't managed. 'Beginner's luck!'

I didn't disagree with him. It was beginner's luck. I took it as a cue to leave, but not before getting him to promise to drop off my share later. I intended to share my prize with Eve and Rowan and who knows possibly even with Claude. I crunched my way to the top of the ridge of pebbles, when I heard a child shriek with joy as he was chased by an incoming wave. I turned to watch. There were the three of them, two boys and a girl, having the time of their lives, their parents keeping an eye on them sitting higher on the bank. The more I watched, the more I didn't seem to be able to prise myself away from the scene. It was ordinary enough, an everyday event but there was something about it, transfixing me. Then, I remembered.

ROWAN

Tuesday was always the day Claude went into town on the local bus. I don't know what he did, nor did I care. All I knew was that he would reappear about five in some sort of pissed state. We had bags of time to do what we wanted. Spot on time, Rachel arrived at my house.

Of all the times, we were on the point of leaving when up walked Zac. He was on one as per usual and barged past me into the house. It would have been a complete waste of time trying to stop him.

'She's frigid!' he announced in his usual style, not giving a shit that Rachel was there.

'Who is?'

'That psycho woman-bitch. I told her my feelings and she said it was impossible. We could never be anything other than doctor and patient.' Zac was already in the kitchen, popping open a beer. 'Who cares a pig-fuck about doctor and patient. Last time I looked we were human beings!'

I told him who Rachel was and he loosely shook her hand. He wasn't interested in her and began rolling a joint. As if poor Rachel was invisible, he carried on about the "psycho bitch." In the end I had to tell him to shut the fuck up. I didn't have time for his crap, so I sat him down and told him our plan. He was only half-listening as always.

'Your job is to stay here and keep a lookout.'

'No worries, sister. I can do that. Who am I looking out for?'

I knew he would be a hopeless scout but allowed myself to be convinced.

I had told Rachel that the focus of our break-in was

the hatch in the lounge floor. We didn't need to bother about the rest. We needed to know what was in that cellar. We left via the back door and, despite ourselves, started to giggle. This stopped when we came across our first obstacle. Claude had unusually closed his top kitchen window. We stood there wondering what to do, when, to my own surprise, I picked up a brick and launched it at the glass. Rachel looked at me with shock. I shrugged.

'Why the hell not? What's he gonna do about it? Kill us?'

Rachel jumped through the window and opened the door. As before, it smelled of tobacco and middle-aged male stuffiness. He wasn't one for decoration, there was hardly a picture up or an ornament in place. The place looked unlived-in, like he used it to doss in and nothing much else.

In the lounge I dragged the mat away and revealed the hatch. We paused a little before taking a deep breath and opening it. It was much heavier than I remembered from my first visit and Rachel had to help me lift it fully back. We were instantly assaulted by the stink of old dried earth and, of course, it was dark.

'Did you bring a torch?' I asked Rachel, knowing she hadn't.

'No, did you bring one?' Rachel asked me, knowing I hadn't. All this planning and we had forgot the most obvious thing.

'You first, then.'

'No, you first, Rowan. You're the oldest.'

'Ok, you stay here while I go down and see if there is a light. Keep holding onto that hatch for God's sake.' Standing there we could see the narrow ladder disappearing, the bottom rungs lost in darkness. I was shitting a brick I got to tell you but cautiously edged onto the first step.

'I'm a bit nervous, Rachel.'

'Don't worry, it will be alright,' said Rachel, reassuringly touching my arm. I started to descend. With every step, the darkness became more impenetrable and the stench more overwhelming. As I proceeded step by step, I was fumbling on each side feeling for a light switch.

'How you doing?'

Despite Rachel whispering, her words were enough to make me jump out of my skin.

'Can you give me a warning if you are going to speak.'

'How can I do that?'

I had descended about ten steps when I seriously thought about bottling it and giving up. How deep was this place. Perhaps there's nothing here anyway. What the hell were we expecting? After the eleventh, I hit solid ground. Still no light. I froze and wondered what to do. Rachel called me in a loud whisper and, being so hyper, I jumped again.

'I think we may have to abandon it. I can't see a thing. We need a torch.' As soon as I said this, I felt a length of string which I pulled straightaway and everything was suddenly illuminated. Seeing the light was now on, Rachel followed me and was soon at my side.

'Weird!' was the first word Rachel used to describe the room we had found ourselves in. I say "room" but really it was a central space with about six alcoves at regular intervals, each covered by a makeshift curtain. In the main space where we were standing was an old mattress to one side folded and held together with a belt. Against the far wall, there was a small table and chair with a solitary book on it. It looked like one of those old ledgers which may have come straight out of Charles Dickens. It was a heavy volume, covered in dust.

Opening the book up randomly I could see it was indeed a log of sorts, but in code: dates with initials followed by a few letters. The first date was July 7th, 1981. I would have been nine then. I skipped to the latest entries and came to a date last week. My initials followed by a few letters and a star. I was about to look for more, interested to see how often my initials appeared, when Rachel called me over.

'By God, Rowan, this man is sick!' Rachel had pulled one of the curtains back and there on about six shelves were various dead animals in pickling jars of differing sizes. 'Why would he collect such things?' We counted twenty in all: seagulls, a couple of foxes' heads, a few moles and rats, a squirrel.

'Let's look in the others,' I said, getting quite excited. We were moving to the next when suddenly the hatch slammed shut like the blast of an explosion. Both of us screamed, remembered where we were and listening for any sound or movement from above.

'Fucking shit. Must have been the wind or something.' I said, after a few moments.

It took both of us to shove the hatch open again. As there was very little space, it proved rather trickier than you may have thought. When finally, it was wide open again, we placed a chair against the open lid to stop it happening again. 'Ok, let's not panic. Let's calm down and focus on what we are about. We have plenty of time. Claude isn't due for hours.'

Somewhat shaken, we walked back down the steps. We agreed which alcove would be next and pulled the curtain to one side. In this one there was a stack of old cardboard boxes. Rachel ripped open the first one. It was full of women's clothing. Musky with age, they had obviously been there sometime. Tearing into the next one, we discovered more clothing, all women's.

'Do you think he's kinky and likes dressing up?' Rachel asked.

'No, can't see that. It isn't his style.'

'This place really gives me the creeps, Rowan. I mean what is it doing here anyway, this place? No one else along here has a cellar, have they?'

'Good question. Everything is a clue, don't you think? For starters, I'm stealing that book. I reckon it's full of secrets. Claude has such an ego that he can't stop himself recording what he does. I bet you your name's in there.'

Rachel wasted no time and went straight to it.

'Look for your initials.'

While she did that, I pressed on with the search. In the next alcove there was a solitary large wooden box. Unfortunately, it was firmly nailed down. I tried to prise it open with my hands, but that was useless.

'Is there anything around I can use to open this box? A chisel or hammer or something?'

'There were some tools in the kitchen,' she muttered, totally engrossed in the book. 'But,' she added, 'You're not leaving me here alone. So, if you go up, I go up.'

I decided to leave it and move onto to alcove number four. This proved disappointing as well, as it turned out there was a similar box there, looking older than the last one but sealed just as firmly.

The next alcove was in the shadow of the light and so I could see very little. I couldn't make out anything and I assumed it was empty until I caught a glint of something on a shelf in front of me. I pulled the curtain aside as much as I could and gradually my eyes adjusted. It seemed to be another specimen in a jar. What was it? I remember hearing Rachel in the background saying something like 'My God! My initials are all over the place.'

I looked closer. At first, I thought that it was a monkey until I realised that the face looking back to me was that of an infant child. I screamed and turned abruptly, ready to run. Claude was standing there, smiling, and with one powerful blow he hit me hard in the face.

CLAUDE

I decided to go into town as is my routine on a Tuesday. Commonly, on arrival, I would start the day right and take my cappuccino in a little cafe called Stanley's. This was a wonderfully quiet, relaxing place where I could innocently flirt with the proprietress, Pam, whilst catching up on the news via one of their newspapers. Pam was always obliging and helpful, but of course, not my type - by about forty years. I would then visit the bank, post a few parcels and invariably buy a few essentials. I would meet up with a few mates of like mind in the Black Dog and we would exchange tales play pool and plot some new joint venture. The gang were all good friends, but in my business such as it is, you always have to be a tad on the cautious side as a friend can easily become a rival or, even worse, a squealer. Please note, that toad Hamilton, may he rest in pieces. Anyway, on this occasion, I decided to return home earlier than usual. I have something of a sixth sense and recently had noticed young Rowan sniffing about. Normally, I do not see her from one day to the next. She avoids me until I come knocking for ransom. Yet, in the last weeks I have seen her hovering about. As Jesus is our saviour, these things play on my suspicious mind. I don't want this loon becoming too familiar with my habits. I am wondering if she is up to no good. Bring it on, I say. There is nothing to worry on. She is no match for the great Claude Mayfellow.

When having a pee, I had a moment of clarity and decided to return home earlier than was my wont. I made sure that I didn't dip out on my usual intake of ale and doubled my rate of consumption. As I was on a mission, I was sharp and focussed and beat every last one of them at pool. Porky challenged me to darts to try and get his own back and ended up losing a 10g pack of home-grown grass. By the time I got back on the bus, I must say I was feeling rather smug with myself.

I have come a long way. I can only thank my father again, and again for being so disciplined with me. His unpredictability made me sharp. When he beat me black and blue, he was teaching me all the while, how to look after myself and defend myself against a world which was equally unpredictable. I can honestly tell you that I have never lost a fight in my life. I am not so much strong as determined. Just as I see a woman and know instinctively what she would be like in the sack, I see a man and I know his weaknesses and sense his vulnerability, which I'm not afraid to exploit. I remember one sports day, I must have been twelve, I was in the hundred yards dash. I came second. Dad took me to one side and praised me to high heavens, the rest of the family looking on. I felt on top of the world. Then he kicked me in the balls as hard as he could. Which was hard, considering he didn't have any run up. The next year I won the counties, breaking the course record. My Dad was a mastermind. And, to boot, considering the poverty in my childhood, now I have a very healthy bank account, thank you very much, thanks to my lucrative now world-wide business in DVDs and other related materials.

I gave the bus driver a hearty wave as I strolled back home. Guided by forces unknown and holy, I went around the back. I stopped dead. I was taken aback to discover the kitchen window smashed and the door open. My first thought was to congratulate myself on my perfect instinct. I crept into the house and could hear voices. I had caught them red-handed, what could be better. I couldn't guess who the two were but one little missy I was positive of. In the lounge I found that my secret place had been uncovered. I was as quiet as a mouse and listened intently. And guess what. I was tickled pink to find that not one, but both of my two favourite people had climbed into my underground den. What luck was this. I tiptoed down one little step at a time. Rachel was reading my ledger. Rowan was in one of the alcoves. F-Christ…this was one of my most desired fantasies coming to fruition. Like it is always with me, I knew exactly what to do …exactly!

As soon as Rowan turned towards me, I gave the bitch a neat fist full in her pretty face. I whipped around to Rachel.

'At last!' says I to the rather shocked young lady. 'I knew that eventually you would come to me, through one means or another. There is no pretending now, Rachel, your fixation with me was becoming embarrassing. Don't look like that, my girl. You do not want to kindle my wrath, do you? Now I suppose our main problem is how do we proceed? Let me see, what must happen next.' I had no doubt what would happen next. God had given me this precious gem on a plate, and I would not make a mistake and flunk this blessed opportunity.

'What have you done to Rowan?' she said as I was blocking her view.

I gave Rowan a cursory glance. She was lying on the floor completely knocked out, curse her. Sometimes, I don't know my own strength.

'Rowan is absolutely fine. Madness is stronger than you think. Give her not another thought, Rachel, my love. Let us return to the business in hand.'

I moved closer to Rachel. Her fear of me was to be expected and was clearly written on her face. Being honest, she was after all a youngster with not much experience in the world of life, let alone love, so I had to make allowances. What had happened to her, to date? A few kisses from some wretched pubescent lads, possibly a quick feel or flash, nothing more than that. Their loss, I say. Rachel was a splendid gift. I eyed my exquisite prey and could see how beautiful she was regardless of which emotions were clambering from her heart to her face. Her apprehension, if anything added to my fascination with her. I decided to give her a little peck, but she turned away from me.

'Don't do that, Claude.'

'Don't do what, my darling?'

'You have no right to do this. You must let us go. My family will be looking for me.'

I stifled a laugh, thinking of the retards she was referring to. 'Oh, dear, Rachel, let's not play games, shall we?' I was picking up the need to emphasise my point. I gave Rowan a nifty kick in the belly to which she replied with a soft groan. I got my kiss. I was doubly intoxicated. With the booze and with the challenge in front of me, I felt as divinely chosen as any man could. However, I realised that I needed to capitalise on my catch because, although I thought this unlikely, I could not be one hundred percent certain that some untoward event may interfere with my pleasure. Seize the moment etc. Once she had tasted Vintage Claude, I was fairly certain she would want more.

'Just accept that I know what you need before you know yourself. You will give yourself quite willingly.' I gave Rowan another kick to underline my meaning. She nodded her head in absolute obedience. 'So, when I do this, for example,' I said touching her little hard breasts. 'Or this,' touching her between her legs. 'You will raise no objection.

In this way, Rachel, you will begin to understand what is happening and before you know it my lady, your enjoyment will promptly follow. Are you getting it, Rachel?'

'You're not allowed to do this,' she told me, pulling back. This was excitement beyond imagination.

'That's where you are wrong, my dear. This is what I was born to do!'

I turned around again, intending to give Rowan another boot, when Rachel placed her hand on my arm.

'No, please don't.'

'Seeing reason, are we? Have you decided to partake of the wonders on offer?'

She bobbed her little head up and down a little faster than she had previously. Clearly, I was winning her over.

I was just going in for my second kiss, this time intending more passion, when, to my great annoyance, her bloody phone went off, maybe not entirely inappropriately, to the Arctic Monkeys song, *I Bet You Look Good on the Dance floor*. 'It's Gran. She's probably wondering where I am.'

'Better answer it then. Make any old excuse. Don't want to make the old bag jealous, do we? Any sly stuff, Rachel, just try to think about your friend lying there' I nodded my head towards Rowan, who was still peacefully unconscious.

'Hi Gran, I'm with Mandy.'

I could hear the old trout say, 'Whatever for?' followed by more questions.

'No, will be home later. No, no, Gran, everything is fine. I will get home by myself.' The old trout was obviously giving her an earful, so I indicated to Rachel to end the call. 'Got to go Gran - see you later.' Much later, I hoped.

'Ok, let's have that phone.' I took it from her before she could object and slipped it into my jacket pocket.' Right, where were we? Before we were rudely interrupted.'

Not all was perfect, of course. Nothing ever is. I had my angel there with me but may have been happier if we had been two stories higher between the sheets of my king size. Additionally, I wish Rowan hadn't been moaning beside us. She was an encumbrance to proceedings. I could not let the moment pass and progressed with my mind on high alert. If God has placed me in this position, I should ride with it and think of delightful ways to involve Rowan in the proceedings should she come to.

I was aware of a certain indeterminate tension in the air, a tension somewhat at odds with the wonderful prospect life had unfolded for me. I thought again about disembarking to the bed upstairs but that stupid bitch Rowan would be down here. I couldn't afford any cock-ups or interference. I did have a thin mattress down here anyway, folded into one of the corners. It was tatty and dirty. I had used it a few times in my educational clips, as I prefer to call them, to create the intensive sexual atmosphere associated with cellars, crypts and basements. I pulled it out roughly and placed it on the floor. I asked Rachel to join me on the bed and she obeyed with what may have been construed as increasing anticipation. It dawned on me that I had that wee pack of dope in my jacket and decided that this would be the most suitable way to break the tension and put the lost girl - soon to become woman - at her ease.

Being home grown skunk, this was weed at its best. We leant against the cold earthen wall while we smoked. I forgave Rachel her coughing and spluttering and even managed to get a sort of laugh out of her. This was a day of firsts for her and I was overcome with feelings of pride for being part of it. To be on the safe side, I got Rachel to drink the brew I took from Eve's Book, which I had stored in one of the alcoves for this very occasion. She balked at her first sip, but I persuaded her to take two good mouthfuls. It is said to put the "maid into a swoon." Its main components were honey, a teaspoon of salt-water and a drop of gull's blood. I personally, didn't believe in it, but it was worth a try.

'Rachel, allow me a question, be honest, have you not thought about me? In *that* way, I mean? Think carefully now as this is important to me.' I placed my hand ever so gently around her neck to reassure her.

'I have,' she said, after a pause.

'Good girl,' I said, congratulating her on her newfound candour by taking her hand and pressing it against my demonstrative member. 'So, I conclude, that you are willing for this to happen?'

'I am.'

Christ Jesus in heaven, I had done it once more. As you know, I have honoured and adhered to my sacred code. In all my days, no female of any age - bar that one on Tophill and she hardly matters - had not given themselves to me of their own volition. This was essential for me. I would never ever want to be accused of taking advantage of another person as this would clearly be an infringement of my ethics. This was the fundamental difference between me and the Hamiltons of this world. I pulled her down beside me and started on my handiwork.

'How about Rowan?' says Rachel.

'Well, looking at her I don't think she will mind. Just forget that she's there. Or are you worried she isn't having any fun of her own? That is not a problem, young Rachel. I am sure she has told you about our mutual arrangement. I guess that was the spur to your snooping around. After this, we shall have two arrangements going on or one arrangement involving three. Sorry, I am getting a little carried away at the endless possibilities. My advice my young filly is to relax.'

'I can't, it's that.' she said, pointing over my head to the ceiling near the hatch.

'Just relax, sweet-pea.'

She pointed to the ceiling again which I took as a distraction. She must have been crapping herself about the prospect of her deflowerment. She kept looking up so, out of common courtesy, I had to look up. Initially, I couldn't see what she was on about. I was going to say that it was nothing when I too saw what was disturbing her. The wall was shiny with water, bubbling along its surface, pouring mysteriously from somewhere above us.

'What the hell!' I stood up to have a closer look and as I did so, the flow of water became stronger. Bits of mud were beginning to tumble down, and I could see that the integrity of the wall on that side of the cellar was being compromised. 'Jesus, shit and fuck!' There was the girl of my desire and once again fate was interrupting. Or should I say Jack Powys was at fault as it was his side where the leak was obviously coming from. That man had been a fucking pest since day one.

What to do?

'I am more than sorry to say Rachel dearest, but I am going to have to investigate. I am, of course, going to have to take some precautions. Don't take offence, but I am doing this for your own safety and well-being.' I was not so entirely stupid or besotted as to compromise my own safety and knew that Rachel was probably still prone to doubt and reservation. She had yet to get to that tipping point where everything would make sense and her unexplored pleasure would be released. I applied duct tape to her hands and feet. In the spirit of cooperation, I thought about leaving her pretty mouth free, but then taped it anyway. I loved her completely, but she was a female after all; trickery being their second nature.

I bolted up the stairs and shut the hatch behind me. I calmed myself for a moment, conscious that I was re-entering the world and didn't want to arouse any suspicion. I went straight to Jack's door and gave it a hammering. Jack wasn't at home, bloody fool. I scanned the shore, only a few fishermen. I went to the pub, which was virtually empty, and asked the bar maid and Mitchell, the resident bar fly, if they had seen him. They hadn't. Meanwhile I had mixed visions, one of water pissing into the cellar and the other of Rachel, all primed up and ready for the taking. Holy son of Jesse and David, fuck and shit, indeed. I didn't want to call the water board or the plumber, and definitely not the police. For once, I was at a loss as to what to do.

I ran back to the terrace and bumped into Rowan's key worker, nurse or whatever she was. I asked her as calmly as I could manage if she knew Jack and where he might be.

'Yes, I know him, but haven't seen him today. You could ask Rowan, but I can't find her either. Maybe they are together.' she said in a chuckle. 'I'm just hoping Rowan hasn't gone into town pubbing it or something like that. We did have an appointment, you see.'

'Sorry, can't help you love, 'I said, quickly, trying to get rid of her.

'We haven't met, have we? You seem familiar. Do I know you from somewhere or other?' I had had enough.

'Can you shut the fuck up? I have a genuine emergency on my hands.'

I left her on the pathway and went straight back to Jack's door. Surprise, surprise. The daft bugger hadn't even locked it. Why hadn't I tried that before? I rushed through the house, noting a clutter of paper and books everywhere. In the downstairs bathroom I could see there was a leak of some sort as the bathroom was soaked, but there was no way you could get to it without pulling the whole thing up. Fuck and Shit!

Still with no plan in mind - what had happened to my faculties, my old reliable? - I returned to the street and thankfully Jack was coming towards the house, looking worried on seeing me coming out of his place. If I could get him to contact the water people and they could get to it from his side, I could return to my prey and all would be well.

'Thank Christ, Jack. Your property has sprung a leak and it's coming in my side.'

'Bloody hell, this is the third time in a month!' He was saying the words, but I had the feeling that the man was not quite right. If I was a betting man, I would say the big baby had been crying. As it wasn't important at this particular moment, I chose to ignore it.

'This may be the worst Jack. Looks much bigger than before, my friend, you really have problems this time. Now be a good boy and get a move on and call the Water Board. Think they need to come out *tout suite!'*

'I'm on it!'

Eve emerged from her house. She seemed bothered and beside herself and was fingering her mobile phone.

'Has either of you seen my granddaughter today?'

'Teenagers will be teenagers,' I said, flippantly. She jumped down my throat at that. 'She isn't a teenager. Rachel is only twelve!'

Before I could do anything, she was phoning her up. Would you believe it? Out of my pocket ran the inane refrain from that annoying band. Sacred Mary, fuck and shit!

EVE

'Claude, how have you got hold of Rachel's phone? I only spoke to her half hour or so ago. Where is she?'

He took the phone out of his pocket and I could see that it was Rachel's the red and black stripe on the back was unmistakable. Before he had been a bit edgy, now Claude came towards me in his familiar way, that is, calm, collected and smiling.

'Eve, just been into Jack's. He has another leak and I went in to see what I could do. When I saw he wasn't there I picked up what I thought was his phone to call the water board myself.'

I turned to Jack and demanded an explanation. 'Wait.

Before you soldier off, what in the devil's name, are you doing with my granddaughter's phone?' Claude gave the phone to Jack who took hold of it immediately in a way I thought was over-confident.

'This is Rachel's?'

'Yes, Claude found it in your house. Please explain?!'

'I can't, I'm afraid. In my home, you say? I have been with Henry over there all morning fishing. Ask him. I haven't seen Rachel here since…yesterday, or the day before. I can't remember to be honest. The days here all fuse into one.' Jack began babbling as was normal for him. 'True, she was in my house last week.'

'Oh, was she now?'

'Yes, she brought me that dinner you made me.'

'Yes,' I said, reluctantly coming down from high ground. 'That's true, I will give you that, but it still doesn't explain why her phone is here and yet the girl is not!' I took possession of it and I could see my last call recorded within the last hour.

Claude began to laugh, putting his arm around me.

'Eve, Eve, Eve, do you think the young girl is playing games? She's with her friends, then she isn't. She's up Tophill and then she isn't. Her phone is suddenly at Jack's, but Rachel is nowhere to be seen. I am feeling a prank, aren't you? Maybe, she is watching us now.' We all look around and the only person we see is Rowan's social worker in her car, staring at us.

'Any rates, man!' Claude said with force. 'The water. The water!'

'Yes, yes, I will contact them on the emergency number,' said Jack.' I know it off by heart now!'

'It doesn't make any sense, Claude.' I resumed.' You know Rachel, this is most unlike her. I'm calling Harry. He needs to know about this. He may call in the cavalry.'

'I think you may be behaving a wee bit hastily, Eve. I'll tell you what let's go in and have a nice cup of tea and discuss what may need to be done.'

We did just that. I told Jack that he wasn't off the hook yet and, when in the house, I apologised to Claude for being in such a mess. 'I'm all in a tizzy, Claude, I am not myself at the moment. I keep having these nightmares and feeling like something bad is about to happen. It's like a premonition without seeing any of the details. It's like all me emotions are out of sync.'

'All will be well, Eve. You are worrying far too much.' He picked up my hand from my lap, opened it and kissed the palm.

'You have been very kind, Claude. You are a true support. One thing you don't know about which is eating away at me is the fact that I have a condition.'

'A condition?'

'A physical illness which is killing me slowly,' I told him, relieved to tell someone, especially someone I could trust.

'What sort of condition are we talking about, Eve?'

'A tumour of some sort.'

'Ah, they're easily treated these days, my darling. I'm sure it's nothing to worry about. What do the doctors say?'

'I haven't been,' I said shyly.' Part of being in the Sisterhood is a refusal to go to any modern medic.'

'Really? Sounds slightly absurd, especially these days.'

'See what you think, Claude.' Before he could respond, I had lifted the front of my blouse and I showed him the growth.

What happened next changed my world forever. I thought I may expect an outpouring of tenderness. What I got was something quite different. Claude pulled back straightaway. He rose to his feet as if about to leg it, knocking the chair he was sitting on to the ground. It was the look of utter horror on his face which was most nasty, a terrible stare of disgust. He couldn't hide it or disguise it in any way. I was seeing the man's real and truthful face. I covered myself up at once. My reaction to the strength of his disgust was the equal and opposite; the bitter emotion of humiliation. It soared through my body in one hot rush and, in that moment, I wished to God that the earth would consume me whole and I would disappear back into the darkness from where I came.

'Claude, Claude, it's alright. It's still me!' Despite my pining, I could sense it wasn't me at all he was seeing. He was seeing only an old hag coming apart at the seams. 'It really is OK!'

'Madam, it is certainly not OK. Your very existence fills me with total and absolute revulsion,' he said, turning on his heels and vanishing down the hallway. Not having enough of these dreadful insults, I followed him lamely. When I reached the door, someone had got to him before me, but I couldn't see who because Claude was in the way. As he moved from the door, I saw Katie shouting at Claude. Strange, I thought, she didn't even know him.

'It's you, it's you!' she kept saying to him.

'I don't know who you are, you stupid woman, so I would be grateful if you would just go and shit on another part of this beach.'

Katie started to cry. 'I was nine. I was nine years old. You...you broke me in half. You left me with a bottle of whisky by the side of the road. I was nine.' Claude stopped a moment as if digesting the information.

'You kept calling me Anna...Anna...Anna - and all the time, I was lying there in agony, I kept wondering "why is he calling me Anna when I am Katie." It, is you, isn't it? I have been looking for you for twenty years and all the time you were on my doorstep.'

'Like I said, I have never seen you before nor wish to again!' replied Claude, but this time less forcefully. As he turned to go back to his place, she grabbed him with an iron grip.

'Now I have you, you're not going to get away with it. Eve contact Harry. It's time for punishment, you piece of shit. I would kill you myself if I could muster the strength. I would rip you apart in strips.' Katie began sobbing and, even though I was only beginning to understand what was happening, I went to her and put my arm around her. I could see Claude was lost for words and I saw that the man was afraid. Both things I never thought he was capable of.

When I looked up again from comforting young Katie, Claude was nowhere to be seen. With Claude gone and leaving me holding that poor girl, the scales fell from my eyes. I took her into the house, and she told me her story.

As a child, her house was on the other side of a disused quarry, so it was her habit to cut through on the way home from the shops or from school. Christina, her best friend, lived opposite to her so they had each other for company. Walking that way home became part of their daily routine and they became familiar with its nooks and crannies.

'Christina was a rather sickly girl,' Katie told me. 'She had asthma. When she became ill, she fought for every breath and could hardly speak or laugh despite me putting on my Katie Bush face. In the October of the year when I was going to be ten, Christina became worse and she began missing more of school. Dad being Dad warned me to take the roadway home, and not to cut through the quarry. I wanted to obey him, but the roadway was three times longer and, don't forget, I knew the quarry like the back of my hand. Seems obvious now that somebody had been watching me because on one of the days when I made my dash through the quarry, a man was waiting for me. At first, I couldn't make out what he was until he began moving towards me. I thought about either running back to the road or darting forward. I made the wrong choice. With amazing strength, he hoisted me onto a rock. He started to talk to me as if we were friends and he knew me. He kept calling me Anna. I wanted to tell him that he had made a mistake; I was in a sort of trance when he laid me on the ground. I felt like I was a doll. He could do what he wanted. He told me how pretty I was and that it was "important to him" that I agreed with what was about to happen. Of course, I didn't understand what was about to happen, but I nodded my head in agreement. When he left me there on my own, he made me promise to say, "nothing to no one."

He said that it would be wise, unless I wanted something really bad to happen to my friend. "And you don't want that to happen, do you?"'

Katie paused and I brought her closer to me. She had been carrying the events of that day in her since childhood.

'To this day, I have never entered that quarry. Shortly after, Christina died. It was an asthma attack, but in my childish mind I connected her death with the stranger's threat. I never said anything to anyone. I promised myself to keep my eyes open. You see, he didn't cover his face. I guess his arrogance was such that he felt he didn't have to. I had heard Rowan speak of Claude, but I had only seen him from afar. Today I saw him at close quarters and there isn't a cell of my body which doubted that this was the man. Claude was my rapist.'

I told her to go into the bathroom, splash water on her face and I would put the kettle on. Before I did though, I called Harry. I told him about Claude and what Katie had told me. I laid it on thick by saying Katie believed he would be coming back for her. I added that I was worried about Rachel too. Rachel is missing, I said, dramatically. I haven't seen her all day. I was still on the phone when Katie came back into the room distressed.

'There's something wrong in the bathroom,' she says.

'What do you mean, my dear?'

'Take a look.'

Something wrong was a slight understatement. A crack as wide as a child's wrist and as long as their arm had formed over the sink. I screeched in disbelief.

I flew into Jack's. He was in his bathroom, watching a crack of his own growing up from the bath.

'What's happening Jack?'

'All I can think of is that the water is seeping into the foundations. I have phoned the Water Board and they're on the way, but I'm phoning again.'

I began to panic, recalling my own words, "Rachel was missing." As I hurried back to my place, I could hear some sort of din going on, but couldn't detect where it was coming from. Jack was behind me.

'I heard that earlier. Sounds like it's coming from ground. I presume its some pipes creaking or shifting.' Neither of us were convinced and made our way out to the front of the house. Katie was already there.

'What is that noise?'

'Buggered if I know,' I said. 'Well, the water people will soon be here hopefully. The police are on their way as well.'

'The police. What's going on? What are you talking about?' says Jack, his usual three-quarters of an hour behind everyone else. We gave him a potted history of events.

'Claude? I can't believe it.'

'Can't you?' I said, jumping down his throat.

I could hear the far-off scream of the siren. Or sirens, should I say, as there was definitely more than one.

We kept listening to the baffling noise going on below our feet. Jack went around the back to check it out there. Meanwhile, Katie and I began pacing around, trying to make sense of it. It was an odd racket; the strangest noise. It was muffled, a sort of screeching like an animal was trapped somewhere and it came in waves, rising and falling.

'Eve, the noise it's directly below here. Listen.' It appeared to be coming up through the ground immediately in front of Claude's house.

'Where is that bastard, I wonder?' Katie said; she physically knelt down and put her ear to the ground.

'That's not a noise, it's voices. Someone is under there!'

JACK

The sound of the children's yelling as the waves tried to capture them echoed in my head. Before my eyes, the scene began to change, the sky became heavier, grey with rain clouds. The wind picked up from a slight breeze to a vicious gale. The sea went from a serene blue to black ink. The waves transformed from a lazy shuffle, becoming higher, more forceful, loud and menacing.

This is what I remembered.

I must have been really young, maybe three or four, as I was stumbling on the pebbles. It was a grey and windy day. My family was around me. I was throwing pebbles into the water or trying to. I was little and the waves were huge and noisy and terrifying. Rosie was showing me how to throw the pebbles.

'Not overhead, you ninny. Sling it from the side. Like this!' I couldn't do it properly and she called me an idiot.

Further up the beach, I could see my parents. They were waving at me. I waved back. I remember it being cold. My hands and fingers were freezing. The noise was deafening and made it feel exciting and unusual. Rosie was having to shout.

'Come on Jack. You're not even trying.' She picked up a pebble and told me to use it. I managed to reach the waves. 'Even James can make a better job of it than you!'

A little way down the beach, there was a little boy playing by the water's edge. He had a stick and was stabbing the air with it. Rosie gave up on me and turned away. I was pleased as I was fed up with the stress of throwing. I found a stone with a hole through it. I held it up and looked through it. There was the little boy with the stick. There was Rosie walking up the bank of pebbles. There was Mum and there was Dad. It fascinated me that all the big world twirling around me could shrink to the size of the hole. I put it in my pocket for keeps.

I began to follow Rosie up the pebbles. It was hard work. The pebbles kept shifting and taking my feet away from under me. I was about to shout for Dad's help when I could hear him above the noise shouting for me. Suddenly everyone was running about and screaming. Dad was on the top of the mound of pebbles shouting and looking over to where the boy had been. Rosie came from nowhere and was crying. I wondered if I had done something wrong. Rosie was hugging me when my Mum tore us apart and started shaking me violently. 'Where's James?' she was screaming. 'Where's James? Where is he? Where's your brother?'

My brother.

I looked around and the little boy had gone. I am not sure how long I had stood there. When I came to, the afternoon was returning to its pleasant reality and I was stumbling along the beach towards my house, my face wet with tears. As I approached the terraces, I was intrigued to find Claude coming out of my house. My confusion didn't stop there. Eve soon joined us, and Rachel's phone went off in Claude's pocket. Claude said that he found the phone in my living room. What was he doing there in the first place? I soon found out. Another leak had started, this time starting somewhere under my bath. Leaks were the bane of my life here. I was much more perturbed by the phone and had no explanation whatsoever for it being in my place. Fortunately, nobody saw that I was in a bit of a state.

When I got into the house, I became conscious of the mess and wondered what Claude thought of all the paper strewn all over the place. The good news was that it was actually coming together nicely, now I had Old Flann on board. We reckoned to have a first draft in six weeks. Just as well, as Weller had emailed me saying that he wanted to see some "proof" of my endeavours.

Then the bathroom. It was obvious that water was pissing out from underneath the carpet as it was completely sodden. There was further evidence that it was soaking into the wall cavity as random patches of dampness were spreading up the walls. I uselessly threw down some towels and went to phone the emergency line. As I was leaving, I happened to look up and was taken back to see a massive zigzag crack running from one side of the ceiling to the other.

I became aware of some distant muffled screeching and wondered if a gull had got lodged in the chimney or somehow in the roof. As I leant to the wall the sound appeared to be coming from below rather than above. I resolved to go and tell Eve and Claude, but first things first, I telephoned the emergency line. They knew who I was before I could inform them of my name.

ROWAN

I could hear the voice of the Wolf. He seemed to be at some distance, and I could barely hear His words. Slowly, He was moving towards me. Was it from the darkness of the forest? Into the plain of snow. Hard to tell. He was coming to me mouthing the same words over and over again. I was becoming frantic, straining to hear what He was telling me. Then I heard.

'Wake up, Rowan, wake up!'

I knew with total clarity that I had to obey him and saw myself lifting little by little from the cold and then I was soaring above, ever higher. When my eyes flickered open, I could hardly believe what I was seeing. My first sensation was one of sharp iciness, I was shaking with cold. No wonder, I was sitting in a foot of cold water. My first thought was about the baby I was carrying.

Rachel was hovering over me and moaning. Her mouth, hands and feet were taped shut with duct tape. I could see the terror on her face as she was trying to call my name. Tears were squeezing out from the corner of her eyes. As soon as she saw that I was coming to, she tried to bombard me with urgent words. They were muffled and all lost on me. I couldn't make out a single word. I was struggling to come to. On the other side of the cellar, water was gushing through without restraint and making a horrible gurgling sound. The far wall was in the throes of collapse. Lumps of earth were tumbling down and building up into a mound which was visibly moving into the middle of the room.

Once the shock had passed, I was tearing off the tape from Rachel's mouth, hands and feet.

She hugged me so hard it took the wind out of me.

'Thank God. I thought you were dead!' she whispered in my ear. She began babbling. 'Claude left us here when the water started pouring in. He left us here, Rowan. He left us. We're trapped. I heard him put something across the trap door. We can't get out. What are we going to do? What are we going to do, Rowan?'

I had no idea, but I could see that Rachel was beside herself with fear. I stood up, pulling her up with me. Staring at her with as much calm as I could muster, I said, 'Don't worry, Rachel. It will be alright. We need to think now, how are we going to get out of this hole? Put your panic to one side and let's do some thinking. Take a deep breath.'

Bless her, here she was a little twelve-year-old girl, standing knee deep in the cellar of a madman. Keeping eye contact, she took a deep breath.

'OK, we have to think.'

'Yes, we have to think.' The problem was that I wasn't thinking, let alone about her. Looking about me at the anarchy, my head was empty of thought. Except the thought that we were both going to be buried alive.

'We have to think,' I repeated, more to myself than to Rachel. Just then the entire far wall folded over on itself and toppled into the room. This pushed the water level up to nearly our waists. We both started screaming, not a sensible thought in either of our pretty heads!

The water was now above our bellies. The room, which had seemed quite large, now appeared crammed. The water was still rising and the earth walls disintegrating in large bucketsful of mud. We tried the trap door again. It was as tight as before and we wondered if Claude had bolted it shut on the other side. We hammered and shouted at the trapdoor, but it was totally silent in the world above. We agreed to stay on the ladder (which was tricky enough), to keep above the water level for as long as possible. The ladder began to move. Slightly at first, then we both felt a convincing movement. Maybe it was our combined weight with the corrosive effect of the water. Whatever it was, the ladder was coming away from the wall.

'Rowan, I'm frightened. I'm really frightened.' I knew she was because she wasn't shouting anymore.

Then the Wolf spoke to me: 'Go to your baby, Rowan. Go to your baby.'

I looked across the room to the alcove. To throw ourselves into the black water would be madness. I couldn't do that to Rachel. It would be suicide. 'Fucking no way!' I said out loud.

'What?' replied Rachel.

'Trust me, go to your baby.' In the shadow, I could see Him. For the first time, I saw the Wolf. I was shaking, not out of fear, more like purest love I have ever felt.

'Trust me, go to your baby.'

I looked over to the alcove, where my baby was. The water was high now and the curtains which shrouded it were floating.

'Rachel, we must go over there.' Rachel followed where I was pointing.

'Over there?' she said weakly. 'It's dark over there. I can't go there, I can't!'

I turned to Rowan and held her as tightly as I could. She was trembling and her face was wet with tears. My heart went out to her.

'It will be alright, Rachel. It will be alright.'

'I'm scared, Rowan. I'm not sure I can do this.'

'You can and you will. Hold on to me, Rachel. Do not let me go. Promise me?'

CLAUDE

How the hell did she recognise me after all this time. I acted as indignantly as I could, but as she continued her rant, the facts she alluded to, began to piece together. When I did finally take a good look at her, I too could recognise in this rather weird-looking banshee as the little girl who had obliged me so willingly years ago. I thought there and then that it would be for the best to make myself scarce, especially if she fulfils her threat to call the "Old Blue." Mother of God, this was becoming complicated. I suddenly had a few dilemmas I needed to sort. A moment away from the action may help me fathom out my next step. The water guys were on the way and now maybe the cops. In my cellar, amongst several other souvenirs I would rather remain secret, were two treasures, one of whom I was about to unburden. I appreciated that I may have to let some of these things go, as matters were coming to a head. Possibly to a headache. The wisdom I had developed over the years has at its cornerstone the phenomenon of letting go. Expediency and pragmatism are its siblings. I thought about my losses and, most vitally, I thought about my ledger, my tome of memories as precious to me as the magic book of that old goat who lives next door. This was essential, but the crucial key I deduced was not to get caught. In short, I needed to get the hell out.

My mind finally re-engaged itself and was thinking in its rapid spontaneous way, always ahead of me and totally reliable. I went straight to Lacey's boat, the one from which Hamilton had inadvertently fallen, pulled it down the beach and launched it without ceremony or fuss. On the water, with all the indifferent acceptance of the sea lapping hungrily about me, I felt suddenly at peace. It was lovely out there and for a fleeting moment, I wished I had my fishing rod with me. I could sense that I was quickly regaining my exceptional sense of perspective. Looking back, the little row of terrace houses appeared almost idyllic. I had spent over twenty years in that place, and on the whole, I have had a most excellent time there. My father would have been well pleased with me. I am well pleased with me. I have very few regrets. Indeed, what regrets I do have is not what I have done, but what I have not. This sadly included my angel Rachel. That girl, that absolute wonder, surpassed all who went before her. Those dark, dark, eyes, the black hair, the olive skin…no, I must stop, I am driving myself a little crazy with her image.

I stopped rowing for a moment as nothing seemed to be happening. The bay was as quiet as a church. I couldn't see anyone on the near shore by the houses, nor near the road. What I took as a chase may not be so. It may all blow over after all. Perhaps fate will somehow resolve the matter for me. Evidence may literally be buried. That yelling bitch Rowan may be seen as the nutcase she clearly is and get the blame for the lot. I rolled a fag and had hardly taken the first drag when the scene changed in an instance. Jesus, Jew of Israel, fuck, shit and piss!

My peace was shattered. I watched the troops come across the causeway. I counted three police cars, a fire engine and two water company vans, sirens blaring, lights flashing, the full works. You could smell the testosterone all the way out here in the bay. At the terraces I could see all the protagonists coming into view, plus a few onlookers and neighbours all gathering around. The pub door swung open and the usual batch of boozers and losers were running over to find out what was going on. I resumed my rowing with renewed vigour. This was serious stuff. Then my eye caught sight of Lacey's old motor, trailing lifelessly from the stern. After a few tugs followed by an almighty kick I released it from its rusting clamp. My instinct was spot on as per usual and there remained some petrol in there. With that a plan popped into my head. I doused the boat with petrol until I was almost overcome with its smell.

'So, this is how it ends?' I said to the sky. 'Claude Mayfellow, entrepreneur of the human condition, conqueror of women, manipulator of men, master of his own universe!' I could hardly stop from laughing. 'Farewell, goodbye, adieu and au revoir, fair world. I treated you as well as I could. Unfortunately, you blew it!' One last glance at the land and the unfolding drama led to one final surprise. In a sudden abrupt jolt, I could see my house somehow shift and its roof collapse. At the same time, a hole appeared in front of it. I chuckled seeing the old banger, Bessie, upend slightly. I could only guess that the water had accomplished its grand finale; its last trick on all four of us!

My handiwork undone; I began singing my favourite Sinatra song. *It was a very good year.* I never finished it. I took one last puff on my last cigarette and threw it into the boat.

EVE

Katie was right, they were voices we were hearing. Who was down there? With Rachel still nowhere to be seen, I feared the worst. Thank God, I could hear the police cars on their way. They couldn't get here soon enough. The ground started to move and we all instinctively moved back a few steps. A moment of silence was swiftly followed by an almighty groan, like distant thunder. The earth was trembling. The house sighed heavily as if it were was breathing its last breath. Everything shuddered and then everything dropped. Claude's roof collapsed, and the rest of the building fell into ours. As it did so the ground right in front of us appeared to buckle and sink. In a second, we were peering into a mucky crater. We were all standing round it in sheer astonishment.

The police were jumping out of their cars, the fire engine pulled up in a skid on the shingle. Two ambulances assumed a pincer movement as they came from both sides. They joined us, all of us looking down into this muddy watery hole. Both Katie and I were crying and didn't know why.

Then through the mud, there was a movement, then another, then another which was accompanied by the collective gasp of the crowd, as two beautiful faces emerged.

AFTER THE WAVES

Now is the time for the truth.

Why was this island "blessed with a curse" and, why is the rabbit such a loathed creature? Neither can be mentioned without summoning misfortune, mayhem or even death. Fisherman and smugglers won't go to sea if either were spoken. Weddings would be postponed, and baptisms cancelled. What's the reason for this? Some say that the curse on the island came before the curse on the rabbits. Untrue. They came together. Some theories support the idea that rabbits were cursed because they had poisoned the islanders through myxomatosis or that they ate through supplies when the precious island went through droughts or famines. Both untrue. Most believe that the fear of rabbits is based on the fact that quarrymen would often see rabbits emerging from their burrows immediately before a rock fall, causing injury or death. That's untrue too.

Here's the real reason:

After the death of Christ, Joseph of Arimathea fled from the authorities to England. With him, he may have possibly had the Holy Grail, but what he did have was the thorn crown of the Saviour. Apparently, he and his party were intending to land much further down the coast, but an almighty rogue wave, much larger than the rest, forced the ship to the main beach. They decided to stay a few days until there was more certainty about the tides, allowing the winds to settle. The islanders were most accommodating. Visitors to the Island were few and this was an interesting party. They had their own gods, but this lot was saying that they had found the one true God.

Tents were set up on the lower cliff. As the sun was setting, locals brought the travellers some mutton and a small barrel of mead. During the exchanges, Joseph became aware that a small rodent had got under the flap of the tent and was nibbling at the crown of thorns. After kicking the meagre creature into the next field, Joseph knew this incident required some sort of pious redress. He thought on it overnight. On the one hand, the creature had eaten of the holy relic. On the other hand, the Holy relic was now part of the fabric of this island. In the morning, he knew exactly what to do. In a short prayer session witnessed by flabbergasted islanders, he blessed the island with a curse.

Blessed with a Curse

JACK

I was fishing over the beach today. I watched the sun hit the horizon with an explosion of reds and yellows. In a moment the sky burnt like phosphorus and the sea lit up in triumphant rivalry. A minute later the fireworks were extinguished, and a subtle twilight followed. Everything here is in competition. It's happening all the while. When there's a storm, the drama reaches a climax with each element trying to upstage the other. I've taken to coming out for walks in such weather, battling against the wind, braving the cold, witnessing the sheer force and cacophony of the waves bashing the pebbles with their usual violent indifference.

It's been exactly a year since we dug Rachel and Rowan out of the crater. Seeing their little pale faces emerge from the mud will always be one of the most potent memories of my life. The shock for me and everyone else was tangible. On impulse, we all rushed to help, to pull them out and free them from the muddy hole. The fire crew said that if Rachel and Rowan hadn't been exactly where they were when the cellar collapsed; they would have been buried under tons of earth and would have certainly died. No sooner had we rescued the pair, when one of the policemen pointed out to sea to a rowing boat in flames. A solitary figure was on board, standing on its deck. He may have been waving, but he was too far out to see properly. The officer radioed for the Coastguard for help. All of us already knew who it was.

The houses were condemned as being unfit for "human habitation." What else could have been expected? The council told us everything we already knew. They had been built on moving shingle, the foundations were hopelessly shallow and, needless to add, the water pipes and the electricity supply were archaic and wholly inadequate. During the demolition they found all sorts of things in Claude's cellar. The ledger made interesting reading, so I heard. Most haunting though were the two bodies they found there, one was a baby, and one which was eventually identified as Claude's second wife. The baby turned out to be Rowan's. I can't begin to imagine how she suffered alone, with the stillbirth of her child, and for it to be used by Claude in one of his many games.

After the events of last year, Rowan fell apart for a while. Who wouldn't? But she's not falling apart now. It turns out that she was pregnant during the whole episode. Her baby was born early, a few days after Christmas. It was a boy. She called him Adam, and both are doing well. She won't tell anyone who the father is. They live in a little cottage on the bend on the way up to Tophill.

Rowan has begun working with people who have also suffered like she has. Maybe, what with Adam and her work, the healing has finally started for her. Rachel has been a huge support to Rowan and, having shared an experience like no other, they have become good friends. Rachel has a natural resilience which will set her in good stead for life, and all it throws at her. Interestingly, Rachel's dad Harry is going out with Katie. It seems opposites do attract. Tom is fighting fit and, thankfully, appears to be untouched by events. I often see them out walking, the four of them, sometimes five if Eve can manage it.

And me? Well, I'm living further up the hill. I miss the intimacy of being next to the sea, but I had to find somewhere after the demolition. From my place, I can see the sea and the coastline, and hear it on evenings when the wind is blowing my way. The house unquestionably feels more solid. But I must confess, I remain as twitchy as I was before I arrived at the Island. I haven't said anything to anyone as yet, but come the New Year, I think I will be off on my travels again. There's a restlessness about me which I'm not sure I will ever be able to shake off. I'm not quite ready to go but I'm also, not quite ready to settle down either.

It took me a couple of months before I could call Old Flann Dad. And it took Rosie even longer to pay us a visit. When she did come, she came alone, without her family. After such a family upheaval, I don't suppose you can magic it all back into place. She had been old enough to remember it all and now knew that, until that day on the shore, I had no memory of the incident when we lost James. Holding onto the grief was unbearable and so she used the excuse of Mum's funeral to leave my life. Not telling me the truth was much easier than telling me. The anguish of that first weekend together was agonising. The pain of that memory tore us apart. I am pretty sure I will never cry quite as much again.

One thing the three of us decided was to mark James' memory with a small ritual. Eve, the only other person with whom we shared our awful history, accompanied us to the water's edge. She blessed the Sea of Souls and spoke to James as if he were standing in front of her, asking him in turn to bless us in our imperfect lives. Under Eve's direction, we threw red roses into the waves. We watched them drift out in an uneven line, little bright flames against the inky blue of the sea. Goodbye, James.

We have seen Rosie only on one other occasion. You can imagine, it's always a bit awkward as we ploughed a track through all the crap of our missing years. Healing is going to take some time. It is difficult to tell whether we are ever going to be close again. The jury's out on that one. Rosie has a hubby, Simon, and I am uncle to two teenagers, Roland and Darcy. There are no plans afoot at the moment for us to meet up.

Out of the blue, two visitors from the past turned up unexpectedly within weeks of one another. My old mate Ellis arrived on the Island. His first ironic words were, 'Why in hell's name, did you come to this sleepy dump? This is the sort of place you come to die - not to live!' He quickly changed his mind after our first boozy night when I told him what had happened here. He never really justified why he had been absent for months. He said he had been "deeply involved in one almighty fuck of a domestic" with his girlfriend, Fran. Once on vacation, they had got lost in the Dolomites and were missing for a couple of days. Under the pressure of not knowing where the fuck they were, he told me that he swiftly found out what this holier-than-thou convent girl was really like. Ellis was meant to stay a weekend with me and ended up hanging for over a fortnight. He too fell in love with Rowan. Easy to predict that one. As only Rowan can, she had no trouble in ignoring him. Truth be told, she was too absorbed in Adam to take much notice.

One foggy morning, about a month after I moved into Artist's Row, Trish visited. I opened the door to her smiling face, her little wave and an exuberant 'Hiya, Jack!' We went for a drink, a meal, a few more drinks. She tried to frame our separation as a "break." Her new relationship was an affair, a distraction, a mistake.

I knew I was listening to horseshit, but I also knew I wanted to listen. The roller coaster of our relationship should have been a warning for both of us. It wasn't. Seeing her there in front of me, the same old feelings were whipping through my veins.

'What was the amazing news you had for me?' I asked her after a few drinks.

'I thought I was pregnant. I wasn't. A case of pseudocyesis.'

'Sounds serious.'

'Phantom pregnancy.'

'Oh,' say I, avoiding eye contact.

It was great to see her. It was great making love to her again. But the spark had died. We had a few weeks together but had to acknowledge that the Seventh Wave had struck again. There was no going back. She eventually returned to Maidenhead with no plans to meet as such, but we agreed to keep in touch.

Both Trish and Ellis came along to Eve's birthday gig. We all gathered in the local and had a fantastic time. Outside there was another storm and all hell was breaking out whilst inside our little haven we were having a ball!

Our book is now with the publishers. Dad and I worked hard in bringing it altogether. It runs into seven parts and tracks the mythology of this island over the last two thousand years. We're very proud of our endeavours. As I write this, we're very proud of living on this sleeping giant, floating on the endless sea, part of the land, but not quite. We have outlined the format for a sister volume. Watch this space. By the way, our commissioner, Weller, despite his initial enthusiasm, eventually lost all interest in the project, lost money, lost the plot and ran off with the local butcher.

As for that bastard Claude, his body was never found. This spawned many stories of sightings, not only locally but as far afield as Scotland. For the girls, for all of us, it would have been best if they had found his burnt and washed-up body on the rocks at Deadman's Bay. This was not to be. The police concluded that he had probably died and ended up fish food, but nobody could ever be one hundred percent convinced.

ROWAN

It wasn't Claude who changed my world. That wanker just told me exactly what I knew about the world. His type of evil was not unique and never would be, but I wish he had never come my way. I hope the bastard is rotting slowly in hell. No, Claude didn't change a thing, but the birth of Adam made everything alive again. As soon as I saw Adam, I fell in love with him, his little body with his shock of black hair. That was also the moment the Wolf died. From that day, I haven't felt, seen or heard from Him. He has vanished. In some way, I miss Him, but I know it's right. He had been with me since I was Rachel's age.

With Adam with me, this was a time to face the future. We had a proper funeral for my baby who Claude had taken and kept in his cellar. All my fears over being arrested or put into the loony bin were groundless. No one gave a shit, to be honest.

The incident was a shock to the islanders and mainlanders alike. We made the six o'clock news. Questions were asked about the stupidity of the police missing vital evidence, about the murder's years ago and about the Tophill rape. For a day or two there were reporters everywhere. Eve and Jack both ended up on TV as eyewitnesses. Needless to say, I hid until they lost interested.

I made the long walk up the hill to visit my parents' grave for the first time. I wasn't brave enough to do this alone and took Katie along. She was incredible and did her job by talking without taking a breath and pushing Adam in his buggy when I needed a rest. There it was, a simple cross with each of their names on either arm and, in the middle, the date of their death and the words "Leaving behind their beloved daughter, Rowan." Katie made up a prayer and we placed a bunch of carnations on the ground. I made a pledge to buy a vase for flowers and visit every week. I did buy a vase, but the visits are probably more like once a month.

When I got back, Rachel was there on the doorstep of my new place. She knew I had been up to the church and wanted to make sure I was OK. I see her a lot. We are somewhere between friends and sisters. It basically doesn't matter what we are. I have no plans of having Adam christened. It might help if I believed in God. If I was though, Rachel would be a godparent to my little man. She loves him almost as much as I do. Almost.

EVE

When it all calmed down, I did a huge amount of soul searching. I had to admit I got so much wrong. I didn't miss the odd thread; I missed the whole kit and caboodle. When Rachel and Rowan were taken to hospital for a check-up, I was in a state meself and Harry insisted he take me to a doctor. It took him one look. I can't remember the word he used to describe it, but he said it was in a fairly advanced state. Rather rudely, he called me a "very silly woman." The very next day I was up in the County Hospital. They gave me every test you can imagine. The results were not good. I may have been misled by the likes of Claude, but I was right about this. It was an aggressive form of bowel cancer and was bubbling up under the skin. They could treat the symptoms, although me card was marked now, and I may have a year if I'm lucky.

What was also plain as plain, was that I had lost faith in the magic of the old days. I came clean with Harry and made my mind up to tell him about the Book. At first, I thought about donating it to the museum. I met with Old Flann to talk about it. In the end though, I didn't give it to him. I had a dream, and, despite Harry's reservations, I passed it to Rachel. Separation was hard but the Book was staying in the family. Rachel being Rachel allowed Old Flann to study it. Jack decided to publish it online and it already got half a million clicks, whatever that means. This wasn't the way we traditionally passed the Book on. There were rituals to adhere to, but times have changed. I heard that the only other living sister, Clara, died the night she found out what I had done.

There's talk of them rebuilding our row of terraces. I am not sure that that is ever going to happen. I'm not that worried. They have re-housed me in the road leading to the pub. The view is not so good, but the sea is hardly any further. Most of all, this house doesn't creak and bend like the old one. It's made of the local stone and has deep enough foundations to argue with anything the sea or wind may come up with.

The terrible events of last year still play on my mind. Why wouldn't they? You could write a book about it. If the image of Claude comes into my brain, I make haste and dodge and dive until he disappears. What it has left us with, is a massive self-made family. The spirit of community no less, just like when I was a kid. Oh, and I'm still on the lookout for husband number seven. Nothing's altered there.

JACK

I am trying not to be sentimental. You may have guessed that I have fallen for this place. If I do move on, I will always been a part of it all and the people I have had shared this adventure with. Some things have an inevitability about them, and you can sense where it is all going and yet you don't know when or how, or even why. I was over the beach with Tom and Rachel the other day and we were pelting this piece of driftwood with stones. One point if you hit it, two if you managed to turn it over. Of course, they were beating me hands down. So, I went right to the edge to increase my chances. I was asking for trouble because the very next wave came thundering in and took me off my feet. The kids thought it was hilarious.

'It's the Seventh Wave!' they yelled at me, helping me back to my feet. I was laughing with them, deciding not to tell them that it was actually the ninth!

THE END

G. W. HAWKER

Gary Hawker has enjoyed a career in Social Work and NHS Training A local author based in Dorset, several previous attempts at writing a novel finally paid off when he completed Inside the Seventh Wave last year. He is currently working on his second novel The Hole at the Centre of the Universe.

Printed in the UK by CLOC Book Print
www.clocbookprint.co.uk